What people are saying

“From the streets of the Br
Margaret, offers a tantalizing glimpse of NYC crime where nothing is ever what it seems, and fighting it is anything but routine.” - NYPD Police Commissioner, Dermot Shea.

“Sister Margaret is a gut punch of a tale that takes the reader behind the crime scene tape and onto an exhilarating tour of the streets, drug dens, dive bars and precinct houses of New York City, with an insider’s view that rarely makes the papers.” -Jessie Smith, Crime Journalist, Kingston Times.

“Sister Margaret is a short, quick, gritty read … that’s a wonderful start to this new series by the Myers siblings with its intriguing characters, nice sense of urgency, and satisfying conclusion.” -Zoe Williams. 8/10 Stars whatsbetterthanbooks.com (Best Book Blog 2017)

“Sister Margaret is a slam dunk police procedural, giving the most on-the-money description of an investigation … If you are on the lookout for a new series of gritty police procedurals, then Travis Myers and Natasha Myers Marsiguerra are definitely names to watch.” -DeathBecomesHer. crimefictionlover.com

“This really is a well-written novel that was an enjoyable and highly entertaining read. I recommend.” -Nursebookie. 5/5 Stars Goodreads.com

“I really enjoyed this book! With just under 200 pages, you have a fast-paced plot, fully developed characters, and a wild glimpse into the life of an NYPD detective … I would suggest grabbing a copy of this book!” -Brianas_best_reads. 5/5 Stars Goodreads.com

What people are saying about Hayden Jon Marshall~

"Devious, intense and disturbing! Hayden Jon Marshall is a twisty, action-packed, satisfying addition to what is undoubtably turning out to be a dark, suspenseful, compelling series by the Myers siblings."
-Zoe Williams, whatsbetterthanbooks.com

"Travis Myers and Natasha Myers Marsiguerra handle police procedurals so well, anyone would think they had the inside track. Oh wait … they do! Authentic and engaging crime fiction."
-Sandra Mangan, crimefictionlover.com

"Out of all the detective-based novels, Tommy Keane is my personal favorite."
-Eleni Madiar. 5/5 Stars lafemmereaders.com

"Hayden Jon Marshall, is an intense and hard-hitting tale, and I was in tears just reading the prologue."
-DiDi Arpayo. 5/5 Stars Goodreads.com

"The crime and its side plots are completely engrossing and entertaining and I found it impossible to put down. Highly recommended for crime fans."
-TJ Rifton. 5/5 Stars Goodreads.com

"Highly recommend to those who enjoy gritty, inner city crime fiction and police procedurals. Seriously, just make a TV series already!"
-Danish Mustardreads. 5/5 Stars Goodreads.com

"A bloody brilliant book that I absolutely flew through! By far the best cop series I've read in a while … there, I said it!!"
-Oriana Blyth. 5/5 Stars Goodreads.com

JENNY BLACK

Also by Travis Myers
&
Natasha Myers Marsiguerra

Sister Margaret

Hayden Jon Marshall

JENNY BLACK

A Tommy Keane Novel

Travis Myers &
Natasha Myers Marsiguerra

Jenny Black is a work of fiction. Names, characters, and incidents are the product of the author's imagination and are used fictitiously. Any resemblance to actual events, or persons, living or dead, is entirely coincidental.

Published in the United States by Bully Press Corp.

Bully Press Corp
P. O. Box 404
Wingdale, NY 12594 United States

Cover design by: Phred Rawles

ISBN-13: 978-1-7343370-6-8

For all the independent rockers, musicians, lyricists, and artists in general, who help keep the world a more bearable place to live.

We thank you for your efforts and for everything you do.

***

Dedicated to every Cop and Detective, in every city, in every country on the planet. Thank you for standing on the side of right, and for fighting the good and never-ending fight against those who would destroy all we hold dear.

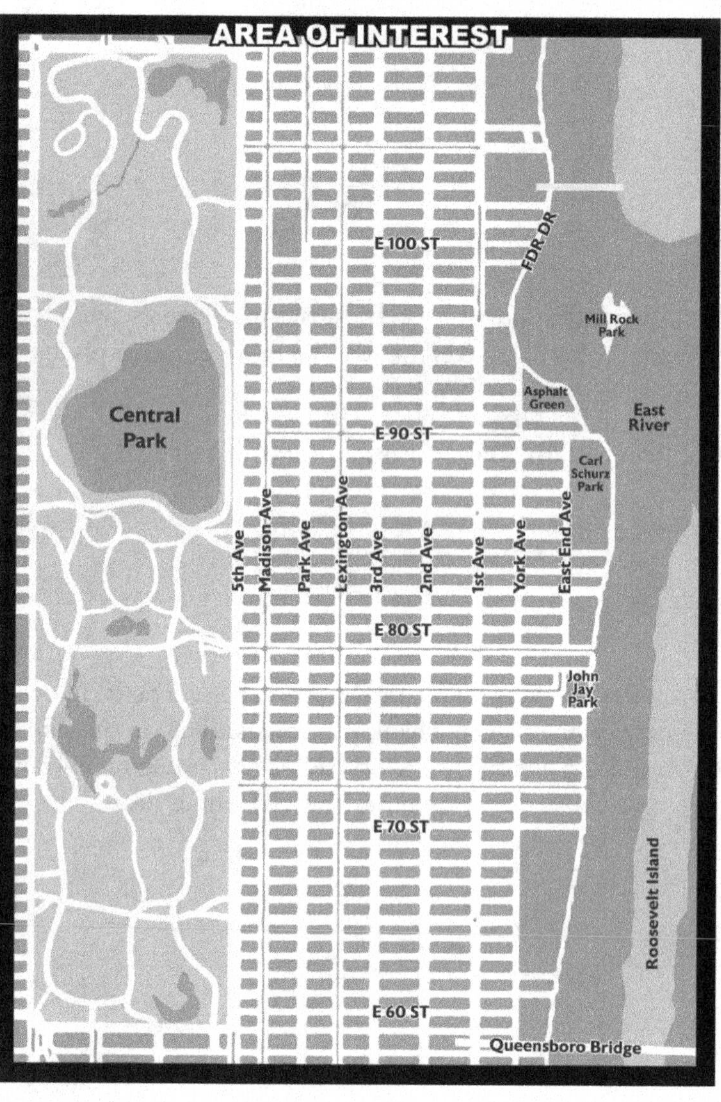
AREA OF INTEREST
Central Park
E 100 ST
FDR DR
Mill Rock Park
Asphalt Green
East River
E 90 ST
Carl Schurz Park
5th Ave
Madison Ave
Park Ave
Lexington Ave
3rd Ave
2nd Ave
1st Ave
York Ave
East End Ave
E 80 ST
John Jay Park
E 70 ST
Roosevelt Island
E 60 ST
Queensboro Bridge

"When I got the music…

I got a place to go."

Song: "Radio"

Band: Rancid

Prologue

When Tommy Keane was a young man, growing up in New York City and running around the streets with his best friend Terry Callahan and their crew, there was always a radio guy. Back in the eighties and early nineties no one listened to music on their phones. Cell phones and iPods would not arrive on the scene until the early 2000's, so you had to have a radio guy on the block, and on occasion a crew might have even had two or three.

Tommy's group of friends had two - Mikey and Tony-Rad. Having two meant there was a considerable chance that music would accompany them during their long days and nights, hanging out on the stoops and street corners of their neighborhood. Whether they were throwing a football, playing some stick ball in the streets, or scrounging a few quarters together for a quart of beer (Yes beer, at least in the eighties, still came in quarts), music was always playing.

Of course, with groups of teenagers in numbers from five to twenty, and at times as many as thirty, hanging out on the same block, the question was always: what to listen to? This was a constant debate and an occasional argument.

Obviously, the radios belonged to their owners, but that meant little. After all, this was America, and the kids in Tommy and Terry's crew liked to consider themselves a democracy. With so many differences in taste, things often needed to be hashed out and so one never knew what one would be listening to on any given night.

Tommy and Terry, as well as Tony-Rad, preferred punk and new wave music, and luckily Tony-Rad was the neighborhood punk rock aficionado. His box was always stocked with a new mix tape of eighties punk and new wave artists, and Tony-Rad prided himself on always turning the guys onto whatever he considered to be cutting edge. He was an enormous influencer within the crew, as well as with a broad spectrum of the neighborhood kids, when it came to what was cool in both music and fashion.

Mikey on the other hand preferred classic rock, and occasionally old school rap, and seventies soul. His box would jump around from older bands like the Beatles and Stones, to the Sugar Hill Gang and Run DMC, occasionally showcasing something from the Stylistics or the Commodores, and even some Doo Wop if his mood was right.

Both of these de facto DJs were loved and appreciated for their contributions on a daily basis. Large radio "Boom Boxes" were not cheap, and neither were the batteries that kept the music going and the block hopping all night.

Back in the day, a corner DJ was something to be.

The corner DJ was, in essence, creating the soundtrack to your life. A song could be twenty years older than you, but if it was in the regular rotation of tunes it was certainly one of your songs, even if it also belonged to your parents' generation. Or it could have been an obscure song or artist which the masses may never have known about. Tons of artists in all genres of music enjoyed unknown success on stoops, corners, and rooftops all over New York City and well, the world, all because a lone radio guy/corner DJ liked the track and stuck it in a mix.

Music in general was, is, and forever will be a refuge and safe haven for youth all over the world and is perhaps the most accessible of all forms of entertainment. A song, no matter how popular or how obscure, can become someone's, anyone's, own personal property in their minds eye. A story or anecdote, set to a simple tune can magically change a life and create a lasting connection, so when you hear the tune some decades later, you are instantly brought back to the memory. For whatever the reason we relate to these songs on such a personal level. They forever influence us and mark the chapters of our own books which we write during our short time on earth.

And this holds true for all of us, regardless of where we grew up, or what we grew up listening to. Whether you were a poor kid from the streets, a middle-class kid from the suburbs, or a wealthy kid in a prep school; we each have those songs that define moments and stages of our lives, that freeze images in time for us forever, like an old photo album.

Music can excite us, soothe us, inspire us, and define us. Although it may belong to everyone, it can also be the most intimate and personal of things, where only the listener knows how it makes them feel inside, and how important a few chords and some truth can be.

Chapter One

There was a cold snap, what they had recently been calling a "Polar Vortex." It was no doubt a proper scientific term, but one of those popular new terms which had suddenly appeared in the news lexicon and had been repeated by everyone ad nauseam whenever a winter in New York was surprisingly cold.

It was absolutely freezing outside, and the city was still a mess from the mid-December snowstorm, which had dropped ten inches of snow on the ground just two days prior. Because of the mess the city was in with the slush and ice, Tommy had taken the Metro North in from White Plains rather than drive down. He got off the Metro North at 125th Street to change over to the 6 train, which he rode to the 68th Street station. He arrived at the squad room about twenty minutes before his shift.

As Tommy walked into the precinct this freezing cold afternoon, Sergeant Ruffalo, the desk sergeant, greeted him with a hearty, "Afternoon, Keane! Cold enough for you?"

Tommy smiled and nodded and made his way up to the squad room on the second floor, where he removed his coat and the heavy sweater he had under it. He had just arrived and already found the squad room too warm to bear. 'Why is this place always so ungodly hot,' he thought to himself. He loosened his tie and rolled his sleeves halfway up his forearms before he sat down at Doreen Doyle's desk, where he opened and reviewed a few of his open cases.

One by one, the rest of B Squad began to roll in, and first through the door was Mark Stein.

"Cold enough for you out there today, Tom?" He said as he removed the gray scarf he had wrapped around his neck.

Just as Jimmy Colletti stepped through the door, "God damn it's cold outside." Came out of his mouth with loud disbelief as he walked in.

Lieutenant Bricks entered next with Doreen Doyle right behind him.

"Good morning, men. Cold enough for you today?" He inquired followed by Doreen's exclamation.

"Jesus Christ, it is cold out!"

Then from beyond the door came more of the same.

"My lord, my lord, my lord… Why oh why is it so cold today, lord?" Charice Tate's, the Squad's PAA (Police Administrative Assistant), unmistakable voice rang out from the front. "Can you believe this? Not but two days ago it was fifty degrees outside, and now we sittin' in this vortex nonsense in the single digits, freezing our you know whats off… Lord, let me make it to retirement so I can move myself to Florida!" Charice continued.

Finally, Sergeant Browne walked in.

"Good morning, all. Damn, it's cold outside today, isn't it?"

Tommy smiled to himself as he was the only one to realize that each member of the squad had just given the same shocking weather report. As if no one knew it gets cold in New York in December, or just how redundant each of them was.

A minute passed and Charice stepped back into the office from her desk with a stack of folders in her arms. She had recently removed the braids from her black hair and now wore it straight.

"One blessing about this cold, it keeps things mellow and slow… Alls I got is four cases here from Patrol and looks like they're all easy ones for ya'll… Here is one for each of you to start your morning with," she said and continued,

"One… Two… Three… Four," as she dropped one in front of each detective respective of where he or she was seated at the time.

"And Detective Keane, you is catching today right, handsome man?"

"If I'm next on the list then yes ma'am, I am," Tommy responded.

***

About a half an hour had passed, with nothing of interest added to the small talk about the polar vortex, when Sergeant Browne stuck his head out from his office.

"Tommy, you're up today, right?" Sergeant Browne asked.

"Yes, sir I am," Tommy said.

"There's a D.O.A. (Dead On Arrival) over at Carl Schurz Park. Take a run over there and find out what the story is please, patrol is on the scene."

"You got it, Sarge… Who wants to take a ride?" Tommy questioned the room in general, as he walked to grab his sweater and coat.

"I'll go with you," Jimmy Colletti said, "My case load is pretty boring and I can't take the heat in here. A little frost bite may help me appreciate this office when we come back." Jimmy stood and grabbed his coat.

"Thanks, Jimmy, I got a ton of stuff here to work through," Doreen added.

Stein just took a sip of his coffee, his eyes never leaving whatever case he had his face buried in, either oblivious to the conversation or uninterested as a whole.

"Body is on the north side of the park, probably up around 89th or 90th Street from what it sounds, and on the river or FDR drive side of that area, not sure exactly, but you'll know when you see the patrol cars," Sergeant Browne added.

"Got it, Boss. Thanks." Tommy said as he buttoned up his coat.

Chapter Two

4:12 PM John Finley Walk, Carl Schurz Park

Detectives Keane and Colletti arrived at Carl Schurz Park and found two patrol cars parked on John Finley Walk, the promenade which bordered, and faced out over, the East River.

Tommy and Jimmy exited their vehicle and as they did Sergeant Diaz, a tall, slim, dark-skinned man with his hair slicked straight back, exited his. He placed his hat on his head, straightening it just so, before he approached the detectives.

"Afternoon, Sergeant, what you guys got for us?" Tommy asked.

"Afternoon guys… Cold enough for yous?" The Sergeant replied, "There's a body of what appears to be a young woman just over the rail there… Here, come take a look." Sergeant Diaz motioned with his head toward the river and the iron railing that ran along it. He walked the detectives around his patrol car and pointed over the edge, "You'll have to step up on the railing and look down."

Both Tommy and Jimmy stepped up onto the crunchy ice-covered snow the plow had left and simultaneously put a foot upon the rail's cross bracing and lifted themselves up onto the rail. They both peered down and saw a young woman partially covered in snow. Half of her face and black hair was exposed. Her left arm and gloved hand, as well as part of her left leg and boot were visible. The rest of her was shrouded in snow.

"Jesus!" Jimmy exclaimed, "How are we supposed to examine the body?"

The woman's body lay on a concrete and stone abutment that stuck out about eight to ten feet from the continuous wall that came up from the East River to the promenade. Looking over the rail, one could see there were a handful of these abutments that protruded somewhat randomly along the stone wall and would only be visible if one were to lean over the railing to see them, or from a boat out on the river.

"Well, it's not that far, Jimmy. We can climb down and take a look. Fuck I wish everything wasn't covered in snow and ice," Tommy responded to Jimmy's question, and he threw one leg over the rail and then the other.

"Tommy… what are you crazy! If you fall into the river, you'll be dead from hypothermia before we can pull you out!" Jimmy protested.

"Relax, I'll be fine, plenty of room here for me." Although he said that with all the confidence in the world, the ice which covered everything he touched, and the bitter cold wind whipping up the river did have him question his decision for a moment as he dropped himself down the seven or so feet onto the abutment. The center of it seemed to be about eight feet wide, and it triangled itself back to the walls at either end over a span of about twenty feet.

Tommy landed soundly in the twelve-inch snow drift that had piled up against the stone wall and covered the dead woman. He then shouted up to Jimmy and Sergeant Diaz.

"Has the Medical Examiner been notified? Also give ESU a call. Let's find out if they have some equipment that can help us retrieve this young lady… Fuck, I wish I wore some proper boots today… Put a call into Crime Scene as well please, I don't want to get too close or disturb her body until we have the okay from everyone."

"You think she's a homicide, Tom?" Jimmy shouted down to Tommy.

"No way to tell," Tommy yelled back, as he squatted next to the body and poked it gently. "She's frozen solid though, completely solid… no way to know right now until after crime scene and the Medical Examiner show. Could be a homicide, perhaps she tried to jump into the river and landed here instead, and later froze, maybe a drug or alcohol fueled accident? … No way to tell or even make a guess right now."

Tommy stared at what was visible of the body and the scene that surrounded it.

Young female twenty to twenty-five years of age. Pretty looking face, the one eye that was not covered by the snow was wide open and brown. She wore makeup; her eyebrows were manicured, dark red, almost maroon lipstick, jet black hair with one blue highlight that was noticeable. On her body was a black Alpha brand nylon MA-1 flight jacket, zipped up to the top over what appeared to be a black hooded sweatshirt, black skintight denim jeans cuffed up to show off her black Dr. Martens 1490 boots.

After about six minutes Tommy hollered back up, "Alright, I'm coming back up." He jumped up to grab the edge of the stone wall but slipped off, then tried a second time and was able to hang on long enough to pull himself high enough to reach the iron railing.

He pulled himself all the way up and climbed over the top of the railing back to the promenade.

"You're a fuckin' nut," Jimmy stated flatly.

"Hey, we gotta check out what's going on here, Jimmy. How else was I supposed to take a look?" Tommy responded, as his body shuddered from the cold, "Let's go back in the car and wait for the others to arrive."

Sergeant Diaz was already tucked back into his patrol car and Tommy and Jimmy climbed into their vehicle as well, to ward off the cold. Tommy sat silently and made some notes in his notebook and afterwards he took the notes Jimmy had made.

"Did Sergeant Diaz say who discovered the body?" Tommy wondered.

"Yeah, it was a 911 call from a passing tugboat that said they saw what seemed like a body lying in the snow. That was earlier in the day. I guess it took the patrol guys a couple looks to find it. I can understand why, who would think to ever peer over the rail, especially on a day like today?" Jimmy answered.

***

First to show was a truck from NYPD Emergency Services, Truck 2, but they could not do anything until Crime Scene and the Medical Examiner's office were finished with the body, so they sat and waited along with Tommy and Jimmy and the officers from Patrol.

Second, about thirty to forty minutes later, Crime Scene arrived at the park. They set up their equipment and started to take photographs and measurements. Emergency Services helped by supplying a couple of ladders, some rigging and two giant spotlights that lit up the abutment brighter than daylight, as it was now dark out. They used the rigging to tie everything together and make everyone's work a little safer than attempting the climb Tommy had made earlier.

Finally, the Medical Examiner's office made its appearance, Jimmy immediately making note of it for the unusual report.

"Oh, look who's here. Do you know what we call her?" Jimmy asked.

A tall, attractive woman with short slicked back blond hair and a long black wool coat, high-heeled boots, and a stainless-steel document case exited her vehicle and glanced toward the detectives.

"The Vampire." Tommy answered.

"Oh… so you know her?" Jimmy was a bit disappointed he was not able to share that bit of information.

The detectives exited their vehicle and walked toward the woman, meeting her halfway.

"Evening, M.E. Marcus, how you doing today?" Tommy nodded at her.

"Not bad, a bit cold, Detective… Keane, correct?" she asked, knowing exactly who Tommy was from past cases.

"Yes, you are correct."

They had worked on numerous homicides together in the past, but Ms. Marcus had a stone-cold, matter of fact way of speaking that always seemed dismissive and borderline rude. However, she was, without a doubt, one of the premier examiners at the M.E.'s office.

She walked ahead of the detectives, over to where the rail was and the ladders that went up and over it.

"So, what do we have? A jumper?" she asked.

"We have no idea," Tommy replied, "Young woman, I'd say early twenties, mostly covered in snow, appears to be frozen solid."

Angela Marcus attempted to peer over the rail and realized she could not observe from that vantage point, so she did as Tommy and Jimmy did and stepped up on the rail and peered over. In her monotone voice she declared, "She's dead." Then stepped down and made her way over to the ladders.

"Are you alright? Will you need a hand?" Officer Dowd from Emergency Services asked.

"No thank you, Officer, I'll be fine."

She unbuttoned her long wool coat so it would not interfere with her ascent and climbed the four rungs of the first ladder then swung her right leg over to the second. As she did, she resembled a swashbuckling pirate climbing a tall ship's rigging from some old Hollywood film, as her long coat blew in the wind. Once she was down, Tommy followed her and the remaining Crime Scene officer removed himself from the scene saying, "We're pretty much done here, let me move out of your way and give you some more room so none of us fall into the drink," as he climbed back up the ladder.

Marcus first surveyed the area and then the body while Tommy surveyed both the body and Marcus as she made her initial exam. He watched Marcus to ascertain what was going on in her mind through her facial expressions and eye movements. Tommy got nothing from Marcus though, she was like a poker champion, and he could read nothing on her face. She was not trying to keep anything from Tommy, it was just her way.

She scraped the snow and ice off the body as best she could and attempted to feel through the young woman's jacket and pants.

"She seems to be frozen solid, which unfortunately means we won't be able to do an autopsy for at least a week until she thaws out fully… I'm sure you understand and realize we can do nothing to change that. To properly thaw a body, frozen like this, will for certain take about seven days. From what I can see here I can't tell you much, Detective. Let's take her up top to the pavement where we can flip her and I can give a more thorough examination of her clothing, and a better look at her body."

They left the girl's body and made their way back up to the pavement. The Emergency Services officers took over and dropped a basket down to pull the body up. Along with a couple of guys from Patrol, the Emergency Services guys used the ropes and rigging they had attached to the metal body basket and pulled the young woman's body up and over the rail. The sound of the basket's stainless-steel banging and clanging, as the wind blew it into the stone wall and against the railing as it rose, was chilling.

Now that the body was laid out on the pavement of the promenade, Angela Marcus took another look, slowly and deliberately brushing off all the snow. She searched the body, along with Tommy, for any bullet or knife holes in her clothing; they flipped the stiff body over and did the same along her back, carefully looking for any holes or clues. Once they were satisfied, they again flipped the body onto its back.

Angela Marcus unzipped the young woman's outer jacket and inspected it for any signs of damage; next she unbuttoned the black denim vest that was under it, and lastly the zippered hooded sweatshirt that the girl had worn over a t-shirt. M.E. Marcus then stood from her squat and stared directly at Tommy.

"I'm sorry, Detective, I really won't be able to tell you anything today. I, as you, see no visible wounds, no visible broken bones, this here in the eye appears to be a slight petechiae which could be from any number of reasons, but in this frozen state it will take a full autopsy to tell you more about her cause of death. Here is my card, may I have yours please? I will call you before the autopsy so you can come witness it."

They exchanged cards and Marcus began to walk off, "Our techs here will remove the body as soon as you are finished, Detectives," she said over her shoulder.

"We done?" Jimmy asked, shaking from the cold.

"No, we're not done, Jimmy… C'mon, we have to search the body still."

"Oh. Right, of course. I think this cold is freezing my brain, sorry."

They squatted on either side of the body and Tommy began to go over it as best he could, methodically, from head to toe. He took note of anything and everything he thought might be of assistance to his investigation. He wrote down the sizes of the clothing tags that he could reach and brand names if he saw any. He searched every pocket, entirely disappointed to find nothing that would identify the young woman. No wallet, no identification, and the only thing in her jeans was sixty-five cents, made up of two quarters, a nickel, and a dime. In one of her flight jacket's inside pockets was a wooden token with the words "Free Drink" around a martini glass on one side and "Snapper Magee's" around a bulldog's head on the other.

"Jimmy, take note of all these band names I'm going to read out to you now, okay?"

The young woman's black denim vest was covered with a bunch of band patches, and little one-inch buttons that Tommy read aloud for Jimmy to write down.

"The Business, Two Fisted Law, Born To Lose, The Queers, Hudson Falcons, Dwarves, The Jukebox Romantics, Damn Broads, OC45, Cry Havoc, Riverside Odds, Fantastic Plastics, Casket Architects… Help me roll her over."

They gently flipped the stiff body and Tommy lifted her nylon bomber jacket as high as he could so he could view the back of her vest and continued to call out names.

"Street Dogs, The Interrupters, Barb Wire Dolls, Svetlanas, The Sharp Lads, Frances Dean, The Adolescents, New Red Scare, Dr. Beardface & the Spaceman, and the big back patch in the middle says HEELS." That patch was white on black with an image of a skeleton riding a horned tiger and carrying a pizza. "Girl had some superb taste in music."

"You know these bands?" Jimmy asked.

"Most of them."

Tommy pulled open the vest and took note of the left breast of her hooded sweatshirt, which had 'Teenage Bottlerocket' with a skull and two crossed rockets printed in white ink, and her black t-shirt, which had a red and white image of a dead bird falling from the sky, with the name 'Say Hello To The Angels' on it, all of which he announced to Jimmy to be noted.

He also noticed and removed a black cord from around the young woman's neck that had a red guitar pick attached to it with the name The Split Seconds printed on it in black.

"Now, Jimmy, now I think we are finished here. Man, I wish this girl had some I.D. on her. Let's hope we have a missing person's report in the system on her we can find." He stood and motioned to the techs who were still sitting in the Medical Examiner's meat truck, trying to keep warm, that they were done with their search and to come and take the body.

Chapter Three

Tommy and Jimmy had spent the better part of the afternoon and evening waiting at the crime scene for all the different units to arrive, do their part and leave, and now they had done their part. Tommy sat in the driver's seat and stared out the window watching the M.E. techs load the young woman into their truck and drive away. And then, that was it, all activity was over at this scene for the time being.

"I'm hungry, Jimmy. You wanna head over to the Mansion Diner on 86th and grab something before we head back?"

"Hell yeah, I'm starving. If you didn't ask those were going to be the next words out of my mouth."

The detectives rode over to 86th and York to the Mansion Diner and parked outside in front of a fire hydrant. They entered and Tommy asked the hostess to sit them next to the window where he could look out and keep an eye on the car.

They were seated at a black booth with a wooden tabletop as a small, round, young woman with black hair, wearing a white shirt with a black vest over it and black jeans, approached the table with two glasses of water. "You guys ready, or you need a minute?" she asked.

"I'm ready, are you?" Jimmy asked.

"Yeah, I'm ready, go ahead, Jim," Tommy said, never opening the menu.

Jimmy ordered a bacon cheeseburger deluxe and a cup of coffee. Then Tommy ordered a turkey club with sweet potato fries and a Coke, the waitress thanked them and left to place their orders. Once they were alone, Jimmy put his elbows on the table and leaned in towards Tommy.

"So, what do you think?"

"About what? This girl in the park?"

"Yeah, what else? The girl in the park."

"Actually, I don't want to think… With the absence of any kind of evidence at all, trying to find a cause of death, would, or may, cloud my vision and get in the way of what the actual evidence is once something is available and presents itself to us."

Jimmy paused, "Yeah, but, but you must think something?"

"No, no Jimmy, I don't think anything. What I'll do, what I am going to do, is try to find out who our dead Little Miss Jane Doe is, begin an investigation by questioning her family and friends, and regrettably wait a week or so to find out what Marcus tells me at the autopsy. And then, I will hopefully have enough information to either close this Jane Doe D.O.A. and or continue an investigation in the event we think there is any foul play going on here."

***

Tommy and Jimmy ate their meals then returned to the station house and the near eighty-degree sauna that it was.

"Long night out in the cold, wasn't it boys?" Sergeant Browne asked, "So what do you have… Any idea yet?"

Jimmy, who had entered first, spoke up, "Some frozen stiff Goth girl dead in the park, almost in the river but she never made it," Jimmy answered.

"Punk girl," Tommy stated as he removed his coat and sweater.

"What's that now?" Sergeant Browne questioned.

"She's a punk girl, not a goth girl, and we don't know or won't know the cause of death for about a week. M.E. said it will take at least that long for her body to thaw… Also she's a Jane Doe at the moment, she had no I.D. on her, and we have no idea who she is. Going to check the computer and see what Missing Persons has. With any luck we'll find out who this girl is," Tommy added.

"Ahh fuck, you landed yourself a mystery date there, didn't you, Tommy?" Sergeant Browne chuckled as he turned to go back into his office.

"Looks that way, Boss."

"Nothin' worse than a CUPPI (Case or Circumstances Undetermined Pending Police Investigation) to throw a monkey wrench into your week is there, Tom?" Sergeant Browne continued as he stopped at the threshold, then laughed again as he shut the door.

"No, Boss, there ain't."

Jimmy continued, "I thought she was a Goth with all that black and dark makeup?"

"No… no she's a punk rocker, entirely different subculture altogether. Musically some of the bands may kinda hold hands, and I can understand how it may confuse you, especially with her being dressed all in black, but they're totally different scenes."

"Okay… and how do you know this stuff and who are all those bands that were on her jacket?"

"Well, I'm a music fan, Jimmy, and I grew up here in New York City, not under some rock somewhere. I'm familiar with lots of music and different cultures and subcultures simply by living here in New York. I'm surprised you didn't recognize any of those bands yourself and actually a little surprised you didn't know the difference between a Goth and a Punk either. You're a young guy, I'm sure you had a few of both running around your high school or college a few years ago."

"Yeah, we did, but I never paid any attention to them."

"And what do you listen to music-wise?"

"Eh… well nothing in particular honestly. Some Billy Joel, Neil Diamond, sometimes some Bon Jovi, and Queen but really I've never been a big music buff I guess… Just listened to whatever anyone else had on."

"What do you put on in the car?"

"I listen to sports radio or the new country hits station."

"You're killing me, kid."

Jimmy seemed saddened that he somehow disappointed Tommy by not knowing any of these things, but Tommy did not think twice about it. He sat down at Doyle's desk and logged into the computer to discover what he could find as far as any missing persons fitting his Jane Doe's description.

After two hours of searches and a couple of phone calls to Missing Persons for possible hits, Tommy found himself coming up empty of any possibilities. Yet he knew this young woman was a healthy adult and it was most likely that no missing person's report had been made by any family, friends, or employers yet, and that he may have to wait a day or two, perhaps even longer, for one to be filed, if one would be filed at all.

Next, he turned his attention toward the little he knew about this young woman, which was next to nothing.

His Jane Doe was clean and neat; she wore makeup that she applied with care, and it appeared her hair was most likely professionally done. As far as Tommy could tell she was of healthy weight and took good care of herself, although frozen and her skin slightly blueish, what little he could catch a glimpse of, appeared healthy. She was also clearly an avid punk rock fan.

Tommy opened his notebook and reviewed the list of bands he had Jimmy write down from the patches she wore; maybe, he thought, there'd be a local act that knew her. So first he began to check off bands that he knew were not local and were in all likelihood too prominent to know his Jane Doe personally. Anyone he did not know instantly he read up on, on the internet, and made a note: a check mark, if he thought they were unlikely to know this woman, and a P if he thought that band may be a possibility.

And the list went like so:

The Business… English band, √

Two Fisted Law… Connecticut band, P for possibility.

Born To Lose… Texas, he thought, plus they had broken up years ago, he remembered – √.

The Queers… Older New Hampshire band, still active. We'll give them a P for possibility.

Hudson Falcons… New Jersey, definitely a P.

Dwarves… California, √.

The Jukebox Romantics… New York, possibly Long Island band? A P.

Damn Broads… Connecticut, a P.

OC45… Boston, possibly a P.

Cry Havoc… Another Connecticut band, P.

Riverside Odds… Philadelphia, a could-be P.

Casket Architects… Upstate NY band, a P.

Fantastic Plastics… Peoria IL. √.

Street Dogs… Big band out of Boston, √.

The Sharp Lads… Brooklyn band, P.

The Interrupters… California & extremely popular, √.

Barb Wire Dolls… California, √.

Svetlanas… Russia, definitely a √.

Frances Dean… Upstate NY, P.

Adolescents… California, √.

New Red Scare… Upstate NY, P.

Dr. Beardface & The Spaceman… Philadelphia, P.

HEELS… Popular Memphis band, √.

Next were the only other three items his Jane Doe had on her that could be a lead at all.

The guitar pick around her neck, The Split Seconds… Washington DC, smaller band, a conceivable P, but most likely a check. He put a question mark.

Her t-shirt, Say Hello To The Angels… Texas, √.

And last, the wooden token for a free drink at Snapper Magee's.

Tommy typed in a search for that name and several things popped up. He found no website but did come across a Facebook page for a location in Kingston, New York and another location in Torrington, Connecticut. After looking over both it was apparent that the Torrington location had been closed for at least two years. The Kingston page was still active, and the location was indeed still open. The description read, "Dirty little rock and roll dive bar, come in for a beer and make some friends… Open 365 days a year from noon till 4 AM."

Tommy smiled to himself and thought, 'What a great place to continue my investigation.' His thoughts were broken by Stein and Doreen as they both shook off the cold, Jimmy asked them, "Cold enough out there for you today? Tommy and I froze our asses off with this Jane Doe D.O.A. over at Carl Schurz all day."

"Yes yes… Christ it is so cold outside today," Doreen answered sarcastically, obvious she had been asked similar questions about the cold a few too many times that day.

Stein chimed in, "Cold is an understatement… What's the story with your D.O.A., Tom?"

"Young woman, frozen solid, lying on an abutment that sticks out into the river off the promenade over in Carl Schurz Park. No signs of foul play that we can find yet. My current job is trying to figure out who the hell she is. She had no I.D. or anything on her to help me out, and I've found nothing through Missing Persons either."

"Yeah, probably too early for a missing person's report to be filed… be patient, one should show up in a day or two," Detective Stein replied.

"Yeah, that's what I'm hoping… Hey, Jimmy, what you got going on tomorrow? I'm thinking of taking a road trip up to Kingston to ask around the pub where that wooden token came from."

"Nah, it's a no can do for me, I have to get out of here early tomorrow, I got a family thing with my sister."

"I'm down," Doreen immediately interjected, "Love to leave the neighborhood for some new scenery, and I am happy to say after today's desk appearance ticket for an old assault, I have no serious cases to worry about at the moment."

"Alright. Let me tell the boss what we're up to."

Tommy got up and walked over to Sergeant Browne's office. The door was open and Browne had his nose in some paperwork. Tommy knocked on the door frame lightly with his knuckle.

"Hey Boss, I have a lead on our Jane Doe. Doreen and I are planning to head up to Kingston tomorrow night to check it out."

"Uh… Oh, well go make sure it's cool with Lieutenant Bricks. It's cool with me."

"Sure, Boss, thanks." He turned around and thought to himself, 'Cool with him, see Lieutenant Bricks. No, go ask Lieutenant Bricks means I don't want any responsibility for you being outside of the city… go ask daddy, it's okay with mommy… lame bastard.'

Tommy walked across the squad room to Lieutenant Bricks' office.

"Hey, Lu, how you doing? Doreen and I are going to head up to Kingston to try and find out who our dead Jane Doe is tomorrow, if that's cool with you?"

"Cool by me, be careful. And of course, if anything comes up, be sure to get with the local PD up there. We don't want to step on any toes."

"Of course, thanks, Boss." Tommy thought to himself, 'See… that's how it's supposed to be.'

As he stepped out of the office he winked at Doreen, "We're in business, Dee. Tomorrow night we're going to check out a little place called Snapper Magee's in Kingston. Dress casual, no pant suits required."

"Fun!" she proclaimed, clapping her hands.

Chapter Four

Tommy's eyes opened in the complete darkness of his room at his mother's apartment on 88th Street. He felt little JoJo, the Boston Terrier, pushed up against the back of his neck. Tommy moved as gingerly as possible so not to wake the little pup, while reaching to check the time on his phone on the nightstand. If JoJo knew he was awake he would jump all over him in excitement, and he would be forced to leave the bed and take the little dog out for a walk in the cold.

Tommy's efforts at stealth failed and little JoJo, disturbed by either Tommy's movement or more probably by the light from Tommy's phone, sat up at attention and stared at the back of Tommy's head. Tommy slowly turned his head and saw JoJo's face not three inches from his own in the dim light from the still lit cell phone, and once the two made eye contact all bets were off. JoJo leaned in and licked Tommy across his cheek. He jumped back into a let's play position and then jumped back at Tommy, both of his front paws landed on Tommy's neck, and he again licked him feverishly with excitement.

"Okay, okay," Tommy said as he pushed the little dog back off him. He swung his legs out from under the blankets and placed his feet on the floor, sitting up on the edge of his bed. Little JoJo now placed both of his feet on top of Tommy's right thigh and shook his entire body in excitement.

"Okay-okay," he repeated and laughed a little, "You are a tenacious little guy, aren't you? … I'm up now buddy, let me get up and we'll go out."

Tommy got in the leaning rest position on the floor and started to do his fifty morning push-ups with little JoJo running around him in the dark licking at his face, his ears, and his feet.

"All right already you pest, let me put something on, will ya?"

Tommy turned on the lamp and quickly threw on a pair of sweatpants, a hooded sweatshirt, and his coat. He stuffed his Smith and Wesson .38 caliber Centennial revolver in the pocket and put the leash on the dog. He took the stairs down and stepped outside of his mother's apartment building. It was 28 degrees out, but it felt almost spring-like after the last three days of single digit temperatures. Tommy looked left and then right, scanning the block while JoJo pulled at his leash to hurry down the steps of the front stoop.

They walked up the north side of the street, crossed over and headed back down the south side of the street, where little JoJo took care of his business in front of the Church of The Holy Trinity's courtyard.

"JoJo, you dirty little dog, have you got no respect?" Tommy said with a laugh as he bent over to pick up the dog's mess. From the church the two cut back across the street and headed indoors to find Tommy's mother, Maria, awake and fixing herself a cup of coffee, still wearing her paisley blue flannel nightgown.

"Morning, Ma, how you doing this morning?"

"I'm doing fine, Tommy, just fine. How are you, Tommy? And how is that little traitor today? Yes you, I'm talking to you," she said, looking down and pointing her finger at little JoJo, "My bed was good enough for you when Tommy Boy was gone, but as soon as he returned, I'm yesterday's news… Fine for you, JoJo, I can tell where your loyalties are."

"So did the two of you make out fine the last couple of days without me?" Tommy asked. He had spent the last two nights of his RDO's (regular days off) in his own apartment in White Plains.

"Oh yes, Tommy, JoJo is a good little boy, Tommy."

"Excellent, glad to hear that, Ma. I think he's turning out to be an awesome little dog."

"He's getting to be a big little guy now too, Tommy, I put him on the scale yesterday, and he was 19.4 pounds, Tommy. He's put on some weight for sure since he's been living with us, Tommy."

"Well, maybe you stop giving him ground meat and fried eggs, Ma, let him stay with the dog food so you don't make him fat."

"Fat? Tommy just look at him, he is a perfectly fit and handsome dog, not an ounce of fat on him, Tommy."

"He is a handsome boy isn't he, Ma… but still, watch what you feed him, all that people food probably isn't so good for him."

"What do you know from what's good for dogs, Tommy? You never had a dog before, Tommy."

"I never had one because you wouldn't let us have one, Ma."

"That's not the point, Tommy. Real meat and real eggs won't hurt our little JoJo, Tommy… Will it JoJo?" she said again addressing the dog.

"And what are you doing, Tommy? You're going to be late for the precinct, Tommy. Why aren't you dressed and out the door yet, Tommy?"

"I'm going in for the late shift again tonight, Ma."

"Oh sure, Tommy… I guess that makes sense then, Tommy."

"I'm gonna change and head out for a couple-few hours Ma, can I pick you up anything while I'm out?"

"No, Tommy, I'm good, Tommy." Tommy's mother replied as she took her place in her recliner in front of the television, lit up a cigarette, and turned on the TV to the news channel.

Tommy went into the bedroom and got undressed with JoJo right behind him, then to the bathroom where he showered and shaved, still with JoJo right behind him, waiting for him on the bathmat until he exited the bathroom, and right back to the bedroom where Tommy got back into the sweats he had on before, this time with some underwear and an undershirt. He put on an additional layer of one more crew neck sweatshirt, his Adidas Superstar sneakers, and his coat, all the time JoJo sitting and staring up at him.

"Listen, little guy, I'm going out for a bit and the weather's a little too cold for you to come with me, so you stay here and keep the old girl company, yea?"

Tommy picked the little dog up and walked back out into the living room. He kissed his mother on the head and sat JoJo in her lap and headed for the door.

"I'll be back in a couple-few hours, Ma."

"That's fine, see you later, Tommy."

Tommy left the building, looked left then right as he scanned the block, before making his way down the steps and turning left towards First Avenue. It was now almost 9:00 AM and with the sun shining and the temperature at 34 degrees it felt absolutely wonderful to Tommy, especially after how brutally cold it had been the last few days. He made his way east towards Carl Schurz Park and back to where the young woman's body was found.

Tommy's pace slowed once he entered the park, and he fell into that meditative zone in his mind, where everything was cleared out, to allow anything that may be pertinent to his investigation in.

As he approached the area of Finley Walk where the abutment was, he stopped and stood; he slowly turned around and looked in every direction, looking at nothing and everything at the same time. He slowly walked closer to the river and stopped again and once more turned around, looking in every direction, trying in vain to pick up anything at all that may help him identify this woman.

Tommy slowly made his way to the rail and looked over the edge. He remembered when he was a teenager running around the park after dark and hiding on this exact abutment while playing catch-one-catch-all with his friends. That was something he decidedly did not share with Jimmy Colletti, as he was doing his best to keep his ties to the old neighborhood, and the fact that he was now basically living in the precinct zone at his mother's apartment, a secret. Living in the precinct you worked was not allowed due to the possibility of conflicts of interests in your case load.

He peered down at where the young woman had laid dead the morning before, the snow and ice now completely disturbed by all the police activity that had taken place during the removal of her body. He lifted himself up onto the rail and swung his legs over and made the seven-foot drop down to the abutment. Once steady, he looked back up to where it was she would have fallen from, then made his way to the far north end where the abutment tapered back into the wall, not so far as to make slipping into the East River a possibility but just enough to gain a different perspective of the scene. Next, he walked the few steps to the other side, where the abutment again tapered back into the wall and squatted and stared for a minute or two, again just to gain another perspective of the scene. Tommy took a few short steps to where the woman's body had been; he lowered himself down and laid right down in the spot where her body was discovered. Here he stretched out and stared up at the sky and up at the wall above.

'What happened here?' he thought to himself, 'Was this a suicide? Did she jump expecting to land in the river but instead knocked herself unconscious, or break her neck or back and froze to death right here in this spot?' He felt the ice-cold of the hard ground beneath him seep through his clothing, at first through his thin sweatpants and next through his thick leather coat and sweatshirts. But the cold didn't affect him, as this young woman was now becoming an all-consuming mystery to him. 'Who was she… What was she doing here… Was it a suicide, or did someone throw her over the railing?' Tommy stayed there, in an almost meditative state, as he pondered what in the world happened to this young woman. The calm, collected, almost dream-like state he had put himself into came to an abrupt halt.

"Hey! What the fuck are you doin' down there?" A loud, barreling voice shook him back into the moment. "Get the fuck back up here before I call a cop, you fuckin' nut!"

Tommy looked up and a Parks Department worker, a large man in a Carhartt jacket and an orange knit cap, was visibly upset to find Tommy lying on the abutment.

"Don't worry, I am the cops," Tommy responded, still lying on his back. He stared up at the Parks Department man who scowled down at him; he reached into his coat pocket and pulled out his shield.

"I'm a detective over in the 2-1. I'm investigating the death of an unknown woman whose body was found here yesterday afternoon."

"What?" The man blurted out, "That's fuckin' weird… So, you're okay, yeah? And not a nut?"

"Yeah, I'm fine… Just trying to figure some shit out."

"That's fuckin' weird," the man restated, "Well okay, some lady grabbed me and told me some guy… You… jumped over the railing, and after yesterday I was thinking maybe this is now gonna be a new trend… Well good, I'm glad you ain't dead, and I'm glad you're not a nut."

"No, I'm fine. Hey, give me a second, I wanna ask you some questions."

"Sure." The Park's employee answered.

Tommy got up and brushed the snow and ice off himself before he jumped up and grabbed the wall and then the rail and pulled himself up and over.

"What can I do for you, Detective?" The broad stocky man asked through a thick black mustache that covered his mouth.

"Well, clearly you heard we found an unidentified body of a young woman here yesterday. Have any of you, any of your people been talking about it? Any rumors, thoughts, ideas as to who she is or what may have happened to her?"

"Nah… nah, I got nothing. I'd tell you if I did, we heard about it and of course people were talking about it, sounded like someone threw themselves off the promenade and missed the water… but nah, no one that I know of knows anything about that. I don't think any of us knew about it until you guys showed up yesterday."

"Alright thanks, pal, I appreciate it. I'm in sweats here and don't have any cards on me but my name is Keane, Detective Tommy Keane 2-1 Squad," he said as he put his hand out to shake the man's thick, meaty hand.

"Tommy Keane? I think I heard of you before… You been in the papers?"

"Once or twice."

"Well nice to meet you, Detective, and if I hear anything, I'll get ahold of yous at the 21st Precinct, no doubt. Good luck finding out who this girl is and what happened to her, sounds like some kinda tragedy no matter what happened."

"Yes, sir, I'm sure of that, and thank you, sir, I appreciate it."

"No problem, Detective, and don't call me sir, I work for a living," the man grinned at Tommy.

"Alright brother," Tommy smiled. He hadn't heard that 'Don't call me sir, I work for a living' saying in a while; it was a phrase often used by veterans, but also by working men in general when responding to another working man to show they were of the same class, "You have a good day, pal."

As the two parted ways Tommy went back to the rail and once again peered over the edge looking down upon the abutment.

"Ahh you poor honey, what happened to you? What is your story?" he said out loud, but softly, to himself.

Chapter Five

Tommy was to meet up with Doreen Doyle at the precinct at 5:10 pm; he went up to the squad room to sign in and then went back down to the front reception area to avoid the unbearable heat. Doreen walked in dressed in tight blue jeans with holes in the front, red high heels, a short leather jacket, and her hair and makeup done for a night out on the town. Tommy looked at her and could not help but comment.

"Look at you, Doreen… I'd give you the old line 'You clean up nice,' but actually you dress down nice, don't you? I don't think I've ever seen you out of business attire before. I like it," Tommy said with a broad smile.

"And look at you, Tommy, you look the same as you do almost every day only in boots and jeans and a - what is that a plain black sweatshirt? Out of your slacks, jacket, and tie, but the same leather jacket as every other day. I guess your sporting the finest in doorway attire tonight. What are you looking to pick up a shift checking I.D.s tonight if we don't land any leads on your Jane Doe?"

"Oh, so we're gonna start the night off that way, are we? I complement you on just how fetching you are tonight, and you insult me… Alright you, I see how it's gonna be."

They smiled at one another as if they were somehow getting over on the job this night rather than going to work.

"Go sign in and I'll wait here for you."

"Okay, I'll be right down," Doreen replied as she intentionally bumped into his shoulder as she passed him by heading for the stairs.

***

7:38 PM North Front Street, Kingston, NY

Tommy and Doreen had made the two-plus hour drive up to Kingston, New York with relative ease, getting to learn about one another a little more while sharing anecdotes of family and friends along the way.

Once they arrived in Kingston, they found the location of Snapper Magee's Pub on North Front Street. It was perhaps a mile from the exit off the thruway. They pulled into a public parking lot right next to the location, got out of the car, and walked about thirty yards to the front of the pub. They both stared in through the large plate glass windows to spot a dozen or so customers sitting at the bar drinking and a short-haired woman bartending, while "Mr. Crowley" by Ozzy Osborne was audible through the glass.

"This is a dirty little dive bar, isn't it?" Doreen stated.

"Yeah. Looks like my kinda place," Tommy replied, "Let's grab a quick bite before we check this place out."

"Yeah, I'm getting hungry myself; do you think they have food here?" Doreen asked.

"Doesn't look it… and I don't think I'd want to eat here if they did," Tommy replied, "Come, let's check out what else is on the block."

Two doors down from the Pub was the Wing Shui Chinese Restaurant, the pair stopped in front of it, but Tommy said he was not interested in Chinese. Another door or two down was a small luncheonette called Dallas Hot Wieners.

"What do you think? Looks clean and it looks quick," Tommy suggested.

"Sure, it looks good to me," Doreen replied.

Tommy opened the door and let Doreen in first. Once they stepped into the luncheonette, they stood for a moment to check the place out. It was a long narrow place, thirteen or fourteen feet wide and forty or fifty feet long, with a long counter to the left with about eight or ten old-style rotating stools bolted to the floor. There were also four booths along the wall to the right. All in all, it had an utterly charming 1950's atmosphere to it. Tommy took note that the three people working the place were all cleaning the already immaculate place to a high shine.

"Are you open? … Are we too late?" Tommy asked.

"No no, come on in please," a light skinned Hispanic man of about fifty years said with an inviting smile and attitude, "Come sit down anywhere you like and tell us what we can do for you," he continued.

"Thank you, sir," Tommy replied.

"What you want, Doreen, the counter or a booth?"

"Let's do the counter, that looks like more fun."

"Okay… Let's head on down there to the end then."

Tommy and Doreen walked down to the end of the counter and sat at the last two stools. A thin, pretty, Hispanic girl of about twenty years old, dressed in tight blue jeans and the same navy polo shirt with Dallas Hot Wieners embroidered on the front as the man who greeted them, at once asked, "What would you like to drink?"

"I'll take a small Pepsi, please," Tommy replied.

"And I'll take a coffee, please… Black," Doreen answered.

Doreen read the menu on the wall behind the counter while Tommy picked up a plastic covered menu that was on the counter itself.

"Wow," he exclaimed, "They've been in business since 1928… What a nice run."

"Must be good," Doreen answered.

"Are you ready yet?" The counter girl asked.

"Yes, I think I will have an order of chicken fingers with fries and one Dallas Hot Weiner, please," Doreen said, pointing up to the menu on the wall.

"And I'll take two bacon cheeseburgers, with lettuce tomato and onion, please… and a side of onion rings if I may," was Tommy's answer.

"Of course," the counter girl replied and walked over toward the cook who stood by the grill. She loudly told him the order as she handed it to him on the note pad she had just written it down on.

"Cool little place," Tommy said as he swung around on his stool to take the place in.

"I love it," Doreen replied, "It reminds me of a little soda shop my father used to take me to in Sunnyside when I was a little girl."

The food came quite quickly and the two ate and enjoyed their meals. Once finished they both stood up. Tommy dropped a $5 bill on the counter and made his way to the register at the end of the counter, where he paid, and both Tommy and Doreen thanked the staff, and exited the restaurant.

"Fun! I liked that little place, and this is such a cute little town," Doreen stated.

"It is a cute little town, isn't it? … So picturesque," Tommy replied.

"Yes, picturesque. Good word, Tommy, it describes it perfectly."

***

Kingston, NY is a quaint and charming town; located just off the New York State Thruway about halfway between New York City and Albany, NY. It became New York State's first Capital in 1777, after the battle of Saratoga, and there are still many buildings dating from the early 1600's still standing today.

North Front Street, where Tommy and Doreen stood, is part of what is called the Stockade District, which is the home of many old structures from the seventeenth and eighteenth centuries, including the state's first Senate House. The area once had tall stockade fencing surrounding it, like one would see in an old frontier movie like *Drums Along The Mohawk*.

North Front Street, and Wall Street which adjoins it to the north, have wooden canopies that run along all the sidewalks, giving that area of town an old-fashioned and pleasant look that is quite unique and has an almost New Orleans vibe to it. The area, with its older buildings and unique canopied façade, along with the Christmas lights and colored neon, coming from some of the businesses, along with the snow hanging off everything, made it genuinely a "Picturesque" setting. Both Tommy and Doreen felt a little Christmas spirit leaving Dallas Hot Wiener's, despite the fact that they were on the search for the identity of a young dead woman, whose body was found some ninety plus miles south of where they now stood.

Chapter Six

8:19 PM Snapper Magee's

Tommy and Doreen made their way back over to the entrance of Snapper Magee's Pub. They passed some of Kingston's residents who were out to dinner or for a few drinks on this Friday night.

"Looks like Kingston is a hopping little town, too," Doreen said as Tommy stepped passed the entrance to first peer into the plate glass windows and scope out the place one more time before entering.

"Yeah, it does seem like a happening town, doesn't it?"

He was surprised to discover the crowd of over a dozen that were there prior had dwindled down to three, in the thirty plus minutes he and Doreen had spent next door at Dallas Hot Wiener's, enjoying their dinner.

"Alright, Doreen, let's see what we can find out about our girl in this little hole," Tommy said as he stepped into the entrance way and opened the glass door for Doreen, allowing her to enter first.

"Why thank you, sir, I see chivalry is not dead," Doreen said as she stepped inside.

Snapper Magee's was a dimly lit place, and as he stepped inside, Tommy at once felt right at home. The room had that stale beer odor of an old pub. 'A Rainy Night In SoHo', by the Pogues was playing on the jukebox, and there were prints of 1940's pinup girls, old tattoo flash, and boxers on the walls. Amidst the tin tackers advertising different beer brands, a large mahogany ship's figurehead, with amazingly robust breasts, hung on the wall as well as a few bras, no doubt left by overserved female patrons, and dozens and dozens of sneakers and shoes nailed onto the walls and ceiling as well.

At the very front of the pub, as soon as you walked in, there was a Foosball game, next to which was a stand-up video game machine called Buck Hunter, where for $1.50 you could shoot some deer, moose, or elk with a plastic pump shotgun. An old CD jukebox was mounted on the wall next to that.

To the right was the bar, which appeared to run twenty-five feet or so along the wall, where two older men sat at the first two of a dozen or so barstools mumbling incoherently to one another. A tall, thin man with glasses, an obvious construction worker of some kind, sat in the middle of the bar and stood as Tommy and Doreen approached. He asked the bartender - a small woman of about twenty-five, with a short, choppy, red and black Mohawk and multiple tattoos, "Am I good? Do I owe you anything?"

"No, Tom, you're good, have a good night and make it home safe," she replied.

As the man walked toward the door, he said goodnight to "Larry and Rich," the two older gentlemen that sat at the front of the bar, and zipped up his jacket, pulling his hood up over his head before he stepped out into the cold.

At the far end of the pub stood an old school pinball machine, the kind where you had to pull a plunger on a spring back to fire the stainless-steel ball into the works. This one was gorgeous, it was the Elvira, Scared Stiff edition by Bally, and it was a beaut.

Opposite the pinball machine, at a stand-up table, was the female bartender that Tommy had seen the first time he looked in the window. She was a nice-looking woman of about thirty, with short dirty blonde hair. She wore a white ringer t-shirt with red cuffs and collar, that read “DON’T BE AN ASSHOLE” across her chest. She looked up and smiled at Tommy and Doreen with a welcoming “Hello” as they passed her by, while they perused the place and took everything in.

Towards the back there were three real, steel tip dart boards to the right. More pinup art, beer tackers, and over a dozen old show posters in frames from bands who had played the pub in the past. There was what appeared to be a few photos of regulars who had died. This seemed obvious because the frames around them had phrases like “In Loving Memory Of” painted on them. One large poster of a bulldog in front of a union jack said, “In Memory Of Anthony William Davies … A Bar Room Hero Who Is No Longer With Us.” Tommy liked that.

Just past the dart area was a small platform. At 4-5 inches off the floor, it probably did not qualify as a stage, and at about nine feet wide and maybe twelve feet deep, there was not much to it at all, but it was obvious that this is where bands would set up and play. It was backed by mahogany-stained oak plywood, which was covered in hundreds of band stickers. A large box-light hung over the small stage, with ‘SNAPPER MAGEES’ lit up in red, and an open bottom that shone down upon all the stickers.

'Cool place,' Tommy thought to himself, "I'm going to use the men's room," he said to Doreen, and stepped to the left of the bars make-shift stage area, where an incredibly old wooden phone booth sat just before the entrance of the men's room.

The restroom was all of four feet wide and consisted of two beer kegs bolted to the wall, with holes cut in the sides to serve as urinals, both were filled with ice - no doubt an attempt to keep the smell of stale piss down to a minimum from what it could have been, rather than where it currently was, and a lone toilet to the rear of the small 12-foot-long room.

The entire room was painted black, in patchy bits, where some of the paint was flat, some satin, and some gloss. It was obvious that over the years, all management had done was paint over bits of graffiti, which was also a vain attempt since there still was graffiti, as well as stickers, all over the walls and ceiling of the tiny restroom. Tommy smiled at a bit of it. One piece written over his beer keg urinal read, in silver sharpie on the black paint, "If God hates gays, why did he make so many of them?"

'Yep, this is my kind of place,' he thought.

Tommy washed his hands and, finding no paper towels, shook them dry and patted them on his jeans. He rejoined Doreen who was standing in the dart area. As he approached her, she motioned with her head at the wall, to look above a large Guinness Mirror where there was a hand painted sign that read "TATTOOS - while you wait."

"Looks like a fun place," she said.

"Yeah, I like where this investigation is going," Tommy replied, "What do you want to drink?"

"Drink?… you wanna drink?" Doreen asked, slightly surprised.

"Yeah, well we want to fit in, right? I'm not suggesting we become shit faced, but yeah I'm going to have a couple beers, what would you like?"

"Well damn? If we gotta fit in… I guess I'm gonna have me a drink."

"Very good then, may I buy you a drink, my lady?" Tommy asked, leaning forward, and putting out his hand palm up, leading Doreen towards the bar.

"Why yes, sir, I do believe I shall partake, thank you so very much."

They took the last two barstools at the end of the bar, Tommy grabbing the stool at the butt end of the bar where he could look straight down to the entrance, with Doreen right next to him on his right, at a right angle facing into the bar.

"Fun!" Doreen began, as she and Tommy both removed their coats and hung them on the backs of their stools, "I love this place… so much character… look at that sticker there," she pointed to a sign, "Get a Tattoo You Fucking Pussy" it read.

"Fun," she said again with a broad grin.

"Let's be cool and feel the place out for a minute before we start asking questions, okay?" Tommy asked.

"Of course, this is your investigation, I'm just along for the ride, and so excited to be out of the precinct tonight."

"So, what can I order you, Doreen?"

"No no, you don't have to get me anything, Tommy, I can buy my own drinks. Besides, you just bought dinner."

"Shut up and tell me what you want, I got this round."

"Well okay then, Mr. Man, I'll take a Jack and Diet, please."

"Jack and Diet, it is." Tommy removed a fold of cash he had in his right front pocket, wrapped in a rubber band. He took out a $50 bill and placed it on the bar.

The bartender on duty, seeing Tommy and Doreen take their seats and Tommy put cash on the bar, left her conversation at the far end of the bar, "Good night, Larry, Rich. Catch you guys next week," she said over her shoulder as she approached.

She was a small woman, wearing a red Snapper Magee's t-shirt with a rip off of a beer label design on the front, and the quote, "Work, The Curse Of The Drinking Class" ~Oscar Wilde, printed on the back.

She had on short black shorts over fishnets, with long black athletic socks that came up over her knees to her thighs, with white stripes on top of them, and on her feet a pair of Cherry Red Arcadia Doc Marten boots, which matched her red and black hair.

"Hi. What can I get for you guys?" she asked as she dropped a coaster in front of both Doreen and Tommy.

"I'll take a bottle of Bud, please, and a Jack and Diet for my Aunt here, please."

With that Doreen slapped Tommy's arm with the back of her hand.

"Oh… so we're going to have one of those nights, is it?" Doreen quipped.

The young woman behind the bar smiled and turned to grab the drinks.

"Oh no wait, I'm sorry, Miss… May I have a Rolling Rock in a bottle instead, please?" Tommy said, when he saw it was available on the back bar where about thirty plus different brands of bottles and cans of beer were lined up.

"Of course," the bartender replied.

As she returned with the Jack and Diet in a large pint glass, she grabbed a bottle of Rolling Rock beer from a cooler under the bar.

"Here you go," she said as she sat the pint of Jack and Coke in front of Doreen and popped the top off the Rolling Rock, casting it off to the side and onto the floor.

"Oh, wow, what a big drink," Doreen stated aloud.

"Yeah, well welcome to Snapper Magee's… That's how we do em here," was the bartender's reply, "That'll be $10.50, please."

"$10.50? Serious?" Doreen asked, "A drink half this size in my neighborhood, without the beer, would cost just as much."

"Yeah, Snapper's is a pretty cheap place even for Kingston. It's your first time here, I guess?"

"Yes, yes, it is," Tommy replied, "Looks like a cool little place. Have you worked here long?"

"Maybe… I don't know, maybe a year and a half now?" she replied.

"Yeah, how you like it?

"Well, I have a love hate relationship. I love hanging out here and the money is good. I genuinely like most of the people and have made some amazing friends, but it's the people you don't like that can make it difficult, especially the stupid, obnoxious, drunken girls at three or four in the morning. That can be a bit much to take night after night. But you just got to remember you're here to take their money and nothing else."

"How's the music scene here? Looks like you do some pretty good shows?"

"Kingston has a fairly good music scene! From what I understand it's not as cool as it used to be, and here we don't do many shows anymore, maybe a dozen or fifteen a year, if that? The boss is tired of dealing with bands, and from what I understand, the newer, younger crowd simply doesn't come out for music the way the older crowd did. He will sometimes do a show for bands he is friendly with, as a favor when they are stuck for a night on tour. I'll tell you what though… when Snappers does do a show, you can be certain it's gonna be a good one!"

"Looks like a lotta punk stuff?"

"Yeah, mostly all punk, a little psychobilly, some rock and roll. Rarely but on occasion, a metal band, but again it would be a rare favor the boss may do for a friend."

"Cool, sounds like a cool place."

"It is… Actually it honestly is… Hi, I'm Kristina," the bartender introduced herself as she stuck out her hand to shake Tommy's and then Doreen's.

"Tommy," said Tommy, as they shook hands.

"Doreen," said Doreen.

"You guys up from the City?" Kristina asked.

"Yes, we are."

"Just getting out of the City for the weekend, or are you up for an occasion?"

"Well, my new friend Kristina, since you asked…" Tommy turned in his stool and reached into the inside pocket of his leather coat and removed an 8 ½ x11 head shot he had of his Jane Doe.

"I hate to ruin this nice get-acquainted session we are having, but we are actually here for work. You see, we are looking for someone, actually some information on someone… We are Detectives, from the 21st precinct, NYPD," Tommy leaned back and showed Kristina his shield clipped to his belt, "And we are trying to identify a young woman… a, well a dead young woman who was recently found in a park in our precinct. She had no ID on her, but she did have a wooden free drink token in her pocket from here… from Snapper Magee's. I'd like to show you a photo of her, if I may?"

"Oh wow! Well yeah, you do look like a cop with that haircut. But yeah, yeah of course I'll do anything to help. Is the picture - is it, bad?" she asked with a hint of hesitation in her voice.

"She is dead, yes, but she doesn't look bad. It's not brutal or gruesome in any way."

"Uh sure, uhm, yeah… let me look at what you have."

Tommy handed her the photo.

"Oh jeeze, the poor thing… You know,… I don't recognize her right away… No, I'm sorry… Amy! Come over here a minute, please," she called out to the day bartender who at this point had her jacket on and was getting ready to leave.

"What's up?" Amy asked when she approached.

"These are a couple of detectives up from the City and they are trying to identify this dead girl. She had one of our drink tokens in her pocket. Have you ever seen her before?"

"No, I haven't," Amy answered, looking down at the photo, "Gee, poor thing, look at her with her eyes still open."

"I know, right," Kristina replied.

"No, no I'm sorry I don't recognize her… What happened? Was she… was she murdered?" Amy asked in a lower voice even though there was no one else in the bar that could hear her.

"We are not certain yet," Tommy answered, "The autopsy hasn't been done and the cause of death is still unknown. We're just trying to find out who she is right now so we can get ahold of her family and start an investigation."

"Wow. No sorry. I do wish I could help," Amy replied. She turned and said goodbye to Kristina, giving her a little hug, "Good luck guys, I hope someone can help you find out who she is," said Amy, as she left the bar.

"Do you mind at all that we ask around tonight? Or do you have someone you think we should ask about this woman?" Tommy asked Kristina.

"You can ask anyone you want; I don't care. And our door guy, Matt, will be in around 10:00, he knows everybody. We have another bartender, Mike, who will be in at 11:00 and he's friendly with just about everyone as well, so hopefully one, or both, will be able to help you."

"A door guy and another bartender? You plan to get busy tonight?"

"Oh yeah. Fridays usually kick ass here. And since it's not too cold, and no snow in the forecast, we should do pretty well tonight."

"Cool, I saw the place had emptied out from when we first arrived around 7:30," Tommy said, taking a sip of his beer.

"Yeah well, we call it Unhappy Hour. When I walk in Happy Hour is over, and all the prices go up, so the day crowd all leaves and we don't really-truly get busy again until about midnight, 1:00 AM."

"Yeah, I can understand that. And thank you," Tommy replied.

"Yes, thank you so much, Kristina, we truly appreciate it," Doreen added.

"Of course, anything we can do to help, please ask," Kristina replied.

***

Tommy and Doreen sat and drank their drinks and took in the atmosphere. Slowly, one or two people began to show up, and by 10:00 PM, all the barstools at the bar were taken, and four people were playing darts in the back.

About this time the music stopped and remained off for three to four minutes. Kristina approached Tommy and Doreen and placed a fresh drink and a fresh beer in front of them and then asked, "Would you two do me a favor please?" holding out a five-dollar bill, "Can you please play some songs on the jukebox for me?"

"Sure thing," Tommy said, "But please keep your money, we'd love to donate to the cause. Come on, Doreen, let's see what they have on this jukebox."

The two of them made their way down the bar to where the jukebox was hung on the wall; above the jukebox was a black and white poster from the film *Quadrophenia* which showed the cast against a wall and the words "Quadrophenia, a way of life" printed above and below their image.

Tommy was immediately enthralled with the selection on the jukebox. He thought it was a terrific mix of old and new punk, ska, rock and roll, with a few oldies and standards thrown in as well.

"My God, this is a magnificent jukebox," Tommy said to Doreen, as they flipped through the pages of available CDs that were in it, "What would you like to hear, Doreen?" Tommy asked as he stuck a five-dollar bill into the machine. "And look at that! 15 songs for $5 Bucks! Now that's what a jukebox should give you!" Tommy exclaimed with a childish excitement.

Tommy straight off punched in The Operation Ivy song "Sound System," and then one from The Mighty Mighty Bosstones. Doreen punched in a Joan Jett tune, then a Distillers song.

"Nice choices, Doreen," Tommy said with a bit of amazement in his voice.

"Don't sound so surprised, Tommy… I know about some cool shit too," she said, giving him a smirk.

"Obviously, you do," Tommy replied.

"Yeah, my older sister, Noreen, was really into punk music when we were growing up, so I had it playing in my bedroom every day."

"Wait… Noreen? Noreen and Doreen?" Tommy asked as he stepped back and looked at Doreen with disbelief.

"Yes, Noreen and Doreen. You got a problem with that, Mr. Man?"

"Ahh, nope… not at all," Tommy said as he punched in a song by Eric Burden and the Animals.

"And my little sister's name is Loreen."

"Go fuck yourself. Now you're just fucking with me, Noreen, Doreen, and Loreen?"

"Yes, my hand to God, Tommy, the three of us: the infamous Doyle sisters, Noreen, Doreen, and Loreen."

"Wow," Tommy said, shaking his head a little, "Very well, if you say so, I'll believe you."

"Oooohh stop there!" And Doreen punched in a song by Lost In Society and one by The Bouncing Souls.

"Look at you go, Doreen. You know your shit, don't you?"

"I told you. My sister listened to all of this stuff, and I looked up to her, still do a little. We listened to this music together, sometimes she'd drag me out to shows with her, too. Were good times for sure… and let me tell you, she would positively love this place."

Tommy glanced at her for a moment, he was really starting to like Doreen in general, and now with this shared love of cool music, he felt he had discovered a kindred spirit in Doreen Doyle he did not realize existed.

"Oh, hell yeah!" Doreen exclaimed, "Are you a fan of American Pinup, Tommy? Have you heard these guys?" She asked as she punched in one of their songs.

"Yes, I know them. In fact, they are one of my daughter Caitlin's favorite bands."

"Well Caitlin has some good taste in music then, 'cause they are one of my favorite bands also. I've seen them a few times and let me tell you they are even better live than recorded if that's even possible I don't know… but man, that girl can sing!"

"Right? She is the complete package; she writes, she plays guitar, she sings, and she's good to look at as well. I saw them once at the Knitting Factory in Brooklyn maybe, I'm not sure, three or four years ago."

Doreen stood up straight, "Was it at Upstart Fest? Maybe like, I don't know 2013… with the Koffin Kats and Turbo AC's?"

"That's the one! Were you at that show?"

"Yes!" Doreen exclaimed excitedly, "With Noreen, and two of her best friends Kelly and Joanne. Man, what a great night, and what a great show, I can't believe you were there too! Wow, what a small world."

"Hell yeah, it is - " And before Tommy could finish his thought a man tapped him on the shoulder. Tommy turned.

"Yeah?" He asked the man.

"Excuse me, Kristina behind the bar wants to ask you a question."

"Oh, okay, thanks pal, appreciate it," Tommy replied and made his way over to the bar, where Kristina pointed to the door.

"That's Matt, our door guy."

"All right thanks," he replied and made his way back to the bar stools where his and Doreen's jackets still hung. He retrieved the Jane Doe's head shot from his jacket pocket.

He nodded to Kristina behind the bar and asked, "Our stuff will be fine here, yes?"

She nodded yes and said, "Absolutely."

Tommy and Doreen made their way to the front door where the doorman, Matt, sat on a stool reading a book. Matt only stood about 5' 8", maybe 5' 9" tall, but was built like a human fire plug. He was dressed like a working fisherman, in a heavy wool sweater, heavy double knee construction pants, work boots, and a cadet's cap with a Triumph Motorcycle logo on it. He had wavy brown hair coming out from underneath the cap and a very full and heavy beard. Matt struck a rather menacing appearance at first look.

"Hello, Matt?"

"Yes?" He looked up at Tommy and Doreen from what he was reading, "What can I do for you?" He replied in an extremely low and monotone voice.

"How you doing? Kristina sent us over to speak to you. I'm Detective Keane, Tommy Keane, and this is my partner, Doreen Doyle. We're up from the City. We're trying to identify a young woman whose body was discovered in a park in our precinct. She had no ID, and we have no idea who she is, but she did have a wooden free drink token in her pocket from here. Can I ask you to take a look at a photo and tell me if you recognize her, please?"

"Of course, Detective, anything to help," Matt the burly fireplug of a doorman answered. Tommy passed him the photo.

"Ahh shit… the poor thing. Look at her… Yes, I have seen this girl before, a few times… but no, I can't tell you who she is, I'm sorry," Matt replied, handing the photo back to Tommy.

"Can you tell us anything about her, maybe she had some friends you know of or could describe?"

"Not right away, no, let me think on it a bit. I'm going to say she seemed nice, unquestionably never a problem or I would remember that. I think she's been in maybe two, three, four, times if that… and probably, I'm going to say, only for shows. She's definitely not a regular, for sure or I would know her."

"Okay, well thank you, you've given us something."

"Like I said, give me some time to think about it a little… Can I see her picture again?"

Matt stared at the picture for a minute.

"Man, it's haunting the way she looks back at you… Nothing comes to mind. Ask Mike though, he's the other bartender working tonight. He'll be in in about an hour, he may have more information than I do."

"Thank you so much, Matt, we appreciate it."

"Of course, not a problem. I'm sorry I couldn't be of more help to you guys."

"No don't worry, you did help us some."

***

Tommy and Doreen stepped back into the bar and made their way back to their stools.

"These people are so nice and polite in this town aren't they, Tommy?" Doreen asked.

"Yeah, they are fuckin' great so far." Tommy answered.

They sat and finished their drinks at the bar and as they did Kristina walked down the bar and asked, "Can I get you two another round?"

"I'm not sure… What do you think, Tommy?" Doreen looked up at Tommy.

"Well, I always like to think if a woman doesn't say no right away to a drink, she must mean yes," he said to both Doreen and Kristina, in his best playful and charming barroom banter. And then, directing his attention to Kristina said, "Yes please, Kristina, we would love another round."

Kristina smiled and turned away before promptly returning with their drinks again, setting Doreen's pint of Jack and Coke in front of her and popping the top off Tommy's Rolling Rock, letting the top fly off to the side and onto the floor.

"I want to introduce you two to my friend, Erin. Erin knows everyone around here. Maybe she can help you out, if you want to ask her about the girl you're looking for."

"Hey, Erin, how you doing?" Tommy asked.

Erin, a tall, attractive, slim woman looked to be in her late twenties, possibly thirty years old. Her hair was dyed a bright electric orange, and she wore skintight black jeans with a black spaghetti strapped tank top and a long, thin, light grey sweater that almost reached the floor. She leaned in closer, between the two detectives, in order to hear them better.

"Hey, Detectives, how yous doing," Erin replied with a large attractive smile. She mimicked Tommy's accent, making fun of the way he spoke, "Up here from the City, are you?" she asked.

Tommy smiled back, immediately recognizing that Kristina's friend, Erin, was a party on wheels.

"Yes… yes, we are, and Kristina told you why we are here, yes?"

"Yeah, she did. Let me see what you have, and I'll see if I can help," Erin replied, still with that large, pretty smile on her face.

Tommy pulled the headshot out of his coat pocket again and unrolled it for Erin. Her smile instantly left her face as she looked at the dead woman's photo, Jane Doe's opened eyes looking right back at her.

"Oh my God, how sad," Erin paused… "She looks so young."

"Do you know her?" Doreen asked.

"No… No, I don't. I can say she looks familiar, but no, I'm sorry. I don't know who she is," she handed the photo back, "What happened to her? Was it - murder?" Erin asked with a genuine curiosity.

"In truth, we don't know, Erin. There were no visible signs of any trauma that we could see, and there hasn't been an autopsy to determine a cause of death yet. Right now, we are just trying to find out who she is, so we can start our investigation, and notify her family."

"Wow, you guys have a kinda hard job, don't you?" Erin replied in a much more serious tone.

"It can be difficult at times, yes," Tommy answered her.

"And do you find it hard, you know… being a woman and being a police detective?" she asked Doreen.

"Like Tommy said, it can be quite difficult at times, but it can also be quite satisfying."

"I always thought doing something in forensics would be super cool. Do you guys do any of that work?"

Tommy stood up from his stool, "Here Erin, take a load off the floor and sit down and join us." Tommy pulled his stool over a bit and let Erin sit in it.

"Well thank you, aren't you the gentleman?" She commented as she settled herself on the bar stool between Tommy and Doreen.

"Let me buy you a drink also. What would you like, Erin?"

"Really? … well sure, thank you," Erin replied.

"Kristina," Tommy raised his hand to get her attention, "I'll take one more Rolling Rock, please, and give Erin here whatever she would like."

"A can of Porkslap Ale, Erin?" Kristina asked.

"Yes, please, darling."

"So, in answer to your question, Erin, no we don't do any forensic work ourselves, that's all done by techs in the different labs, some are detectives and others are civilians. What Tommy and I do is investigate crimes," Doreen said.

"What kind of crimes do you two do?"

"Well, we are squad detectives who work at the precinct level, so we do just about every crime imaginable, from small petty crimes with a known perpetrator, all the way up to the big one?"

"The Big One? You mean murder?"

"Yeah, murder is the big one… as big as a crime gets," Doreen said.

"Have you… do you do a lot of murders?"

"Any murders are a lot, or too many, I guess I should say, but over the last fifteen, sixteen years - well longer than that - ever since Rudy Giuliani was Mayor, crimes and murders have gone way down in the city. Overall, the city is a surprisingly safe place, so no, not a lot… This dinosaur here," she motioned to Tommy, "though, has been around forever, and spent the last twenty years in the Bronx where business was, well it was busy. He has arrested dozens of murderers."

"I guess you're right, the city is so much safer than it was years ago. Have you ever worked on a big murder?" she asked Doreen.

"All homicides are a big deal for us, but I understand what you mean, and yes just about two months ago, the squad Tommy and I are in worked the Sister Margaret case that was all over the news. Did - "

"I heard about that one! That was the nun murder! Oh wow, so you guys are kind of famous then."

"No. Famous no. Well, Tommy here is a little famous. He's worked on a lot of big cases over the years."

"Really? Like what? What would I - "

Kristina once again interrupted their conversation, "Sorry guys, this is Mike. He's my partner tonight and he may be able to help you."

Tommy and Doreen turned and looked up at Mike, who was a mountain of a man. He stood well over six feet tall and weighed at least 280 pounds, and he sported another long full Grizzly Adams beard. He was wearing a sleeveless black t-shirt with the name Modest Mouse printed around an image of a buffalo, with several tattoos running up and down both arms, and he stood looking down at the trio sitting at the bar.

"Hey, Mike, how you doing? I'm Detective Keane, and this is Detective Doyle, and this is our new friend, Erin, if you don't already know her. We're up here from the 21st Precinct in Manhattan and we are attempting to identify a woman whose body was discovered dead in a park yesterday. We know nothing about her other than she likes good music, and she had a Snapper Magee's drink token in her pocket. Can I show you a picture, sir?"

"Sure, I'd love to help you out, if I can," Mike replied.

"Okay great," Tommy again removed the headshot from his coat and unrolled it and handed it to Mike. "Here she is, do you know this woman, Mike? Take your time."

Mike paused as he looked at the photo, his lips tightened, and his eyes widened for a moment, he took a deep breath before he began, "Yeah… uh, yes. Her name is Jenna or Jenny, I'm not sure. She's been in at least three times that I can remember. Once to see The Split Seconds, that is for sure. And she was also here to see Kyle Trocolla and the Strangers play, she was friends with him and with the band. I'm certain of this because they all hung out late, till closing, sitting right here where you are sitting now. I'm sorry, I don't know if it's Jenna or Jenny though, and I never knew her last name either. But this is without question that girl. She has "HOPELESS ROMANTIC" tattooed across her knuckles, right?

"We couldn't tell, she had gloves on."

"You didn't take her gloves off? Don't you guys search -"

Tommy interrupted, "She was frozen solid from the cold and her hands were closed, so we have to wait for her to thaw out before we can remove her clothes."

"Holy shit!" Mike exclaimed, as both Kristina and Erin made shocked faces at the sentence that just came out of Tommy's mouth, realizing some of the realities of Tommy and Doreen's work.

"Okay - well this conversation calls for a round of shots! What's your poison, Detectives?" Mike asked with a blustery, more positive attitude.

"Jameson is my drink of choice there, young Michael, but I'll be having none of that tonight, because I have to drive back to the city, and I have already hit my limit on alcohol. But my partner here is one drink behind me."

"I'm drinking giant pints of Jack and Coke, Tommy, how can I be behind you?"

"Shut your cake hole, Doreen. She, and our new friend Erin here could also use another beer - what is that a Pork Slap? Never heard of it. But yes, sir, my good man, a round for these two ladies, and something for yourself and young Kristina here would be nice, thank you."

Mike reached behind his back grabbing a bottle of Jameson without even looking at it and poured four shots of Irish whiskey into four shot glasses. Each of them, Doreen, Erin, Kristina, and Mike took one in hand, and they all lifted it as Mike toasted.

"Here's to the NYPD!"

And Tommy, holding his bottle of Rolling Rock said, "No- No fuck us, here is to Miss Jenna or Jenny, you poor young thing, you left us too soon."

And to the sound of the Dropkick Murphy's playing "The Rose Tattoo" on the jukebox, they all had a drink for Jenna/Jenny.

***

It was now about 11:30 PM and the bar was beginning to get crowded. Tommy thought they should stay a bit longer to see if Kristina, Mike, or Matt at the door, could help them out with any other leads as to who, if anyone, may know more about his Jenna/Jenny Doe.

As Doreen and Erin continued in conversation, Tommy put another $20 on the bar, and motioned to Mike, "Anything these two want," and he excused himself and headed back up to the door to speak to the doorman again.

Matt had nothing more to offer. Even after thinking about it for over an hour and getting the information that Mike had added, Matt still had nothing. He did, however, introduce Tommy to four other regulars who he thought might be of assistance. Unfortunately, they were of no help either. Checking the time on his phone, he realized it was almost 1:00 AM and he needed to see if Doreen was eager to leave. They did have a big drive ahead of them. At this hour, Tommy felt it would only be about an hour and a half, but still he needed to get them on the road sooner rather than later since it appeared they had received as many leads as they were going to get on this outing.

As he made his way back into the room, he made eye contact with Kristina at the near side of the bar, who was pouring several drinks. She gave him an odd, wide smile, as if she knew something he did not. About halfway through the three-deep crowd to where Doreen and Erin were sitting, he could see Mike, who also was wide-eyed, smiling, and motioning with his head to where he had left them both over an hour before.

Once he finally made it back to the end of the bar, he found both Doreen and Erin, nose to nose and kissing, and kissing heavily, almost to the point of making out passionately, albeit a little more subdued.

Feeling a bit awkward about interrupting, Tommy squeezed himself back into his spot where he stood before, next to and behind Erin, and motioned to Mike.

"Give me a Pepsi, Mike. I may be awhile still."

Doreen opened one of her closed eyes and saw Tommy standing there, looking straight ahead. She then put both her hands on the cheeks of Erin's face and gave her one more long, rather hot kiss, before she pulled back.

"I think it's t-time for me, for us to go, Erin. But it was nice to m-meet you tonight. Are we g-gonna (hiccup) go now, Tommy?"

"Yeah, it's about that time, Doreen," Tommy said with a broad smile, "You ready?"

"Ya-yup… I amzz," was her recognizably drunk answer.

As Doreen stood and put her jacket on, Tommy pulled some money out of his pocket, and waved for both Mike and Kristina to come back to his end of the bar. When they arrived, he handed them a $50 bill.

"Thank you, guys, so much. I truly appreciate all your help tonight. Thanks for the drinks and the hospitality. If I didn't live so far away, this would be my new favorite gin mill… Cheers, guys," Tommy said and took a large gulp of his Pepsi.

"Please come back," Kristina replied.

"And good luck with that girl," said Mike.

"And goodnight, Erin, it was more than a pleasure meeting you, dear," Tommy said to Erin.

"Goodnight, Tommy. Goodnight, Doreen, come back soon!" she replied.

Tommy walked Doreen towards the door and as they approached the exit a young, nice-looking, very gay black man stepped in and announced dramatically to the entire bar, "Hey hey, let the fun begin! Uptown Eddie has arrived! … And may I introduce, fresh off the stage, The Lady Esther Gin!" and with that an exceptionally tall and attractive drag queen walked in. The Lady Esther Gin, as she had just been introduced, must have stood at least seven feet from the top of her remarkably high beehive hairdo to the bottom of her sparkly silver platformed stilettos, and as she entered with an entourage of another three to four gay men, the front half of the bar all cheered for her.

"Just when it starts getting interesting," Tommy said, disappointed to be leaving as he led Doreen past the crowd and shook Matt's hand on the way out.

Matt looked surprised and said, "Hey what's this?" When he was palmed a $10 bill with Tommy's handshake.

"Nobody ever tips the door guy. I know, I stood at many a door for many a year," Tommy replied, "And thank you for the help tonight."

"Thanks, Detective, but I didn't help at all I don't think?"

"Well, you helped more than you realize, Matt. And more than that, you weren't a dick, you were a gentleman, and I appreciate that."

"Thanks, man, I appreciate you. And please, stay safe."

Tommy held Doreen closely around the waist as they made it over the frozen brick and bluestone sidewalks of Kingston back to the parking lot and into the car.

"Well, that was a great night of police work, wasn't it?" Tommy began, after going through the toll booth getting onto the Thruway, "We have a solid lead on our Jane Doe, had a few drinks and a few laughs, and made some new friends along the way as well. I liked tonight, think we need to work this into our regular routine of crime fighting, hey Dee? What do you think? One night a week of Pub inquiries sound good to you?"

"Oh God, I'm so embarrassed," was Doreen's reply.

"Oh stop, you have nothing to be embarrassed about. So what, you had maybe one too many drinks."

"That's not what I'm embarrassed about and you know it."

"Oh what? You embarrassed about breaking wind? I don't think anyone but me noticed that, Doreen. It was pretty busy in there, I knew it was you, but it could have been anyone."

"No… Stop trying to be funny… You, you know what I'm embarrassed about."

"What?"

"You know, Tommy, c'mon… stop."

"Oh what? You playing tonsil tennis with Erin? You stop, Doreen. Why should you be embarrassed about that? You were enjoying yourself, and you made a connection with another human being, what a beautiful thing. And I tell you what, making a connection with another human being while on duty and getting paid for it… fuck yeah! Definitely a great night in my book."

"I didn't embarrass you at all, Tommy?" She asked, looking at him sideways.

"No, like I said I think I was the only one who knew you broke wind. I think everyone else was blaming the short guy with the Black Flag tattoo," Tommy grinned at her.

"No, you jerk! You know what I'm saying?"

"Oh, you're talking about getting drunk and making out with that hot orange-haired beauty at the bar?" Tommy smiled, "Nope, not embarrassed by you at all. In fact, I'm very happy for you. I didn't know you were playing for that team though. I certainly don't care, but in the few months that I've known you you've never let on… Not that it should be anyone's business anyway either."

Doreen leaned away from the passenger's door and into Tommy, resting her head on his shoulder and wrapping both her arms around his right arm. She liked Tommy and now with the alcohol was feeling a little vulnerable to him yet protected by him at the same time.

"Oh God, I don't know what I want… I really like girls, I mean I really like them, but I would also like to meet a nice guy and have kids and a family. You know like an old-fashioned family. To tell you the truth, I wouldn't mind being a housewife. I mean, I like my job, and in about ten more years I'll be looking forward to a nice pension, but you know, this fucking clock thing… tick tock tick, I ain't getting any younger," Doreen sighed, "All these girls I get mixed up with are all head cases. I have not been able to, and probably will never be able to, tell my mom and dad that I like girls, and the guys and the family thing, well the guys aren't exactly beating down the door to get to me, Tommy. And this job, well this job shows me how few real decent men there are out there. So many of them seem weak to me now. I had this guy for a while, a real nice guy right, nice-looking, treated me well, wanted a future. He was a construction worker, a carpenter, built buildings, but man if he wasn't just a pussy momma's boy in the end. Got to where I didn't respect him at all and couldn't even look at him. And everybody loved him so much. But when you lose respect for someone, you never get it back…" Doreen stopped talking.

Tommy began to speak, but he realized the only reason Doreen had stopped speaking was because she was now asleep.

Rather than driving back to the precinct, Tommy drove straight to Sunnyside, Queens, and woke Doreen up after over an hour-long nap to ask her exactly what street she lived on and what building she lived in.

He said goodnight, she thanked him for the "Best night I ever had on the job." He made sure she got in alright, then paused for a second in front of her building and said softly to himself, "You're one of the good ones, Doreen."

Then he headed back to the City.

Chapter Seven

Tommy's eyes opened as the alarm began playing "Talk Of The Town", by The Pretenders. It was day one of Tommy's two RDOs (Regular days off), but he had forgotten to turn off the alarm before going to bed just a few hours before. He laid still in his bed, staring up at the ceiling in the dim light of his cell phone, as the song played out.

Tommy was happy with himself and the little knowledge he had gained with his Jane Doe case. He was also happy he was able to spend a quality evening with Doreen Doyle, someone he was growing more and more fond of with each week he spent with his new squad. He had been unwillingly transferred to the 2-1 precinct, from the 5-3 in the Bronx due to punitive actions taken against him by the department, for taking a prisoner for a drink on his way to central booking after his arrest. It had been a questionable act, Tommy had to admit.

Tommy was, overall, becoming happy with his new assignment. He still undeniably missed the Bronx, and his old squad in the 5-3, but he felt immensely lucky to be working with the people he was working with. Doreen, who was easily becoming his favorite and probably was from day one, was an exceptional and decent person as well as a sharp investigator. Mark Stein was also a solid human being and was every bit Tommy's equal when it came to running an investigation. Tommy felt honored to be working with him. Jimmy Colletti was a genuine kid, but he had a lot of growing to do, both in life and as a detective. Still Tommy could see Jimmy's heart was in the right place, he just needed more time and more experience, and for his father, the retired Chief Colletti, to stop coddling his boy with cushy assignments. The only way to get accomplished at this job was to be up to your neck in it. As far as Lieutenant Bricks, Tommy could not have asked for a better Squad Commander, and he was profoundly grateful to be working for him. As for Sergeant Browne, and the illustrious Captain Pileggi… well, these two he sensed he could work around.

Yes, Tommy had decided to be happy with his new command. It had been about ten weeks now since he arrived, and he was beginning to feel he could make the 2-1 his home. His only concern at the moment was that Doreen would feel weird, or put off with Tommy, after the prior evening's heart to heart on the way back home from Kingston. He was, without doubt, taking a shine to Doreen and did not want her too ever be uncomfortable around him. Ever.

Tommy rolled out of bed and did his every-morning fifty push-ups, without the disturbance of little JoJo, who, due to Tommy's late night out, had bunked with Tommy's mother that evening. Tommy threw on some sweats, some sneakers, and his coat, stuffing his .38 Centennial revolver in his pocket and stepped out into the short hallway leading into the rest of the apartment.

"Good morning, Tommy," he heard from his mother, already up and in front of the television, then the scamper of JoJo's little feet, on the oak floors, rushing toward Tommy, excitedly wanting to say good morning in his own way.

"Morning, Ma, how you doing this morning?" he said as he picked little JoJo up in his arms and nuzzled his face into his, "I'm going to take this little guy out for a walk, Ma, would you like anything while I'm out?" Tommy asked.

"No, Tommy dear, I'm good, Tommy. You're up early, Tommy, you were home so late last night I thought you would sleep in a little?"

"No, Ma, I didn't shut the alarm, and I woke up feeling fine, so I'm gonna take JoJo out, and if the temperature is not too cold, perhaps head out for a run today, depends on how I feel."

***

So far, his RDO looked grand to Tommy. As far as his Jane Doe case, nothing more could be done until the autopsy, and therefore nothing haunted him work wise. The weather, brisk but pleasant, made for a soothing long walk around the neighborhood with little JoJo. He took himself out for a short run, followed by a breakfast of Belgian waffles, two eggs over easy, and some bacon, at the Mansion Diner on 86th Street.

After breakfast, he headed back to his mother's place, first stopping by Glaser's Bakery to pick up half a dozen black and white cookies and an apple turnover for his mother. Once home he showered and sat in his bed for a bit, with little JoJo curled up beside him, while he called his daughter Caitlin.

They chatted for a bit. He enjoyed checking in with her and seeing how her first semester, up at Siena College, had been now that it was coming to an end. By all accounts it could not have been going much better. Caitlin, who was in the pre-med program, had managed to earn a 3.6 GPA, while making several new friends and landing herself what seemed to be a rather polite new boyfriend, who Tommy met for a moment on Thanksgiving Eve.

After finishing up with Caitlin, Tommy put in his weekly call to his ex-wife Cookie. They had a short but pleasant conversation during which they both bragged to one another about how well they had done with their beautiful Caitlin. They talked about how proud they both were of her and discussed plans for Christmas.

Once he finished up his conversation with Cookie, he put in a call to his old partner, Henry Sanchez. Henry had retired on a three-quarters pay 'line of duty injury' pension, after a gunshot by a drug dealer took his left eye during a buy-and-bust operation a little over ten years earlier. Both Henry and Tommy had been a part of the operation while working in the Bronx Narcotics Division.

Tommy did his best to call, and to visit Henry on occasion at his home in Carmel, New York. There he lived with his wife, Damaris, their seventeen-year-old son, Anthony, and fifteen-year-old daughter, Alexis.

Unfortunately, when he called, Henry was asleep. Damaris never woke Henry while he slept. The injury had left him with a constant headache and any sleep, however brief, was welcomed. Nothing, outside of Henry's daily care, was important enough to bother him with when he was able to go down for a few hours. Henry's life, for most of the last ten plus years, now revolved around doctor visits, an occasional surgery, and his daily routine which consisted of four to five naps rather than a full night's sleep, different drugs to ease the headaches that would show up frequently and unannounced, and hours and hours of Netflix.

Damaris now only worked part-time as an RN at Putnam Hospital and devoted most of her time to her husband and her children. Tommy loved Damaris; she was everything anyone could ask for as far as a wife and mother to Henry and the kids. She was as strong as they came, never complained, and worked like a horse to keep everything in her world in line.

Over the years, Tommy had come to think of Damaris as family, and although it was a wholly different relationship than the one he had with Henry, it was no doubt as solid. Together they shared a friendship of their own, built around a man they both loved more than themselves.

Tommy and Damaris spoke for almost an hour that afternoon, discussing everything and nothing at the same time. They wished one another a "Merry Christmas" with the old, "In case I don't see you" attached and followed with an "I love you, Tommy" and an "And I you, Damaris" before they each hung up.

***

By the time Tommy and Damaris were done talking, it was well after two in the afternoon, so Tommy put on some jeans, a long sleeved green and gray Guinness rugby shirt, and his Adidas Superstars. He tucked his .38 Smith and Wesson Centennial into his waist and picked up little JoJo off the end of his bed. He gave him a kiss on the head and a quick snuggle and dropped him off on his mother's lap in the living room, kissing her on the head as well, before grabbing his coat.

"I'm heading out for a few hours, Ma. Not sure when I'll be home so don't worry about me for dinner or nothing, okay?"

"Okay, Tommy, have a lovely day, Tommy. Be careful, love you, Tommy."

"Love you too, Ma."

Tommy made his way down the steps and out onto the front stoop of the building. He stopped and scanned the block from left to right, and left again, as was his habit, and stepped onto the sidewalk, making his way to his favorite haunt - Bailey's Corner Pub, on East 85th Street and York Avenue.

It was a bonny, brisk, four block walk to the pub, and Tommy arrived at about 3:35 PM. He found the place to be fairly quiet, as he liked it, and his favorite stool near the front, up against the wall under the "Failte" (Welcome) sign sat empty and available. He claimed it and hung his jacket on the chair's back and sat down. Molly, a long-time bartender at Bailey's, looked over from where she chatted with a customer at the far end of the bar and smiled at him.

"Hey, Tommy! How you doing? The usual?"

"Yes please, Molly," Tommy responded.

As Tommy sat on the stool, Molly placed a bottle of Budweiser on a coaster in front of him, along with an empty rocks glass in which she poured a rather heavy double shot of Jameson's Irish whiskey.

"Whoa slow down, kid. I appreciate your heavy-handed pour but I wanna spend a few hours with you today, and if you start me off like that it won't be long till I'm done for the day."

"Ahh, come on, Tommy, you ain't no lightweight, I watched you put away at least a dozen of these in a night."

"I like to pace myself, Molly; I'm a professional," Tommy said with a cocky smile, "You heard of the tortoise and the hare? Well, you're looking at the tortoise. I like it slow and easy, that way I can go all day."

Molly looked him in the eye and with a sly smile and a lowered, seductive voice replied, "Slow and easy…so you can last all day, huh? I like the sound of that, Tommy." She left him with a wink as she headed back down the bar to back up some of the other customers.

Tommy took his first sip of beer for the day, ice cold, exactly the way he liked it, and then took a small sip of whiskey and another of beer. He read through the Daily News, as well as The New York Post, page by page and watched Molly walk up and down the bar, interacting with the customers who ebbed and flowed throughout the afternoon.

Molly was an astonishingly cute young woman of twenty-four. A lifelong neighborhood girl, she grew up with her parents and a younger sister a few blocks away, on 83rd Street between 2nd and 3rd Avenues. She had graduated from Saint Jean's High School and did a year of college at CUNY (City University of New York), where she decided she had no interest in college as a whole. So she took a gap year to decide what she wanted to do with herself. She was on her fifth gap year by this point.

Molly was, however, an outstanding bartender. Fast and attentive, she enjoyed her work and her clientele. She was an enthusiastic storyteller and an excellent listener, and man was she easy on the eyes.

Molly stood about five foot, four inches. Her hair was fine and straight, and it was a light red, almost a strawberry blonde. She had huge green eyes, and a few freckles that bounced across her nose and cheeks. She had an awesome, honest laugh and an infectious smile that lit up her face. On this day, she wore her usual attire of tight jeans, sneakers, and a tight baby doll style t-shirt that was just short enough to occasionally rise up to give a glimpse of belly button if she took a deep breath or were to reach for something. Patrons also received a delightful glimpse of her thin, tight waist and the top of her panties whenever she bent over to retrieve a bottle from one of the coolers.

Bottom line, Molly understood how to work the bar and her customers. She was always cute and sexy enough to be alluring to the men, but never appeared overtly sexual enough to annoy or piss off her female clientele. She was easy to talk to, fun, kind and understanding.

Tommy, of course, was not immune to Molly's charms, however, he had no interest in her. She was too young for him for one. He preferred women who were closer to his own age; mature, sensible, and seasoned women. There was also the torch he still carried for his ex-wife, Cookie. Although he had been with a few women over the years that he had had genuine relationships with, Cookie was still his ideal. A sucker for her in every way, he held her above all others, even after being apart for ten years. Tommy had other relationships yes, some he even considered to be girlfriends, and treated as such, but he never could shake the desire to reconcile with Cookie. Even if he himself recognized it as only a fantasy, it was a fantasy he could not shake.

Something Tommy never realized about this torch that he carried for Cookie, the one that made him so indifferent to women, was that it made him exceptionally attractive to many women at the same time. There was an accidental dynamic to Tommy's attitude; he did not care about attracting women, yet he always dressed nicely and was well groomed. He could carry on an authentic and meaningful conversation with any woman, and even be cute and flirty, but never did he hit on women, nor was he in any way sexually aggressive, because his heart still belonged to Cookie.

He certainly liked women and found himself attracted to them as much as any other man, but in the end, he did not care. And this indifferent attitude, combined with his overt confidence and the fact that he was a handsome man made him irresistible to many women. For them, Tommy was simply a man you did not meet every day.

And our Molly was one of these women. She had had her eye on Tommy for over two years now, ever since she first laid eyes on him, sitting right where he was sitting on this day. She had always had a thing for Tommy, and she liked absolutely everything she had learned about him. He was a rough and tumble neighborhood guy who made good for himself, and now that he lived in the neighborhood again, and was in the bar two to four times a week, she was able to learn more about the man. Hell, she could even read about him in the papers. Both the recent Sister Margaret murder, and the Thanksgiving Day rescue of that little Hayden Jon Marshall boy and all those other children, were big news, even in a city as huge as New York. And here he sat, drinking at the end of her bar, a simple, soft-spoken man who wanted nothing more than to be left alone with his beer, his whiskey, and a newspaper.

Molly thought of him as a true hero, although Tommy would certainly argue that point. He, as most active cops in the world do, hated the word hero. Whenever the word came up, he always had the same line: "A hero ain't nothing but a sandwich." Another favorite line of Tommy's concerning heroism was "Today's hero is tomorrow's slob" and he did not just say those words, he believed them.

Police work was his vocation, a job he thought he was destined to do. And he fully believed there was still honor in doing it well and to the best of his ability, simply because it needed to be done. He did not differentiate a great chef creating a fabulous meal, or a carpenter building a beautiful home, from a cop on the beat doing the right thing for a victim, or a detective chasing down and catching the worst of the worst. No, a cop was not a hero. If he was worth his salt, he did his job well, as the chef or the carpenter did. And to Tommy it was that simple.

***

At about seven PM, Tommy was well into his seventh or eighth beer and his fourth whiskey. He had finished both papers, played a few songs on the jukebox, and joined in on a couple of conversations with a couple of the regulars when Molly approached with another bottle of Budweiser and a refill of Jameson.

"No more whiskey, Molly," Tommy said.

"Don't worry about it, Tommy, this one's on me." Molly paused a moment, "Listen, Tommy, can I, can I ask you a favor?"

"Sure, kid, what can I do for you?"

"Well, I'm done here in less than an hour when Jack comes in, and I wondered if you're still here, if you could walk me home? I only live not even two blocks away, but I'm a little nervous…"

"Nervous? For what, Molly?" Tommy asked, genuinely concerned and curious what she was getting at.

"I got a stalker, I think. There's a little creepy guy who I keep seeing when I come back and forth from here. The other day he was sitting on my stoop, so I turned around and walked back up the block."

"What? How many times has he come around? Do you have any information about him?"

"No, nothing. He's just around the neighborhood… young white guy, thin, kinda weird looking guy."

"Has he ever spoken to you?"

"No, nothing. I just keep seeing him is all. If he had ever bothered me, I might have called the cops, but no, he just keeps popping up. And I thought, I thought maybe if you don't mind you could walk me the two blocks… if you don't mind?"

"No, no, of course I don't mind, I'll be happy to walk you home, Molly. And if you spot this guy you point him out to me, okay? And your friend and I will have a little talk."

Molly smiled. Her heart began to beat fast with excitement and her face blushed a bit at the thought of Tommy walking her home.

About another forty minutes passed when Jack Norris, Molly's replacement, walked in and, seeing Tommy from behind, leaned over past another customer and gave Tommy a strong pat on the back.

"Hey, Tommy, how you doing pal?"

"Never better, Jackie-Boy, how you making out pal?" Tommy said as he twisted in his bar stool to look at Jack.

"Living the dream, Tom, living the dream."

Jack was one of Tommy's favorite bartenders. He was a true professional, a career barman, and sharp as a tack. He grew up working in pubs all over New York City and had garnered a worldly education one can only receive with years spent behind the bar. Jack's father was a barman before him as well. Jack appreciated his job, and he did it well, and in return he knew a dependable customer and a decent man when he saw one and had nothing but admiration and respect for Tommy in return.

Tommy watched Jack as he made his way through the bar to the other side, where the opening to behind the bar was. He smiled at the patrons and stopped for a brief hug with a dark-haired woman of about forty, sitting with her friends. He shook hands with one or two more patrons as he made his way through the growing crowd. Jack greeted Molly, giving her strawberry blond ponytail a light tug, as she went over the day's news before turning the bar over to him. Yes, Tommy thought, Jack was a decent and upstanding guy.

Tommy finished his beer, as Molly bent down to grab her jacket and purse from under the bar. As she said her goodbyes, he put his own coat on and waited for her by the door, nodding goodnight to Jack.

Chapter Eight

Tommy and Molly left Bailey's Corner and started to walk toward Molly's apartment located on 84th Street off First Avenue.

"Thanks again, Tommy," Molly began, "I can't thank you enough for this."

"Nonsense, Molly, it's nothing. It's my pleasure to make sure you get home safe, kid. Who do you live with?" Tommy inquired.

"No one. I have my own place."

"No kidding? Good for you, that's unusual these days, in this neighborhood, especially for someone your age."

"Don't I know it! I got lucky and took over my aunt's place. The apartment is a tiny one bedroom but it's super cute. The lease is still in her name and she's had it since before I was born, and with the rent stabilization I only pay $785 a month."

"Impressive! Good for you."

"Yeah, some of the neighbors are paying $3,000 for the same apartment I live in. Rents are out of control in this city."

"Damn straight they are."

Tommy and Molly reached her building, a five-story walk up sandwiched between two identical looking buildings. Tommy guessed that it was built sometime in the 1880s from the look of it. Molly stepped up onto the first step of the stoop and turned to face Tommy.

"Thank you so much, can I please ask, do you mind walking me inside?"

"Inside?"

"Yeah, I'm sure I'm safe now, I… well, I still feel a little nervous. Besides, I'd like to show you how cute my place is. You don't mind, do you?"

"No, not at all."

Tommy followed Molly up the steps and into the vestibule, where she unlocked the door. They climbed up one flight of stairs to the second floor, where she unlocked the three locks she had on the door. Her apartment was half of an old railroad apartment that had been renovated years earlier and turned into two small one-bedroom units.

They entered right into one decent-sized room: a combination eat-in kitchen and living room, about thirteen feet wide by thirty feet long. At the end of the room, a five-foot alcove abutted with a door that led into the bathroom, and another that led into the bedroom. Molly was right; it was an extremely cute little apartment.

The floors were well maintained, refinished original 130-year-old quarter sawn oak, and the kitchen looked like it had been redone within the last five to ten years. It had simple, Shaker style, oak cabinets, with a light gray granite countertop and back splash, up against exposed brick walls. Newer, stainless-steel appliances, and a white, porcelain cast-iron drop-in sink finished off the kitchen. Molly had a quaint, 1940s style porcelain dining room table in gray with red trim and matching red vinyl and chrome chairs.

The living room was a comfortable size and the main piece, a sturdy sectional, dark brown, L-shaped sofa, divided the living area from the dining area. The chrome and glass coffee table and end tables had photos of Molly's family on what appeared to be different vacations, to the beach or on a ski trip, and one of her and her sister at Harry Potter World at Disney, all framed in the same black frames. On the wall, two notably large Edward Hopper prints hung on the exposed brick over the sofa. One was "Early Sunday Morning" and the other, probably his most famous work, "Nighthawks."

Tommy was somewhat impressed. As a man who had been in literally thousands of apartments, all over the city, and saw how so many different people lived, he did not expect young Molly, a twenty-four-year-old barmaid to not only live alone in this big city, but also live so well. But then, she was a neighborhood girl, Yorkville was her turf, and she knew how to survive and take care of herself here.

"Thanks again. Well, this is my place. Cute, right?"

"Oh, the place is beautiful, seriously charming," Tommy acknowledged, trying not to sound too impressed, "I love the Hoppers on the brick with the black frames. Sharp, really sharp."

"Oh, you know him? Yeah, I love them too, and I think they look great on that wall. Do you want a beer or something? Can I offer you something to drink?"

"No, I don't think so. Thanks though kid, I need to be heading out," Tommy stated, almost in an uneasy manner.

"Nonsense, please. Let me grab you a beer to say thank you, only one. Take your coat off and sit down, will ya?" Molly stated in both a light and fun but rather demanding tone. She took two tall boy cans of Pabst Blue Ribbon out of her refrigerator and popped one open, handing it to Tommy as he stood, still in his coat, next to the dining room table with his back to the sofa.

"Give me a minute, I'll be right back." Molly left him standing in the living room as she went to the bathroom for a minute, and after that into her bedroom.

Tommy took a sip from his beer and bent over to look at the photos Molly had on the end table next to the sofa. Next thing he realized, Molly stood right beside him, now wearing nothing but a women's cut pinstriped New York Yankees baseball jersey. Only one button was closed about midway down her torso, so it hung on her perfect young body, showing nothing but giving a near glimpse of almost everything.

Tommy stood up straight, as if he were somehow caught doing something wrong, when in fact he had not done anything at all.

"Oh. Molly," was all he got out.

"Please take off your jacket and get comfortable," Molly requested, taking charge of the moment.

"Woah, listen, I… I…"

"You what? Don't you like what you see? Don't you like me? I like you. I like you a lot," she continued as she grabbed the lapels of Tommy's heavy leather coat with both hands and pulled herself up, kissing him hard on his mouth.

"No, no, Molly," Tommy began but as he did Molly pulled herself back up and again kissed him hard on the mouth. This time Tommy relaxed just enough so she was able to slip her tongue in between his lips. He tasted the toothpaste from her freshly brushed teeth.

As Molly lowered herself from her last kiss, she turned the lapels to Tommy's coat outward and pulled his coat down to his elbows. Here he was stuck, and Tommy again began to protest.

"Listen, Molly. You are a complete doll, but I think you're a little young for me."

"No, Tommy, you listen. I'm a grown woman. I'm going to be twenty-five next month. I can do what I want, with who I want. I'm old enough to know what I want, and I want you, Tommy. I want you, here and now. I want you inside of me… I have been watching you for over a year, and I've been wanting this, wanting -"

Before she could finish, Tommy kissed her back. Her words, the alcohol, the toothpaste in her mouth, it all took over. There was no resisting this beautiful young woman, and Tommy gave Molly a long passionate kiss, a much softer one than the ones she had laid on him. She grasped at the feeling it gave her and held on to it as it snaked down deep inside of her, from her head to her toes.

Tommy's entire body relaxed as he backed away from the kiss and exhaled. The beer and whiskey on his breath, after as passionate a kiss as Molly had ever received, added fuel to her already smoldering desire, and she pulled Tommy's jacket off him, the coat and the can of Pabst hitting the floor. She began to undo Tommy's belt and then unbuttoned his Levi's, as he kicked off each of his sneakers, holding onto one of the dining room chairs with his right hand to brace himself.

She took each of her hands and ran them down and around his backside, removing both his Levi's and underwear in almost a single move while she lowered herself onto her knees in front of him. She pulled each sock off him as the jeans left each leg. Her hands slowly ran up the backs of both his strong, muscular legs until they each held one of his ass cheeks, and she took his now full erection into her mouth.

Tommy stood almost paralyzed for a moment as her warm, wet mouth engulfed him. As she began to move her head up and down, with his eyes completely closed, he removed his rugby shirt and t-shirt, and stood naked in the dining room, somewhat in shock at how this day had turned out.

He reached behind himself and clasped both of her hands in his and brought them to his sides. He gently pulled her to her feet, and as she rose, she kissed his stomach, and then his chest, occasionally flicking her tongue out along his body. She moved back to his mouth where they kissed deeply and passionately again.

He took his hands and ran them over her shoulders, dropping the baseball jersey to the floor and revealing her flawless body.

She stepped back to show herself to Tommy, holding his right hand in her left and letting go with the other one. She stood motionless for a moment to allow him to take her in fully. She turned, still holding onto his one hand, and leaned over the brown sofa, and as she did, pulled him closer. He let go of her hand and placed each of his hands on her hips and slowly but deliberately entered her. Together they both exhaled a heavy breath. He was now precisely where she wanted him to be and doing exactly what she wanted him to do. But as the pace of his strokes began to quicken, Molly softly spoke out, "Slow down, Tommy, stop, stop," she stood, turned, and kissed him again.

"Let's take this into the bedroom. And remember. Remember you are the tortoise. So, I want it slow and easy… and I want you to last all night."

Tommy did not say another word as Molly led him by the hand into her bedroom, where they enjoyed one another, slow, easy, and all night.

Chapter Nine

Being that Kyle Trocolla was a popular musician and a public figure, Tommy had no problem tracking him down. He did not even need to run his name through the NYPD system, since his entire life was basically online.

Tommy, of course, did run him through the system regardless, just to make sure there was nothing in his past he should know, before contacting him and asking him for a meeting.

He found nothing dark or nefarious on the surface, nor buried deep in any criminal data banks anywhere across the country on Kyle Trocolla. In fact, the only thing not average or boring about Kyle Trocolla was that he was an accomplished, well-known, singer-songwriter and guitarist. For about fifteen years he was a member of the somewhat legendary hardcore punk rock band Two Fisted Law, out of Danbury, Connecticut, and now toured the country doing his solo acoustic folk/punk stuff, apparently with some critical acclaim.

Outside of that, Mr. Kyle Trocolla was a simple, average guy. When not touring the country screaming punk rock tunes into a microphone, Kyle's day job was as a social studies teacher at Danbury High School. He was, from all accounts on his social media pages, the biggest New England Patriots fan who ever lived, was one hundred-percent anti-drugs, but seemed to have a strange addiction to Philly cheese steaks. He was married to a woman he described as the love of his life and seemed to be somewhat obsessed with his cat.

Several phone numbers for Kyle came up on the printout Tommy ran, all with a 203 area code. The first number he tried was a wrong number; the person answered with a heavy Spanish accent and no knowledge of any Kyle Trocolla. The second number was out of service, but the third number was current, and the message stated, "This is Kyle, please leave a message." And so Tommy did.

"Hello, Mr. Trocolla, this is Detective Keane from the 21st Precinct in New York City. Your name has come up in an investigation we are conducting. Let me assure you, sir, you are in no way the subject of this investigation, or again in any way a suspect of any sort of wrongdoing. We are trying to identify a young woman and we believe you may know who she is. Please, sir, if you would give me a call back at this number, I'd like to come and ask you a couple questions, in the next day or two, at your convenience of course. Thank you much."

With that done, he opened the case folder that sat on top of the ever-growing number of case folders stacked on the corner of Doreen's desk. He sat for several hours, banging away at his current case load. He closed a case and arranged for an interview with the hopes of closing another one later in the day, when his cell phone went off. "Kyle Trocolla… alright," Tommy said softly to himself.

"Hello, Mr. Trocolla, how you doing today, sir?" Tommy answered the phone.

"I'm fine, sir. I'm sorry it took me so long to call you back, but I turn off my phone while at work, and didn't hear your message until just now."

"No, no don't worry about it, only a few hours have passed. In fact, let me thank you for getting back to me as quickly as you did."

"No problem. What — What can I do for you, Detective? It sounds like you are possibly looking for someone I know. A missing person?" Kyle said, sounding concerned.

"Yes, something like that. Listen, I would like to come and visit you tomorrow, if possible? Is it possible? Maybe we can meet somewhere outside of school. I don't mind meeting you at school, but I understand that can sometimes put people off, you know, having the police showing up and asking for them at their workplace, and I can only imagine the rumors that might fly around a high school if people realized I was asking you questions."

"Sure, of course. What time would you like to meet?"

"Anytime, Mr. Trocolla. You tell me, and I'll come visit you, at your convenience."

"Okay, well I have a break between 12:30 and 1:30, and I can also do something after 4:30… More like 4:45 or 5 PM, if that works better for you?"

"Okay perfect, would you like to meet in the parking lot? Or do you have a coffee shop or a diner nearby? I'll buy you a cup of coffee and take a few minutes of your time?"

"Uh – sure. There's Three Brothers diner on White Street, if you'd like. I'll meet you there at 5 PM. I can, or should be able to, make it by 5 PM tomorrow."

"Okay perfect, 5 PM at the Three Brothers Diner on White Street. I shouldn't take more than five to twenty minutes of your time, sir. Thank you very much."

"Oh no problem. I'm glad I can be of assistance, and I hope I can help you out. Have a pleasant night, Detective Keane."

"You too, Mr. Trocolla."

Tommy was happy. He sensed he was a step closer to hopefully finding out who this Jane Doe of his was. Also, now that he had set up this end of day interview in Danbury, he thought he may have landed himself another little 'get over' day out of the office. He figured he would sign in from his apartment in White Plains, then head on up to Danbury, a city he was quite familiar with, as it was the largest city near Brewster, NY, where he had lived, and where his wife Cookie and daughter, Caitlin, still lived.

'Hmm, maybe a little Mexican tomorrow at El Ranchero,' he thought, 'and I can bang out some Christmas shopping at the Danbury Mall while I'm waiting to interview Mr. Trocolla. Yep, tomorrow is looking like a pretty bright day to me,' he thought to himself.

Tommy hopped up from the desk and knocked on Sergeant Browne's door. No answer. He did an about-face and walked across the squad room and pushed the already ajar door to Lieutenant Bricks' office open, sticking his head in.

Lieutenant Bricks looked up from some paperwork he was working on. "Hey, Tommy, what can I do for you?" he asked.

"I booked an interview with a high school teacher in Danbury, Connecticut, in regard to my Jane Doe tomorrow afternoon. I'd like to sign in from home and go interview him, then sign out from up north as well, if it's alright, Lu? Save me the trip back and forth from White Plains."

"Of course, Tommy, whatever you need to do. Nothing in on that girl yet, huh?"

"No, sir, nothing yet."

"What a shame, I expected something from Missing Persons by now."

"Nope, not a thing yet."

"Okay, yeah, do whatever you need to."

"Thanks, Lu."

As Tommy sat down, back at Doreen's desk, Sergeant Browne's office door opened.

"Did you knock, Tom?" Sergeant Browne asked.

"Yes, I did. Wanted to ask about starting my tour from home tomorrow. I scheduled an interview in Danbury, Connecticut, and I wanted to start from home and possibly end it there also, depending on how long the trip takes."

"Well, I'm not sure, Tom. You did just go on a field trip up to Kingston over this woman, maybe you ask the Lu and check if -"

"Already did, Boss, and he said to do whatever I needed to do… But thanks," Tommy said, interrupting Sergeant Browne. As he looked back down at his paperwork, he thought to himself, 'I went straight to daddy this time, thanks mom.'

***

Tommy woke up in his apartment in White Plains, NY. He had been spending so much time at his mother's place in the City, he almost felt odd and out of place here in this apartment. Although he had lived in it for the last ten years, it had never seemed warm. He had some decent furniture set up in the apartment, and he kept the place neat and clean, but it had never been home to him.

Tommy may not have even noticed it himself, but since divorcing Cookie, and leaving their house in Brewster, he had never had a home. Internally, the only places he ever considered homes, outside of his childhood apartment on 88th Street, were the ones he shared with Cookie and Caitlin, first on East 81st Street in the City and then in Brewster. This place in White Plains was nothing more than a hotel room to Tommy. It may have been an altogether lovely two-bedroom apartment, but no, it was never a home.

Tommy made this day exactly what he wanted. He woke up and did his usual set of push-ups and later called into the precinct, when he knew someone would be arriving at the squad room. Charice answered the phone, and he had her sign him in.

He lounged around the apartment for a bit and made himself some oatmeal the way he liked it with walnuts, raisins, and a little too much brown sugar. Afterwards, he turned on the news, but getting bored with that, he decided to find some of Kyle Trocolla's solo work on his computer. He typed into YouTube and found some songs and videos from the previous year's album *The Stranger*. The first video to pop up was for a song called "Three Chords and the Truth."

Tommy liked it. He liked it a lot, and he turned up the sound and listened to a couple more songs of Kyle's before heading to the bathroom for a shower. As he got dressed for the day, he kept his outfit simple and casual with a pair of jeans, a plain black crew neck sweater, and his Adidas Superstars, while he cranked some more of Kyle's solo work via his computer.

"This kid can write," he said aloud to himself, and the four walls that surrounded him, in his blacked-out bedroom.

***

Tommy made it to the Danbury Mall a little before 11:00 AM and by noon he had finished. He had purchased some white Adidas Superstars with mint green stripes for his daughter, Caitlin, who made a comment recently that Tommy's boring old Superstars were now making a comeback with the cool kids at college.

He also picked her up a nylon flight jacket, another relic that old man Tommy wore for decades, which was suddenly cool again with Caitlin's friends on campus. In Macy's he bought a fetching, somewhat expensive, long black sweater with a belt for Cookie, some Yankee Candles in various scents, and a gift certificate for a manicure and pedicure at one of the mall's spas.

Tommy, always a fan of the holidays, enjoyed shopping for his girls. As he passed the line of children with their parents waiting to meet Santa and take a photo, he was first saddened that those days of waiting on that exact same line, with Caitlin and Cookie, were now past, then the thought of his Jane Doe hit him rather hard. This poor girl would never experience another Christmas with her family, and her family would never share one with her, nor would she ever stand in line with her children to get a picture with Santa. No, there would be no more holidays for his Jenny Doe. Regardless of who she was or how she came to pass, that was it, it was all over for her. Tommy paused and took a seriously deep breath. He could feel some emotions rising and knew from experience that a deep breath or two could usually keep a tear from his eyes.

"Who are you? And what happened to you?" he said out loud in a soft voice to himself. He turned and headed for the exit, his mood changed, and his shopping done.

Tommy checked the time as he left the mall and then raced over to El Ranchero Mexican Restaurant on White Street, about a mile east of the diner he planned to meet Kyle Trocolla at, later in the day.

El Ranchero was one of Tommy's favorite Mexican restaurants. He would eat there around once a month or so with Cookie and Caitlin when they all lived in Brewster. They would come to Danbury on Tommy's RDO's to catch a movie at the Loews Cinemax and sometimes hit the mall. They would often go to a little record shop near the mall called Volt, as well as a little punky shop called Trash American Style, which were right off Route 6, as they made their way back to Brewster. Both Volt and Trash American Style had been gone for over ten years now though, no doubt unable to keep up with the rising rents and changing times.

'Fuckin shame,' Tommy thought, thinking of those places and the trips to Danbury he and the girls used to make, 'Nothing cool ever lasts. I guess if it did, it wouldn't be cool.'

Tommy found a spot and parked out front of El Ranchero, next to a small beer distributor located right next door. El Ranchero was a true Mexican, Mexican restaurant, with about 90% of their clientele Mexican and many of the waitresses speaking little to no English.

He entered the place and as was often the case, he was the only American in the restaurant at the time. He sat in the side room, in the corner, next to a window. A cute waitress of about twenty years of age approached with a tray of chips and salsa and a menu.

Tommy spoke to her in his weak but restaurant-ready Spanish, "Sin menu gracias. Por favor, puedo tener una enchiladas de banderas y tres tacos carnitas por favor" (No menu, thank you. Please may I have an order of flag enchiladas, and three tacos carnitas please?)

The waitress smiled at Tommy and replied "Si" as she wrote the order down, "Y para beber?" (And to drink?)

He paused for a moment until he realized what she was asking, "Pepsi, por favor."

She smiled and Tommy replied with, "Gracias, mi amore."

The food came quickly, and it was everything he had been thinking about since he made the phone call to Kyle the day before. For many a detective, their days revolved around their meal; knowing where they would be working, deciding on what to eat and where, and finally sitting down to enjoy a tasty meal. This was an important part of dealing with the everyday stresses and monotony of police work. Although crime never ended, and there seemed to be something different to deal with and attend to each day, it could become a huge monotonous grind at times. A satisfying meal was always an enjoyable way to break up a tour, with a little time to try and enjoy oneself, even if only for a moment.

Once Tommy finished his meal, he hopped back in the car and headed over to the Loews Cineplex on Eagle Road, one of those giant movie houses that had sixteen theaters in it. He had no idea what was playing but figured there would be something he could watch to kill a couple hours before he met with Kyle at the diner.

He looked up at the choices on the electronic wall display above the registers, and he decided on a 2:15 showing of *Manchester*

By The Sea. He had heard terrific things about the film and had liked Casey Affleck, in the one or two films he had seen him in.

Tommy had never seen a movie alone until he became a cop, and even then, not until he got into S.N.E.U. (The Street Narcotics Enforcement Unit) was a precinct level narcotics team that some of the busiest precincts required. The 5-3 had two S.N.E.U. teams. Members of S.N.E.U., much like officers and detectives assigned to the narcotics boroughs, spent hours and hours a week at court on 161st Street in the Bronx. The courthouse was located directly across the street from a small shopping plaza, which housed the Concourse Plaza Multiplex Cinemas, and it was there where many a narcotics officer would spend time; watching movies, waiting for their time to sit before the grand jury, or just killing a day. Because once you were signed into the court system you were basically lost to time, and on your own until the end of tour.

So, Tommy, during his time in S.N.E.U. and O.C.C.B. (The Organized Crime Control Borough), saw everything playing. Sometimes so many films that Cookie would not only be angry with him for seeing movies she wanted to watch without her, but also often grew suspicious that he must be seeing these films with another woman, or women, he had on the side. How else could someone go to a movie in the theater four, five, or even eight times in a month? But no, it was just the nature of how the court system and the police department worked. Was he supposed to be going to the movies while on duty? Absolutely not. But what else were you supposed to do while waiting hour after hour to meet with an ADA, Judge, or the grand jury, with a multiplex directly across the street?

Tommy loved *Manchester By The Sea*, a heartbreaking tale of a broken man rekindling a relationship with what is left of his family after his brother dies and he finds out he is now his nephew's guardian.

Tommy could identify with the lead character's sense of loneliness and his self-isolation. Tommy thought the writing, the dialogue, and everyone who acted in the film gave a spot-on performance. Although the depressing theme of the film did bring him down slightly, from his mostly happy day of getting over on the Police Department and the City, he did very much like everything about the movie.

With an hour left to kill before his meeting, Tommy walked across the parking lot to Best Buy and wasted time looking at TVs, appliances, and a bunch of other stuff he did not need and had no intention of buying, until he needed to get back in the car and head over to Three Brother's Diner on White Street.

***

Tommy arrived about fifteen minutes early and texted Kyle to reconfirm their time. Kyle immediately texted back, saying he was on his way.

Tommy took a booth next to a window and sat facing the entrance. He knew what Kyle looked like from his online photos, but was aware Kyle would not be able to recognize him, so he wanted to be able to catch him as he entered. Tommy ordered an unsweetened iced tea and waited no more than three or four minutes before he saw Kyle get out of a black pickup truck he had parked outside of the diner. Kyle was a nice-looking man. He stood about five foot eight and had his hair cut short in the classic, traditional style that had made a comeback in recent years: short and tapered and parted on the side. He wore glasses and had a full and neatly trimmed beard, and although it was cold, he stepped out of his truck in only a cotton plaid short-sleeved shirt, blue jeans, and black Converse sneakers.

Kyle was neat and clean, but a little too trendy and hip for a high school social studies teacher Tommy thought. But he was, after all, also a nationally touring musician.

As Kyle stepped into the diner, Tommy put up his hand and said loudly without yelling, "Mr. Trocolla, here."

Kyle nodded and smiled and walked towards the booth where Tommy sat, and Tommy promptly stood up and extended his hand to say hello.

"Hello, Mr. Trocolla, thank you so much for coming to meet me," Tommy said.

"My pleasure, Officer… Detective? How should I address you, sir?" Kyle asked, comfortable but still slightly put off by this very unusual meeting.

"Just call me Tommy. Tommy is fine."

"Okay, Tommy, nice to meet you."

The waitress interrupted their meeting and asked Kyle what he would like, and he asked for a coffee.

"So, Tommy…" he began to ask, not knowing what to expect, "Why did you want to talk to me? What can I help you with?"

"Well, Mr. Trocolla -"

"Please call me Kyle."

"Very good, Kyle. We have a Jane Doe, a woman, a dead woman, who we can't identify. She's a young woman who we were able to trace back to a small rock and roll joint in Kingston called…"

"Snapper Magee's," they both said in unison.

"Yes, Snapper Magee's," Tommy continued. "Well, word is you partied with this woman a few weeks ago, and the staff thinks you may have known her personally. And I'm hoping you can tell us her name."

As he continued, Tommy unrolled the head shot he had, pausing a second to allow the waitress to set Kyle's coffee in front of him.

"What can I get you gentlemen to eat? You decided yet?"

"Nothing for me," Kyle answered.

"Same. Nothing, thank you," Tommy also responded.

The waitress looked rather unhappy, now knowing this table would be a small check, and left them alone.

Tommy revealed the photo.

Kyle paused. A look of sadness came over his face, he breathed heavily then began to speak, "That's Jenny Black - May I?" He reached for the photo and took it from Tommy.

"Wow… Wow, this is so sad. She was a delightful kid, what happened to her?"

"We don't know. She was… her body was found frozen in Carl Schurz Park a few days ago. Cause of death is still unknown. Until right now we had no idea who she was. So, thank you for giving me a name. What can you tell me about her?"

"Wow…" Kyle paused, again taking in the photo and what Tommy had shared with him, as he stroked his beard, "Not a lot. I've known her for a few years but only from seeing her at shows."

"Well, what can you tell me? Does she have friends that you are aware of, a boyfriend, or any family we can contact?"

"I've seen her with friends on occasion. I don't think I've ever seen her with an obvious actual boyfriend. She makes a lot of shows and has put on a few shows down in the City, but that's the only place I've ever seen her… at shows. She seemed smart; I know she's educated. Her father I think makes television commercials, and they live in the City, I believe… She's joined us for drinks during and after shows three or four times, and she was a naturally sweet girl, but to be honest I don't know much more about her. I'm sorry, I wish I had more for you."

"No, no, don't apologize, you're helping me out tremendously," Tommy said, as he took notes in his notebook. "You say she lives in the City, do you know where exactly?"

"No idea, but I'm pretty sure it's in Manhattan. She never said Brooklyn, just said the City."

"No boyfriend, but you have seen her with men. Or no?"

"Yes, I have seen her with a couple of guys. Once with a guy who I believe was a college friend - tall, light skinned black kid, and once with a punk kid who I don't know but also recognize from shows. She would also often show up at shows alone, dance, have a drink, then split… She was a cool girl as far as I could tell."

"She drink a lot?" Tommy asked.

"No, not a lot. I've seen her drunk maybe, but never shit faced."

"Drugs?"

"Not that I have ever seen. She didn't seem to be into any drugs… just didn't have that vibe to her, but man, you never know." Kyle said and shrugged his shoulders.

"Always have money? In other words, was she one to try and get free drinks off guys at shows, or ask to get in free, or anything?"

"No. I mean yes; she always had her own money. She would usually buy the whole band a round, and she would always buy some merch, a CD or t-shirt or something. So yes, she always had some money, and she wasn't cheap. I can't tell you what she did for work, but I do think her father had money. Like I said I think he made TV commercials. What, what do you think happened to her? You have to have some idea?"

"No, I really don't, and we won't for a few more days. There were no outward signs of violence or foul play, and she was frozen solid, so much so that it will take an entire week for her to thaw out before the Medical Examiner's Office can perform an autopsy."

"My God, that's so sad," Kyle uttered, shaking his head slowly, "From everything I know, Jenny was a well-grounded kid. No drugs, no shady friends. As I told you, she was altogether a sweet girl; she was fun and funny, and loved to come out to shows."

"Okay, Kyle, thank you so very, very much. I know you don't think you gave me much, but you have helped me out tremendously today, thank you."

"I hope you can find out what happened to Jenny."

"We will – Let me also tell you while I have you here, I thoroughly enjoy your new stuff."

"My new stuff? You mean my music? Really? Thank you!" Kyle beamed, surprised that Tommy would have a clue who he was.

"Yeah, I liked Two Fisted Law also. I saw you guys a couple of times a few years ago, but I don't know, I think the new stuff is, well, I guess more mature, maybe a little more heartfelt?"

"Wow, I wasn't expecting that, but thank you. Well, obviously I write from a different perspective now at this age, but you know, those were those days, and these are these. I think all my songs are a reflection of what I'm doing, and was about, at the time."

"Oh yeah, I can definitely see that, and it comes through. I'm happy I was able to watch you on stage years ago, and now I look forward to coming to see you sometime in the future."

"Thank you. Thank you, Detective, that means the world to me." Kyle said as he reached into his pocket to pay for his coffee.

"Put your money away Kyle, I got this."

"You sure?"

"Yes sir, more than sure."

"Thank you."

The two men stood up and shook hands. Kyle headed back to his pickup and Tommy paid the bill for their coffee and tea, dropped a five-dollar bill on the table for the waitress, and headed home.

***

Once back at his apartment, Tommy started up his computer and began to search for Jenny Black. He found dozens on every different social media platform; there were singers, actresses, authors, housewives, teenagers, the elderly… but out of the dozens and dozens of Jenny Blacks, none of them were the Jenny Black he was looking for.

His "get over day" turned into a long, uncomfortable, mind-bending night of staring at a computer screen with absolutely zero luck. Tommy decided that he would use the Police Department's system at the precinct to maybe find his Miss Black for him. He resigned himself to the frustrations of still not being able to get a handle on this young lady and decided to turn in for the night and start fresh at the precinct in the morning.

Chapter Ten

Tommy woke, again to "Talk Of The Town" by The Pretenders, which was one of his favorite songs from one of his favorite bands. But on this morning, as he laid in the complete darkness of the bedroom of his White Plains apartment - which he kept the same as his bedroom on 88th Street, with all the windows covered with black trash bags (to ensure zero light enters the room when he is sleeping,) Tommy thought it was time for a new morning wake up tune. He searched out, and programmed in, the song "Strong Bow" by American Pinup, which was on his mind ever since he and Doreen had had their trip to Kingston a few nights prior.

Once he set the song for his alarm, he rolled onto the floor and did his fifty morning push-ups, got showered, shaved, and dressed, before he fixed himself a bowl of Raisin Bran Crunch cereal. He headed out to work, opting to drive in today rather than take the train.

Tommy arrived at the squad room about twenty minutes late, which was something that almost never happened, but something he also never thought of. He simply was always early, if not definitely on time.

His more-than-punctual nature however was something that even in the few weeks he had been at the 2-1, had been noted by all in the squad and therefore his lateness was commented on by everyone, starting with the squads PAA Charice Tate.

"Detective Keane? Late? Is that even possible or is my watch and the clock on the wall off by a few minutes?" She grinned up at him.

"Good morning, Charice." Tommy smiled slyly.

"Tommy! Where have you been, young man? I was getting worried when I didn't find you at my desk when I arrived this morning." Doreen said, in a rather maternal manner, with her arms crossed and then waving her finger at him sarcastically as Tommy entered the room.

"Yeah, Doreen was about to file a Missing Person's Report on you. What's your story? I think this is the first time since you've joined us that you weren't the first signed in for tour," Jimmy Colletti chimed in.

"All right, all right, I'm here. Traffic was a bitch this morning and the parking no better," Tommy replied as he picked up the new case folders Charice had left for him on Doreen's desk and dropped them onto Detective Keogh's desk from A Squad.

As he sat down, he made eye contact with the ever quiet and stoic Mark Stein. Stein looked back down at his case folder and flatly stated, "Good morning, Tommy, so glad you decided to join us today."

And with the morning's greetings and wise cracks over, the squad got to work on their cases.

"How was your day yesterday? Did you find out anything to help identify our, your, Jane Doe?" Jimmy asked as he leaned back in his chair and stretched.

"Actually, I had an excellent day, and yes, I had a positive ID made, which was grand. But from there on I spent hours on the computer at home desperately trying to find something on this woman. I couldn't find anything that matched no matter how I ran it. I'm hoping our system will come up with something I can sink my teeth into. I just want to find out who this woman is before the autopsy."

"Ahh, too bad, that sucks," Jimmy replied.

"Need a little help with the computer, Tommy?" Doreen asked, "I'll be happy to run her if it helps you at all."

"Sure, if you don't mind, that would be wonderful, Doreen, thank you. Her name is Jenny Black, common name as it turns out. I got dozens of hits but nothing that matched, and I tried every variation, Jennifer, Jen, etcetera, but nothing that came up looking like our girl. We can also run her father - going to assume his name is Black also, and all I learned is that he makes television commercials. So hopefully that may lead us somewhere."

"Well, let me plug both their names into the system and try to work some magic for you."

"Thanks, Dee, I appreciate it."

As the computer went to work, Tommy flipped through several of his other cases and thanked the gods that there was nothing currently as pressing as his Jenny Black case at the moment. He was getting attached to this one and wanted to find out who she was to notify any family she may have as soon as possible.

While going over his current workload, he made a point to run a line through "Jane Doe," which he had written on the exterior of the brown cardboard folder, and wrote Jenny Black over it with a Sharpie marker.

After about an hour, Doreen pulled up a chair next to Tommy, who still was sitting at Keogh's desk.

"There are a ton of Jenny Blacks here, Tommy, but looking at them I only find three maybes on all of these pages of shit. And I couldn't find anything on a known Mr. Black who works in TV advertising. Here, I highlighted them for you, and even still I have to say, I'm not feeling them. But here you go, this is all the system had to offer." Doreen placed the list of names in front of Tommy on the desk.

"Thank you so much, Doreen. I certainly appreciate the help," Tommy replied, and he spent the next three hours tracking down the three women on his list of possibles.

The first was alive and well; she was a thirty-year-old mother of three living in Brooklyn.

The second was also alive and well. She was twenty-four years of age, a perfect age match, but was of mixed race and living on 13th Street in Manhattan with her mother and younger sister.

The third was also of the perfect age at twenty-three, but she was also alive and well and had moved from New York to Florida about two years prior.

So there Tommy sat; with nothing, nothing, and nothing, and half of his day shot already. He lowered his head a bit and ran his hands over his hair.

'Think Tommy think,' he said to himself, 'What will be the key here? So far music has been your thread, right? Her clothing and personal affects led you to the pub in Kingston, the pub led you to Kyle Trocolla, and Kyle gave you a name, a name and what else? Nothing but a bit of a back story, part of which was that she does shows on her own… which means she must have venue contacts and promoter contacts. This punk scene is a small scene Tommy. Liz may know her. I bet Liz can give me some information.'

Tommy pulled out his cell and started looking through his phone book. He had an old friend, a Brooklyn woman who had been putting on shows all over the city for at least twenty years.

He typed in "Liz" and nothing pop up.

'Hmm, what is her last name? I don't remember. Did I ever know?' he thought to himself.

He typed "Elizabeth." Again, nothing popped up.

'She called herself Red, Liz Red,' so he typed that in and again, nothing.

Tommy was getting frustrated, and then he remembered doing this in the past, "Lyz, stupid," he said out loud and gained the attention of the entire squad room.

Tommy typed in "Lyz" and still nothing.

Then he typed one word into his phone in all caps: "CANDYAPPLELYZ." Yup, that was it. Candy Apple Lyz, of CANDY APPLE RED PRODUCTIONS, the name of her promotion company, and again he thought, 'A reason to enter things into the phonebook properly, dummy.' Tommy hit the call button and the phone rang, and a message answered, "Hello, this is Lyz, please leave a message and I might get back to you."

"Hey Lyz, how you doing? This is Tommy, Tommy Keane. It's been forever since I've seen you. I'm still on the job, and I have a case with a young woman who I am hoping you may possibly be able to help me out with. Please, if you can, give me a call as soon as possible. Thanks, Lyz, and hope all is awesome in your world, all the best, Tommy."

Tommy went back to work on his case load and not ten minutes later, his phone went off. He looked at the caller ID and grinned.

"Lyz, you beautiful creature, how the hell are you, kid? Thank you so much for calling me back so soon."

"Listen, I have a young woman. A Jane Doe, that we're trying to identify, and it may be possible you have crossed paths with her. Do you think I can come visit you today sometime? … Anytime that is easy for you, and anywhere you want to meet is cool with me… Yeah? 8PM? The Grand Victory in Brooklyn? … Cool, I'll be there… Okay, excellent. Yes, I'll definitely be there by eight… Looking forward to seeing you again."

Tommy had known Lyz Red for over twenty years. They were not necessarily tight friends but had a long-time relationship, going back to before Tommy was on the job, back to when he was still working in bars and clubs around the city. The bar world, even in a city as huge as New York, is a fairly small world when you work in it, especially when you add music to the mix, as few places do music. Once you shrink that list down to bars and clubs that do rock and roll, and punk rock, well now you are talking about just a handful of places city-wide. So it was not unusual for people to recognize one another, even if only by name and reputation from borough to borough.

Now Lyz, or Red, or Lyz Red, had a solid and much-respected reputation throughout the city as a serious and honest punk rock promoter. She had put on shows in probably every rock and roll venue in the city at some point in her career. Bands always liked her because she was always fair and decent to them, and venues always liked her because she put in the work to make sure shows would be well-attended and the venue would make money.

Some called her "The Queen of Punk," a moniker she did not particularly care for, but one that showed how much the punk scene in New York City loved and respected her.

***

Tommy drove onto the block, where Grand Victory was located, ten minutes to eight and was disappointed to find no available parking anywhere near the venue. Two beat up vans were being unloaded by a handful of rag-tag, punk rock band members taking up the street and sidewalk with their gear. He was able to finally squeeze into a spot three blocks away.

As he approached the entrance, he saw several punk rockers standing with their jackets and vests festooned with band patches and buttons, laughing and smoking cigarettes. This scene made him unhappy and a bit disappointed that he was there investigating a young woman's death rather than joining in on the joke and enjoying a show.

Lyz saw Tommy as he entered the Grand Victory. She smiled broadly at him from behind the podium that stood a few feet from the entrance. It had been years and a look of joy came over her face.

Lyz was wearing a pair of dark black jeans and a black tank top that had Refuse Resist printed on it, and a red and black unbuttoned flannel over the tank. Lyz was short and adorable. She had her red hair cut in a fashionable bob that was shaved over her left ear. Her makeup was completely done up but not over the top by any means. She leaned against the podium, as she sipped a cup of coffee, and waited for Tommy to make it through the door and past some more punk kids chatting inside the entryway.

"Hey, Tommy. How you doing?" She asked as he made his way up toward her.

"I'm doing pretty good, how you doing, kid?"

"I can't complain. And if I did, who would listen, right?" She said with a laugh as they embraced. She kissed him on the cheek.

"I'll always lend you an ear. You're a good kid and I always liked you."

"Well thanks, you're sweet. Welcome to the Grand Victory. Would you like something to drink? A beer or a soda? Maybe some water?"

"No, no thanks, I'm fine thanks."

"Okay, well, here you are. Let's grab a seat at the bar and you can ask me what you wanna ask me before it's gets to loud and busy in here?"

"This is fine right here; we shouldn't be but a minute. I realize you're at work and have stuff to do."

"No, we're cool, we have time. So, tell me, ask me. What is it you need me to tell you? You have a Jane Doe? A woman you can't identify, right? … You think I might recognize her?"

"Yes. We have a young dead woman, between the ages of twenty and twenty-five or twenty-six. We have nothing to go on with her; no ID, no fingerprints, no Missing Person's Report that matches her description, nothing. But she is a punk rock girl, and supposedly she puts on shows here in the city. So, I am hoping you two may have crossed paths and you possibly can tell me who she is."

Just as Tommy finished his sentence the band began their sound checks. The room filled with the noise of guitars and drums, as well as the banter between the sound man and the band "Check—Check one! One, Two Three Four Five! Check, Check!"

A cross look came over Lyz's face, as she looked over Tommy's shoulder, towards the stage. "C'mon, lets step outside where it's a bit quieter." Once outside and near the curb she began again. "Okay, so what do you have? A photo of a dead woman that you want to show me, is that it? See if I know her and can identify her for you?"

"Yes. Exactly."

"Is it bad?"

"No."

"Okay. Let me look at it." Lyz said and braced herself for the photograph.

Tommy pulled the 8 ½ x 11 headshot he had of Jenny out of his inside coat pocket unrolled it and handed it to Lyz.

"Oh no, oh fuck. That's Jenny Black," Lyz said immediately and succinctly in a high pitched and surprised voice, "Oh God, what happened to her?"

"We're not sure yet. She was found frozen in a park last week, and we still haven't been able to do an autopsy."

"Aww, no, this poor thing. She's so, so, young, and she is… was, seriously such a sweet girl."

"So, you know her? That's great but now here's the problem I'm having. A fella named Kyle Trocolla ID'd her as Jenny Black as well, but we can't find a Jenny Black that matches her anywhere in our systems, which is odd. Do you know anything about Jenny Black that can help me out here, Lyz?"

"Sure, I do. Jenny Black isn't her real name. Everyone calls her Jenny Black because she only ever wears black clothing, no one has ever seen her in anything but all black. She's kind of like a female Johnny Cash. And you saw Kyle? How is he doing? He's the best. I haven't seen him in a while."

"Kyle appears to be doing well and seems like a genuinely decent guy. So fuck me, I've been wasting my time and searching the wrong name this whole time then. Okay, well that explains that. Can you give us her real name? Do you have any way of getting in contact with her?"

"Sorry, no… I barely knew this girl. She's a bit younger than me as you know, and we had different circles. I can tell you everyone liked her a lot, and she was a super sweet person. Other than that, I don't have anything. I'll tell you what though, if you can find Nicky the Skin, he will definitely know her; I know he knows her or knew her fairly well. They did a couple of fest type shows together at the Knitting Factory. He will definitely know her."

"Nicky the Skin? Awesome, thanks for the lead. Do you have any contact info for this Nicky fella?"

"Actually no, Tommy, I'm sorry. Nicky the Skin is kind of a shady guy. I would imagine you have some kind of police file on him. He's supposed to have underworld ties. I think his father was in the mafia and I'm kinda sure, at least rumor has it, he is also mixed up with organized crime. To be honest, I am not aware if any of that is true, but I avoid that shit like the plague. So no, I absolutely don't associate with him, I am just aware of who he is, and have always avoided him anytime I have seen him in the flesh."

"Okay. Anything more than Nicky the Skin? A last name?"

Lyz shook her head, "No, sorry."

"Okay, well thank you. I so appreciate you giving me a little bit of your time today, and I'm so glad you still have the same number."

"I don't think I helped you much, Tommy, but it was really good to see you again. Please come inside, hang out and catch the show. I'll buy you a beer and we can BS a little."

"I can't right now kid, but I'll definitely come see you sometime, and you did help me out today in a big way, you pointed me in the right direction, and that's what I needed. Thanks."

"Anytime, Tommy," she smiled warmly at him.

Tommy and Lyz reminisced for a minute or two more about old venues and bands. They embraced one more time after being interrupted by a young woman in a short leopard-print skirt with a blue mohawk, who shouted out the door of the Grand Victory, "Hey, Lyz! They need you inside for a minute!" Lyz wished him good luck as she headed back in, and Tommy left and headed back to the 2-1.

***

Back at the precinct, Tommy again searched the computer for this new link in the Jenny Black chain, "Nicky the Skin," and sadly, just as with Jenny Black, came up with nothing, no matching nick names, or possible connections to anyone.

'Was this young woman mixed up in organized crime?' Tommy thought, 'What kind of twist is this?'

So, as had strangely become custom over the last ten or twelve weeks, he picked up his cell phone and called Reif's Pub on 92nd Street.

"Hello, Reif's," a woman's voice answered.

"Hey, how you doing? My name is Tommy and I'm looking for Terry Callahan."

"No one here by that name, honey," she answered.

"Please love, this is important. Just ask Terry to call Tommy Keane. He knows me and will call me. Thank you."

"Sorry, I don't know any Terry."

And then the phone hung up.

About twenty-five minutes later Tommy's phone went off to a number he did not recognize.

"Keane," he answered.

"Hello sweetheart," said the smooth, low voice on the other end of the line, "It's been a few weeks… I'm going to guess this isn't a social call and you're not asking me to dinner or drinks. But as always, if you have a question, I'll do my best to answer it for you." It was Tommy's lifelong friend, and underworld figure, Terry Callahan answering Tommy's call.

"Hey, smart ass, how you doing? And yeah, you certainly have my number. I'm in a spot again and am wondering if you might be able to meet me sometime, somewhere. I got a guy I'm curious if you know?"

"Anything for you, my friend."

"Tell me when and where and I'll come meet you."

"I'm up at Mount Sinai Hospital. Sissy's aunt had a stroke and we're visiting right now. How 'bout I meet you on the park side of 5th Avenue at 101st Street at about midnight? That work for you?"

"Absolutely, I'll be there."

Chapter Eleven

Tommy always had to use backdoor methods to get ahold of his friend Terry. Terry, being an archcriminal, and knowing at any time the NYPD or FBI could be after him for any number of less-than-legal activities he may be involved in, never touched a landline. He only worked off burners, which are relatively cheap throw away phones. He usually had more than one burner on him at a time and made sure it was never the same from one week to the next. This meant he could never be reached, and his phone line could never be traced or tapped. So, anyone wanting to talk to Terry would have to leave a message at one of the bars he frequented on a daily basis, or get ahold of one of his runners, which was also a near impossible task.

At 11:52 PM, Tommy sat on a bench with his back against the dark gray stone wall that surrounds Central Park. He saw his friend Terry standing across 5th Avenue, waiting for a break in the traffic. Neither man waved nor acknowledged the other. Terry walked across the avenue and Tommy stood up. The two embraced in a long, tight hug, their almost matching leather car coats crunched and squeaked against one another.

Tommy sat back down on the bench and Terry sat next to him.

"How's Sissy's aunt makin' out?" Tommy asked.

"Not too bad actually. These strokes are scary things, but the docs think she's gonna recover well. She has the thing where one side of her face doesn't move anymore, but she hasn't lost her speech, and that's a great sign.

"This her Aunt Margaret?"

"Yeah, her mother's sister. It's rough on Sissy, they're awfully close. She's named after her."

"Yeah, I remember that. And how you makin' out?"

"Alright, can't complain. Day in day out, nothing new or interesting to report. But you ain't here to ask me about me. You need some info. Who you lookin' for and why?"

"Right to the point hey, Terry?"

"Well, that's why we're sittin' here, ain't it?"

"Yeah, I guess so. Well, I got this body we found in Carl Schurz last week -"

"Yeah, I heard. Young chick, right? In her twenties? Suicide attempt? Or you think someone killed her?"

"Not sure yet. Medical Examiner hasn't been able to do an autopsy yet and I have been having an awful time trying to ID this girl, hitting dead end after dead end. But a new name has come up. A fella they call Nicky the Skin. Supposedly he's a dicey character, but I can't find out anything about him since I don't know his real name. All I can run is his nick name, and I get nothing back for 'Nicky the Skin' in the computer, no matter how I mix it up or flip it around. I'm hoping you may know something about this guy, or recognize the name?"

Terry paused and looked out at the traffic moving south on Fifth Avenue before he turned back toward Tommy.

"Is he wanted? You think he's involved in this woman's death? Cause you know, without knowing the facts of what went down, I ain't ratting on no one, not even to you."

"No, it's not like that. I just need to find out who this girl is so I can get with her family and notify them. And then start an investigation into what could have possibly happened to her, cause right now we have absolutely nothing… and no, this Nicky isn't a suspect in anything, other than we think they know one another."

"Okay, well then, yes. I can give you a little info on this guy. Now, I have never met this Nicky the Skin, but he is the son of Matty-Boy Lupovich. He's got a decent rep as a stand-up guy. From what I understand, everyone likes him, but he's a ghost. He runs in extremely small circles, mostly stays south of 14th Street, all his shit is shylocking (lending money/loansharking). He's a young kid, inherited a lot of his father's business when Matty-Boy was whacked in Queens a couple years back."

"Yeah, I remember that… Matty-Boy Lupovich, hey? There's a name for you. He was one tough fucker."

"Fuck yeah he was. Matty the Pipe. He was a legend, one of the scariest men in New York for what, forty plus years?

"Alright, so you say this guy Nicky, his son, is a ghost. Any idea how I can get ahold of him?"

"Well again, I don't know this kid personally, but if you go see Stanley Petofski down on 10th Street, at the 363 Club, he will be able to get you in touch with Nicky."

"Stanley Petofski? Stanley Petofski? Do I know that name? Or should I know that name?"

"Yeah, you're a Detective, you should know that name. Listen, I'll send a message. I'll get with Stan, and I'll set something up for you. Maybe, maybe if we're lucky, you'll be able to get with him tomorrow; it's way too late for tonight, he's probably in bed already. You'll like Stan, he's old school New York."

"Thanks, brother. Once again I am in your debt."

"No. I do for you because I want to do for you. You don't owe me nothin' and you never will."

"You're a grand fella, Terry."

"Ha! Yeah, well maybe you remind Sissy of that next time you see her. And tell my probation officer too. I think the both of them are of the opposite opinion," he said with a grin.

Tommy and Terry stood and embraced. Terry hailed a cab and Tommy started to walk the twenty-three blocks from where he stood, across from Mount Sinai Hospital, to Bailey's Corner Pub. Throughout the entire walk, he went over the possibilities of this young woman's life, and death, in his mind. It was now the end of the fifth day since her body had been discovered by a tugboat on the East River. There was still no cause of death, and still no hint as to who she really was.

Tommy stopped along the way to Bailey's Corner for a quick bite at Papaya King, which still sat on the corner of 86th Street and

3rd Avenue where it had been since 1932. It was one of the few places left in the neighborhood that had been there since Tommy was a kid. Tommy ordered himself two franks with mustard and sauerkraut, and a small Papaya drink. 'Damn,' he thought, 'there is nowhere that does a hot dog better than this place.'

Tommy stood at the counter, looking out of the large plate glass window, chewing on his hot dog and sipping on his papaya juice. He remembered when the building across 3rd Avenue stood two-stories tall, and was a Woolworths Department store, a nationwide chain that had been gone for decades now. He smiled to himself as he remembered the time he told his sister, Kathleen, that Santa wasn't real and pulled down the beard of a sidewalk Santa to prove it to her, right there in front of Woolworths.

He glanced across 86th Street to the opposite corner, which was the old Thom McCann's Shoe Store, another shop that had been gone for decades now. And kitty corner from where he stood was once an old hotel. It had been well past its prime when he was a kid. 'Was it the Astoria hotel? Or the Berlin?' Tommy could not remember; it was too long ago now. But Papaya King had lasted, and at the moment, he was truly thankful for that.

Tommy finished his franks and drink, wiped some mustard from the corner of his mouth and left the warmth of Papaya King as he stepped back into the cold. He headed east and walked the next few blocks to Bailey's Corner. When he walked into the pub, he was happy to see the place was fairly quiet. Jack Norris was down at the end of the bar serving another customer, and Tommy wondered if there would be a question about Molly and him leaving together after her shift the last time he was in. Tommy removed his coat and hung it up. He sat in his favorite stool at the end of the bar, and as he got settled, Jack sat a bottle of Budweiser and a rocks glass of Jameson in front of him.

"Hey, Tommy, how's it going?"

"Not bad, Jackie, not bad at all. How are you makin' out tonight, my friend?"

"Eh, little slower than I'd like it to be for this time of night, but other than that, I got no complaints. Did our Molly make it home alright the other night?" Jack asked casually.

"Yes, sir she did. No issues at all," was Tommy's reply.

Jack, seeing there was no gossip to be added from Tommy, simply asked, "You interested in the papers tonight, or you already read them?"

"No, I'm set. Just going to have a round or two then head home for some sleep before I do it all again tomorrow."

"Okay, give me a shout when you're ready."

And with that, Jack returned to the conversation at the other end of the bar.

***

The following morning back in the squad room was uneventful; Tommy and the rest of the squad took care of their respective cases, made small talk, and teased and cracked jokes at one another's expense.

Tommy ran the name Nicholas Lupovich in the Department's system and found two arrests for old assaults, neither of which had convictions. Nothing at all, as far as contact with the police came up for the last several years.

At about 10:15 AM, Tommy's phone rang from a number he did not recognize.

"Keane," he answered.

A smooth and confident man's voice replied, "What do you think, honey? 1:30 at the 363 Club on 10th Street work for you?"

"Absolutely. Do I need to know anything else?"

"Don't be late."

"I won't. And thanks."

"My pleasure, sweetheart." The line disconnected.

"Hey Jimmy, you wanna take a ride this afternoon around one? I have an interesting lead on my Jane Doe."

"Sure. One works for me."

"Cool."

Chapter Twelve

Tommy and Jimmy drove the Crown Vic down to 10th Street and found the 363 Club.

"Here it is," Tommy said, as they stood outside of the building. Tommy looked at the place and immediately liked it from the outside. The 363 was a throwback, a dinosaur from a time in New York City that simply does not exist anymore.

The club was located in the cellar, eight steps down from the sidewalk, in a five story, well-maintained, twenty-four family building built of tan brick. On the large front window, painted in yellow script with a black outline, was "The 363 Club, A Democratic Gentleman's Club, Members and Guests Only." Now it may have read "Democratic Gentleman's Club" on the window, but like most of these old school social clubs, it was anything but.

The 363 Club was owned and operated by Stanley Petofski, who was, in essence, the Lower East Side's answer to Terry Callahan. He was as hardcore as they came, profoundly smart, and highly organized. Stanley had his fingers into all sorts of enterprises, in and around his neighborhood, both criminal and legitimate. He also had a close connection with the Plumbers Union local, which kept him and his crew on the books with no-show jobs. This enabled them all to collect healthy paychecks and health benefits, and additionally bought Stanley Petofski some semblance of legitimacy, as well as a deeply loyal following within his crew and with the surrounding hangers on, in the neighborhood.

Stanley had recently turned sixty and had been a professional criminal and gang leader since the age of sixteen. For forty-four years, he was involved in just about any sort of crime imaginable, barring anything he considered sexually deviant. Stanley was a devout Catholic, who took care of his mother and three younger sisters, as the one and only man in the house. He felt there was nothing worse on the planet than a man that would, or could, abuse a woman. He had no tolerance for the mistreatment of women in his presence, in his neighborhood, or within his crew, which numbered around a dozen members. All were old-school neighborhood toughs who clung to their old ways, and to their leader Stanley Petofski, the way Legionnaires clung to the flag and the glory days of when they once served their country.

Yes, this crew of reprobates was a proud bunch, the last of a dying breed. Similar to Terry Callahan's crew in Yorkville, these few men were the last of the old-style career criminals left on the Lower East Side of Manhattan, and they were proud of it. Made up of a handful of Polish, Irish, and Germans, all of whom had long standing family ties in the neighborhood.

The Petofski crew was legendary in the underground world of organized crime. So much so that even the five families of the Italian Mafia, not only consigned an approximate ten block radius to "Stanley The Pollack's" crew, but would always inform Stanley of any action that they would take on his turf prior to taking it, out of respect, as well as give a taste of any scores that may take place in his territory.

Stanley Petofski, as wealthy and powerful a man as he was, rarely made it more than three or four blocks in any direction from the intersection of 10th Street and Avenue A. To him, nothing in the world mattered outside of his realm. Here, he was King, and he ruled from a wooden barstool, his working man's throne at the end of the bar, day in and day out, at the 363 Club.

***

Tommy and Jimmy walked into the club. It was a narrow, long room, close to fifteen feet wide and eighty feet deep. To the left of the room stood a beautiful, art deco, mahogany bar, with a matching back-bar that must have been at least eight feet tall and stopped about an inch from the cream-colored tin ceilings.

The bar itself was about thirty feet long, with approximately sixteen or so mahogany colored oak stools tucked in close. The place looked like it had not been redecorated since 1920 but was still immaculately clean. The floors were a black and white pattern, done in one-inch hex mosaic tiles. To the right of the room was a twelve-inch rail that ran the length of the bar opposite it, with backless stools beneath it.

Large mirrors with fancy frames hung on the brick walls along with old photos of people from the neighborhood. In the center of the wall, in a heavy black frame, was an old lithograph of the American flag with "These Colors Don't Run" printed above it.

Under that frame sat a jukebox, another older CD jukebox, but unlike the one he had just seen in Kingston at Snapper Magee's, this one was a larger floor model. It was currently playing "I'll be seeing you" by Rosemary Clooney.

Towards the back of the room sat Stanley Petofski, sixty years old and about five feet eight inches tall. He wore a reddish plaid flannel shirt and navy-blue Dickies, with simple black Oxfords. The man was neat and clean and had zero flash. He looked like what he pretended to be, a simple plumber. He had a receding hairline of light brown, graying hair and wore a neatly trimmed goatee.

Next to him sat a man of about forty-five who stood when he saw Tommy and Jimmy walk in. This was Jake Hoffs. Jake stood an even six feet tall. He was lean and muscular, and wore his hair in a tight flat top, which at first glance made him look like a highway cop or State Trooper. With a second look it was obvious he was a hardened criminal, that guy you would not want to meet in a dark alley. Jake Hoffs was one of Stanley's main enforcers. Behind Stanley and Jake, sat two more mean-looking characters. They looked to both be in their late forties, possibly fifties, and sat at a table playing gin and drinking Budweiser. They both stopped all activity and looked intently at who had just entered their domain.

Behind the bar was an unusually small and slight man wearing a plaid flannel, this time in brown and black, with the sleeves cuffed up past his elbows. He appeared to be about thirty-five and was certainly the youngest man in the room barring Jimmy. He stood at maybe five-foot-three and could not have weighed more than 120 pounds.

This man looked up from the sink where he was washing glasses and not recognizing either of the detectives immediately spoke up, "Members only, fellas. Says so right on the glass."

Before Tommy could respond, Stanley Petofski spoke up, in a rather subdued and humble manner.

"It's alright Half-Pint, I believe these gentlemen are here to see me. Are you him?" he said with his eyes on Tommy, and before Tommy could answer, "The mighty Detective Thomas Keane from The Bronx? You are him, yes? I've read about you, Detective. Heard of you and word is you're a decent guy, old school."

"Yes sir, Mr. Petofski, I'm Tommy Keane, and this is Detective Colletti. Thanks for inviting us in, and for helping us out. We appreciate it."

"Don't thank me yet, Detective. I haven't helped you with anything yet, and I don't know if I'm going to. Come on over here, have a seat, and let me buy you fellas a drink."

Tommy and Jimmy walked down the length of the bar, and Tommy took the stool next to Stanley.

"What'll you have, Detective?"

"A bottle of Bud, thank you."

"And you, youngblood?" Stanley said, now looking at Jimmy.

"Nothing for me," Jimmy replied.

Tommy turned and, with a pleasant voice but an agitated look only Jimmy could see, said, "Sit down and have a drink, Jimmy."

And Jimmy promptly took the stool next to Tommy and said, "Okay, I'll take a Coors Light if you have one, please."

And with that, the short man who Stanley called Half-Pint put two bottles of Budweiser in front of the detectives.

"So, do you think you can help us out here, Mr. Petofski?"

"Call me Stan, Tommy. My father was Mr. Petofski, and nobody liked him. And yes, I know I can help you out, question is, will I? I have an idea of what you want from me, and we do have… well, let's just say our mutual friend asked me to help you out if I could, so here we are, and I'm willing to listen. Please tell me exactly what it is you need."

"Well, Stan, I have a dead girl, and from what we can tell so far, a real sweet, decent, educated girl. Probably from a fine family, but we don't know who she is, we think that Nicky Lupovich may be able to identify her. Nicky is in no way a suspect, but from what I understand he knows this girl. But as you may know, Nicky Lupovich is also a bit of a ghost, and we can't find him anywhere. And if this young woman lost her life due to some evil fucker's doings, well I can't let this trail go cold, Stan. Time, time is of the essence, and I need to identify her so I can get on with my investigation. All I'm asking, Stan, is that you put me in contact with Nicky Lupovich, please, if you can."

"I see you're in a spot here, looking to find who this girl is. And she's a decent girl, a regular citizen, right?"

"Yes, as far as we can tell, and from the little we know, yes, she's a regular citizen and a decent person."

"Half-Pint!" Stanley shouted down the near empty bar, and Half-Pint jumped to attention.

"See if you can get Nicky the Skin over here right now, and if not now, find out where that kid is and let him know I want to talk to him right away."

"Yes, Cap, I'll find him." Half-Pint threw on a leather pea coat and a scally cap and headed out the door.

"Hopefully, it won't be too long before Half-Pint gets back, and maybe with Nicky. And if not, we'll hopefully be able to put you two together today or tomorrow, the latest."

"Thank you," Tommy replied as he took a sip of his beer.

"Listen, Tom, I've seen you in the papers several times over the years, and recently with that dead nun and those kids that crazy cult fuck had up there on the East Side. Now you and I, well we might play for opposing teams if you know what I mean, but I would like to tell you thanks. We all appreciate having a man like you taking care of business on your side of the aisle, so to speak. If you get what I mean, we know you're a decent guy and we appreciate you is alls I wanna say."

"Well thank you, I appreciate that, I truly do."

"And you. You, youngblood," Stanley leaned back in his stool and addressed Jimmy, "You're lucky to be working with a man like this. Pay attention and learn, the city needs admirable men keeping an eye out for its citizens."

The door opened and Half-Pint entered the club. He went to the back, behind the bar where Tommy and Stanley sat still bullshitting. It had only been about ten minutes since he left.

"The Skin says he'll be here in less than fifteen minutes, Cap."

"Thanks, Half-Pint."

They continued to talk, and Tommy was happy to have such a simple and civil conversation with Stanley, who seemed to be genuinely interested in his personal life and career. It was obvious to him that there was some honest respect and even admiration being shown from Stanley. Tommy remembered what Terry said, that Stan was a decent old New York kind of guy, and he agreed.

***

Nicky Lupovich, also known as Nicky the Skin, entered the club about ten minutes after Half-Pint had returned. He was an average sized man of twenty-six, about five-foot-nine, and 170 pounds. He had a shaved head, wore a navy-blue Harrington Jacket, with Brass Knuckles and Hub City Stompers embroidered on the left chest, a black polo shirt, with white tipping on the collar, snug fitting tapered Levi's, cuffed up high to show off his highly shined Doc Martens boots.

To his left was a short, very fit, good-looking, blonde girl with a Chelsea haircut. She wore a green nylon flight jacket, a short, bleached denim skirt with what appeared to be thin suspenders hanging from beneath her jacket, fishnet stockings and cherry red Doc Martens boots. To his right stood a taller, dark-skinned Puerto Rican girl, also in excellent shape, wearing a similar Harrington jacket that Nicky wore, only in maroon, also with Hub City Stompers embroidered on the left chest. She had dark navy skintight Levi's on, also cuffed up high and showing off her cherry red Doc Martens.

Stanley leaned in a bit and said in a hushed voice to Tommy, "I love this kid. He fuckin' kills me. Look at him, this fuckin' kid should have his own theme song the way he walks around."

Nicky Lupovich was a hardcore, traditional skinhead, through and through; he was also the son of Matty-Boy Lupovich and a whore mother he never knew. Matty-Boy was deeply entrenched in the underworld of New York City; he acted for years as an independent contractor, working for many, many criminal gangs and Mafia families, as an enforcer and collector of debts.

Before he was shot in the face and killed in Queens, Matty-Boy had such a strong reputation he rarely had to resort to violence. Simply knowing Matty-Boy was on his way, tended to result in the payment of whatever debt was owed.

Matty-Boy's murder was committed by a small up and coming gang who had made the mistake of robbing a hefty sum of cash from a mob connected poker game. Matty-Boy, who had been given the assignment to retrieve said cash, was shot several times in the face, neck, and chest. He died from his wounds several days later at Mount Sinai Queens Hospital in Astoria.

His killer's remains were discovered several months later buried in a potato farm in Hamilton, New Jersey.

Nicky the Skin was raised as his father's protégé and was taught from an incredibly young age how to make friends and influence people. Both, according to his father Matty-Boy, could be accomplished with a short length of iron pipe.

A simple pipe was Matty-Boy's weapon of choice. He had explained to his son that the police could charge you for using anything as a deadly weapon. But in a court of law, a simple piece of pipe that "happened" to be lying on the sidewalk, or poking out of a trash can, was much easier to explain away to a judge or jury as a defensive weapon than a gun, knife, blackjack, or pair of brass knuckles were. Plus, a short length of pipe cost nothing and worked exceptionally well when it came to "influencing people."

Nicky, now twenty-six, had inherited several of his father's accounts, as well as some of his father's reputation as a no-nonsense negotiator. Unlike his father, who was simply a bulldog of a man, Nicky Lupovich earned much of his personal reputation as a tough guy by training in Muay Thai kickboxing under the tutelage of a Mr. Phil Nurse. Nurse was a British and European champion kickboxer who had taken up residence in NYC sometime in the early 90's, and who Matty-Boy had enrolled Nicky in classes with, while he was still in junior high school.

By the time Nicky was sixteen, he was truly a skilled and dangerous fighter, something he proved on several occasions in high school and on the streets of his neighborhood. His own skills with his fists, as well as the legacy his father left him, enshrined him as an up-and-coming player in the NYC underworld.

***

It was obvious to Tommy, just by looking at this kid that he was a fighter. Tommy, who as a teenager himself boxed out of Julio Rivera's Gym, on East 12th Street, not three blocks from where they all sat right now immediately recognized Nicky the Skin's walk, stance, and movements as that of a fighter.

Nicky paused momentarily in the entrance and took in the room before he entered. He spoke to the two girls who were with him, softly and inaudible to anyone else in the tiny bar, then with his left hand he motioned them to take a seat at the bar. He reached into his pocket, took out a wad of cash, and dropped a hundred-dollar bill on the bar then again, motioned with his hand for Half-Pint to give the girls a drink.

Casually, almost in slow motion, he walked over to where Tommy, Jimmy, and Stanley sat. Stanley rotated around in his stool and stood up, and Tommy and Jimmy followed Stan's lead.

"Nicky, how you doing, son? You're looking well, glad to see you're taking care of yourself, kid."

"Yeah, I'm doing alright, Uncle Stan. Life is decent, and I got no complaints. You look the same as ever, all good with you, I hope?"

"Yeah, kid, all is good with me, thanks. Let me introduce you to Tommy Keane of the NYPD. He's got a question or two for you. Hoping you can help him out a little, and hey," Stan's tone took on a more serious note, "You know I wouldn't have called you in here if it wasn't the right thing to do."

"Of course, I know that. How you doing, Detective?" Nicky said, while extending his hand for a handshake, "I've heard of you," he added as they clasped hands.

"Nice to meet you, Mr. Lupovich, I've heard of you also. And let me say I'm sorry about your father."

"You knew my father?" Nicky asked.

"I never met him, no, but we did have mutual friends, and from what I understand he was a gentleman."

"Well thanks, I appreciate that. So, you think I may know somebody you are looking for, or I guess I should say, trying to identify?"

"Yeah, that is exactly what I am hoping. Can I show you a photograph?"

"That's why I'm here."

Tommy removed the headshot from his coat pocket, unrolled it, and handed it to Nicky. Nicky looked at it intently, then moving just his eyes up from the photo, asked, "Someone kill her?"

"Not a hundred percent sure yet, but we are thinking that may be a possibility. Right now, I have no idea, but not knowing who she is has kept us from getting a proper investigation going."

"This is Jenny Black," Nicky said flatly still not breaking eye contact with Tommy.

"Actually, we know that, but we can't find anything about her anywhere. The girl is a complete mystery to us. There are hundreds of Jenny Blacks all over the tri-state area, and none of them are this woman."

"Cause that ain't her real name." He moved his eyes back down to the photo he still held in his hand.

"That's what I heard just yesterday. Do you know what her real name is?"

Nicky looked back at Tommy and handed the photo back, "Her real name is Jenny Lindel. She's a good kid too, well, was a good kid, I guess. She's from uptown somewhere. Her father is a famous song writer, wrote a couple of hits in the late 70's early 80's, for some pop top 40 bands, but made some real money doing jingles for TV commercials. I know her from shows. She was a real class act, put on a lot of shows herself, some here at Arlene's Grocery but mostly in Brooklyn at Trash Bar, Grand Victory, Knitting Factory, all around there."

"Can you tell me anything about her personal life? How well did you know her?"

"Nah, didn't know her too well. I know who she is, knew her enough to say hello and goodbye. We co-sponsored a Ska Fest once, but never really got friendly. We ran in different circles you know. But everyone liked her, I never heard anyone say anything bad about her. She wasn't into anything other than music that I know of, no drugs, not a drunk, just liked to make the scene, you know. Enjoyed putting on her own shows, always had a knack for it -- bands liked her because she always paid them, and the venues liked her because they always made money off her shows. She was well known and well-liked by everyone in the punk scene, as far as I know. I mean I never heard anyone say anything bad about Jenny."

"Boyfriend?"

"I've seen her with a couple different guys, but no committed boyfriend that I know of. She was definitely a cool chick though, I'm sorry to see her go."

"What can you tell me about the guys you have seen her with?"

"One was a tall, black guy, same age, seemed alright. I think he was a musician. But I kind of don't think she was into him, but he was definitely into her, he'd show up to shows and hang around her all the time… friendly enough. I could be wrong, but I think he played Sax or Trombone? Other guy, he was a drummer, white guy, maybe thirty, think he toured with a band called Hudson Falcons, seemed likeable enough."

"Hudson Falcons, the Jersey band?"

"Yes sir, the one and only."

"Let me ask you now, is there anything at all that you can think of, no matter how small, that may seem odd to you, out of place, suspicious in any manner whatsoever about either of these two men you described to me, or about Jenny Lindel, or her life? Anything unusual at all?

"Unusual? Ha, well these are punk rock kids, Detective, fucking everything about them is unusual. But I have to say, I really can't think of anyone that would ever want to hurt Jenny Black, everyone seemed to like her, and as far as those two guys I mentioned, I would say, harmless. I know anyone is capable of anything, but on the face of it, nah, I don't see either of them being suspicious in anyway."

"Mr. Lupovich, I can't thank you enough for putting a proper name to my Jenny Black, thank you so much for coming to meet me and helping us out today."

"Please, Detective, call me Nicky, everyone does. Uncle Stan said you were a good guy so I'm happy to help."

And with that they all shook hands, exchanged some more pleasantries, and Tommy and Jimmy left the 363 Club with a warm invitation to stop by and say hello anytime either of them was in the neighborhood.

Chapter Thirteen

Tommy let out a deep breath as he began to speak on their way back to the car. "Outstanding! We now know who our girl is – finally. Let's head up to the precinct and run the Lindel's, see if we can locate them and get this investigation headed in the right direction."

"Yeah," Jimmy replied, "You wanna grab a bite before we head back? I'm getting hungry. How about a slice before we get in the car?"

"No, I'll do you one better. How about some Polish? You like Polish food?"

"I've never had it."

Tommy stopped in his tracks on the sidewalk. "You've never had Polish food?" he asked incredulously.

"No. What like goulash, right? Nope never have."

"Well, that's it then, you are in for a treat, my friend. There is a place about three, four blocks away. C'mon, I'll turn you onto something new."

They both got into the car and Tommy drove them over to 12th Street and 2nd Avenue and found a spot a few doors away from the Little Poland Restaurant.

"This you're going to like," Tommy said as they entered the place.

Little Poland was a small Polish restaurant that was arranged like an old diner; a counter with stools sat to the left of the restaurant as soon as you entered, and several tables were set up to the right. It probably was, at one time, a simple diner, but for the last thirty to thirty-five years it had been the Little Poland Restaurant and was now one of the exceedingly few remaining Eastern European restaurants left in a neighborhood that used to be full of them.

Tommy and Jimmy took a table towards the rear of the restaurant and waited for what seemed a bit too long for a young Polish woman to come and greet them.

"What you like?" She said slowly and with a heavy accent.

"Hey, how are you? Could we get a couple of menus?" Tommy asked.

"Oh no menu? Okay," the waitress answered and walked away. She then returned with two menus.

"What to drink?" She asked as she placed one of the menus in front of each of them.

"Pepsi for me," Tommy replied.

"I think I'll take a Pepsi also," Jimmy said, and turned his attention to Tommy, "So what do you recommend?" he asked.

"To be honest, I have never had anything bad in this place. There are some things I may like more than others, but never have I ever had anything I wouldn't have again."

"Well, that doesn't help me right now. What are you getting?"

"I think I'm going to get an order of pierogi, half potato, half meat, that I'm going to split with you. Also, a cup of dark bean and kielbasa soup and a chicken cutlet with spinach, carrots, and sauerkraut."

"Alrighty then, sign me up for the same," Jimmy stated, closing his menu.

The waitress returned with both of their Pepsi's and Tommy placed their order.

"Okay, same and same, like twins, got you," the waitress said and turned and walked away, yelling the order in Polish to the overweight elderly woman visible inside the kitchen past the countertop.

"So worthwhile day today? As far as finding out who this dead girl was anyway, yes?" Jimmy asked.

"Yeah definitely, I've been chasing this one all over the tri-state area just trying to find out who she is and now we finally know."

"So, let me pick your brain a little."

"Please do," Tommy replied and took a sip of his soda.

"These men we just met with, they're obviously gangsters, right? I know you told me this on the way down in the car, but how did you know to come see these guys, and how did you set up this meeting?"

"Well, with this job of ours, you're going to meet a lot of different people, from all walks of life, including some rather unsavory types, but I want you to know something and understand something. You can't be a dick if you want to get ahead as an investigator. You see, you don't have to like any of these people, or think it's okay for them to do the things they do. However, if you make an attempt to understand them, understand their way of life, and if you show them some respect, they just may show you some respect back. Now this goes for everyone you may run across in life, as well as on the job. You see it may be that hooker, junkie, drug dealer, scam artist, or corner thug that in the end winds up being your friend. Okay, so get that - in the end, you never know who your friend is going to be. Some mutt may give you a tip or a crucial piece of information, some other miscreant may call 911 while you're getting your ass kicked, or in today's case, some highly dangerous career criminals helped us to find out who our Jane Doe really was."

"Good advice, I get that. But how did we get to meet these guys today? Obviously, you didn't know them before today, right?"

"You are correct. I didn't know them, but I put the word out that I needed this information. I asked another contact if he could help me out, and here we are."

"Okay. So that was it, you just asked around?"

"Well yeah, Jimmy, isn't that what we do all day, every day? We ask around. That's all an investigation is - asking, following leads, asking, following more leads, sometimes it's simple and other times it's impossibly difficult."

"Yeah, you're right, you make it sound so simple, but I know it's not. Now other than don't be a dick, what other investigatory advice can you give me?"

"Pay attention. I know that sounds really basic and simple, but that's it. Pay attention to everything around you, at all times. Pay attention to the crime scene, pay attention to the victim, pay attention to everyone and everything about everyone during every interview. Sometimes it's the smallest things that will shed light on a case. Act as though no one is telling the truth, they may be, but you have to prove it. You see for us, Jimmy. Well at least in my opinion, as detectives, we really aren't in the law enforcement game, we are in the truth game. Do you get what I'm saying? If we can figure out the truth, we can make an arrest, and the District Attorney's office can enforce the law. We, my friend, are all about the truth."

"Ahh. I like the way you put that. Yeah, it makes sense. Now a slightly different topic, do you know how or what the connection is between the older guys from the 363 Club and the Hub City Stompers gang is? Do the young guys, like, pay up to the older guys?"

Tommy paused and smiled.

"So here you go. You were paying attention. You caught that both Nicky the Skin, and that lovely looking Spanish girl, both had Hub City Stompers embroidered on their jackets. First-rate, you caught a link there. I'm sorry to tell you though that the Hub City Stompers is not the name of their gang, it's the name of a Ska band out of New Jersey. And I'm guessing both of them were nothing more fans."

"Well, that's a little embarrassing. And how do you always know all of this stuff?"

"I pay attention, Jimmy, almost like it's a curse. I pay attention and in this case you did too, you would have figured out the truth once you had begun searching it out. If you look you will find, just be diligent. And please understand, if I ever come off preachy, I'm not talking down to you, okay? I learned from older guys on the job, and as a newer detective you're doing the same thing. And know that Stein is never talking down to you at all when he tries to school you, he's just pointing you in the right direction."

"Oh no, I get it, and I appreciate it, believe me," Jimmy replied, then asked, "Nicky the Skin and these girls were Skinheads, right? So, I'm a little confused because I thought Skinheads were racist, but that taller Spanish girl was pretty dark. Were they Skinheads? The kid's name is Nicky the Skin."

Tommy smiled again, "Yes they are Skinheads, but not what you're thinking. Traditional skins, real skinheads, are not the racist thugs portrayed on TV. For the most part, that is all media bullshit. The skinhead scene, in reality, was possibly the first ever multi-racial youth movement not forced upon kids by the government. It started in England and was really all about the music, Ska music in particular, which was almost all put out by black artists, and black and white kids together created the original skinhead scene or what is now called the trad skinhead scene. It was based in a sort of unity among working class youth, but that was later co-opted by asshole wannabe pretend Nazi dummies, and then perpetuated by the media."

"So, what you're telling me is that skinheads are not the racist bad guys everyone thinks of when we hear the word skinhead?"

"Yes, that's exactly what I'm telling you. A true skinhead is not a racist, and a racist really can't be a true skinhead. That being said people are people and there are assholes in every group. And the Hub City Stompers are not a gang, they are a just a fantastic ska band from New Jersey."

"You are an interesting man, Tommy Keane."

As they continued to chat their food came and Tommy and Jimmy ate their fill.

"Damn that was some tasty food, thank you so much for turning me onto this place."

"My pleasure. I haven't made it down here in probably over a year, so yeah, believe me it was my pleasure. Tomorrow, I hope to have to go to the Medical Examiner's for the autopsy. You want to come along for that?"

"Sure, if I'm free as far as no new cases, then absolutely. And what's next today?"

"Well, I'm going to run the Lindels in the computer, find out where they live, and go notify the family that their daughter Jenny has passed. You along for that ride, Jim?"

"Well, yeah, I guess so. I haven't done this yet, but it comes with the territory, right?"

"Yes sir, it does, and it's a miserable fucking thing to do. I hate it, and don't think anyone ever gets used to it."

Chapter Fourteen

4:19 PM 127 East 92nd Street.

Tommy and Jimmy arrived at the Lindels' block and parked at the fire hydrant a few doors down from their home. Silent and solemn, they both approached the Lindels' brownstone and made their way up the tall, thirteen-step stoop and rang the bell.

The notification of a family member when a loved one has died is often called the longest walk a police officer will ever make. Few things are worse than having to be the one to break the news.

The door was answered by a young Central American woman, dressed simply in denim jeans and a white t-shirt.

"Hello, how may I help you?" she asked.

"Hello, I am Detective Keane, and this is Detective Colletti. We are from the 21st Precinct and would like to speak with Mr. or Mrs. Lindel if they are available, please."

"Oh hello, yes, yes, Mrs. Lindel is in. I will get her, one moment, please," the young woman replied and closed the door leaving the detectives on the stoop.

Not more than a minute passed when the door reopened. Lisa Lindel answered it, with the young woman standing right behind her. Lisa Lindel was younger than Tommy and Jimmy expected as she appeared to be in her mid-thirties. She was an incredibly attractive woman, dressed casually in tight black yoga pants, running shoes and a wide, cut-away neck, gray sweatshirt, which fell down her left shoulder, exposing a black bra strap. Her brown hair with blond highlights was pulled back in a high ponytail, and she wore minimal makeup. Her appearance, though casual, was also obviously curated to show off what a true natural beauty this woman was.

"Hello, Officers. I am Lisa Lindel, Charles Lindel's wife, how may I help you?" she asked.

"May we come inside, Mrs. Lindel? We need to speak with you for a moment."

"Yes, of course, I'm so sorry. Please, please come in," she replied, inviting the detectives into her home, "Here - step into the parlor here and have a seat," she continued, motioning the detectives in to the first room to the right, off the foyer.

"Thank you, Mrs. Lindel, but please may I ask you to have a seat, ma'am? Is your husband home, Mrs. Lindel?" Tommy asked.

"No, no he is at the hospital now, he's at Sloan Kettering, awaiting a surgery. And, and okay… you're making me a little nervous now, sir. It's not normal for us to have the police arrive unannounced at our door, and now you're asking me to sit down? What is wrong, Officer? Why are you here?" She sat, perched on the edge of a rather expensive looking settee.

"Mrs. Lindel, we have found a dead body that we believe is that of your daughter, Jenny, and —"

"Oh my God!" Lisa Lindel said aloud, almost shrieking.

"Yes, I'm so sorry to bring this news to you. We have been informed that this young woman is your daughter, and, and I need to show you a photo now, and we will need you or another family member to come down to the morgue to positively identify the body, if it is indeed, Jenny. I'm so sorry, Mrs. Lindel. Do you understand what I am asking, ma'am?"

"Oh My God!" she said again, loudly, and dramatically. She took a few deep breaths. "Yes, I understand," she said in a calmer voice as her hands began to tremble.

Tommy reached into his coats inside pocket and pulled out the rolled-up photo. He held up the photo and showed her the headshot of Jenny.

"Is this your Jenny, Mrs. Lindel?"

"Oh God… oh God, yes, yes, it is," she said, and she began to sob unrestrained. She reached out with her right hand, grabbed Tommy's wrist, and held a firm grip with her small, well-manicured, hand.

Tommy placed his other hand on her shoulder, "I'm sorry, Mrs. Lindel, I am so deeply sorry."

He gave her a minute to pull herself together.

"What happened to her?" She asked after a minute. Her hands wiping tears from her eyes and cheeks.

"We're not positive yet, Mrs. Lindel. She was found in Carl Schurz Park, and the Medical Examiner's Office hasn't been able to do an autopsy yet."

"Oh my God!" she exclaimed again with a loud sob.

Tommy gave her another minute to pull herself together.

"What? What do I need to do now? I need… I need to see her? I need to identify her body for you? Is that what you need me to do?" She glanced over and made eye contact with Jimmy. This look took him by surprise, and almost flinching he looked to the floor to escape her gaze, feeling almost ashamed to be trespassing on her pain.

Tommy responded, "Yes, ma'am. Are you able?"

"Oh God… No… I mean, I mean yes. I guess that's what I have to do. Oh my God. When, and how do I do this?"

"Well, you can go to the morgue at Bellevue Hospital whenever it's convenient and if you'd like, we can escort you today, if that helps at all. Detective Colletti and I can drive you down there – again if that helps?"

"Could you? Would you?" She looked up at Tommy, her eyes beseeching, "Please, drive me there and back. Is that a possibility? I don't think I can do this on my own, especially with my husband in the hospital. If you could take me that would be so kind of you."

"Not a problem, Mrs. Lindel. We'll be happy to take you and all you'll have to do is tell us that she is indeed your daughter, Jenny. Now please, if you're up to it, can we ask you a few questions about, Jenny?"

Mrs. Lindel took a deep breath and let it out, "Hoooo. Yes, yes of course. I'm sure you have questions, what do you need to know?"

"Okay, well tell me a little about Jenny. We know nothing about her."

"Well, she was beautiful, but a handful. She was a bit of a wild child, she loved to party and run around with all kinds of crazy, tattooed, and pierced people. I, I am her stepmother. We had a good relationship I like to think, she drove her father and I a little nuts sometimes, but she wasn't a bad person. A bit crazy, and a little, I don't know, irresponsible. She liked risky behavior."

"Did she use any narcotics to your knowledge?"

"I believe she did," Mrs. Lindel replied and again began to cry.

"Did she ever talk about suicide? Was that ever something you thought she would, could, be capable of?"

"Oh. Yes, without a doubt she was capable of taking her own life."

"Does she, or did she still live here?"

"Yes, yes she did."

"May I ask, Mrs. Lindel, why there was no Missing Person's report filed for Jenny?"

Mrs. Lindel paused for a moment. Jimmy looked up from his pad where he was jotting down notes when she did not answer right away, and her eyes briefly made contact with his. She quickly focused once again on Tommy.

"Well, I've been so busy with my husband at Sloan Kettering, and well, to be honest, we rarely cross paths, you know? She is an adult now, and she comes and goes as she pleases. She often doesn't stay here at home, and even when she does, she comes home in the middle of the night and then sleeps all day. She, Jenny lives almost like a vampire, so, so it really, I really, to be honest haven't missed her the last few days. Oh my God that must sound so terrible?"

"No, ma'am it doesn't, it's understandable," Tommy replied with compassion, "Can you tell me at all about her friends? A boyfriend? Or perhaps a girlfriend? A best friend?"

"Jenny was mostly a loner. I know a couple names and only met a few of her friends. A Max, a Julie, a Jerry, to tell you the truth, I haven't spent any time with any of her friends. She is such a private person. She, she's been an adult as long as I've known her and most of her life is spent out of the house."

"Okay, how about her birth mother? How is her relationship with her mother?"

"Her real mother died when she was seven. She also passed from a cancer, so it was just Jenny and her father before I joined the family. And they, Jenny and her father are, well, Charlie has been her best friend ever since Jenny lost her mother. They share the love of music and adore one another. Oh God, how am I going to tell him?" she again began to sob. Tommy gave her a minute to gather herself. "Do you think, should we go identify her now?" Lisa Lindel asked, cutting her answer short.

"Sure, if you are up to it, we can drive you down now, if that works."

"Yes, yes please. I would like to get this over with, so I can go to the hospital and be with my husband later, if you're okay with that."

"Absolutely," Tommy replied, "Let me give them a call and let them know we are on the way."

***

Lisa Marie Lindel, nee Peterson, was raised in a happy, upper middle-class family in Pittsfield, Massachusetts. Her father made a career as a successful lawyer and her mother, a hospital administrator. She was the middle child of three children. Her older brother was currently working as a lawyer in the Boston area, and her younger brother was the manager of a health food store in Great Barrington, Massachusetts.

Lisa had been a gorgeous young girl, and in high school had won the Miss Western Massachusetts beauty pageant. She had a lifelong love of dance and acting, which both her parents fully encouraged her to pursue, and she ended up graduating from Salem State University with a bachelor's degree in drama.

Although Lisa was attractive, could sing, dance, and act, she soon found that the life of a working actor was a near impossible dream to achieve. Lisa had moved to New York City at the age of twenty-two, and for almost a decade worked as a waitress, a bartender, and a receptionist, while she went out on audition after audition, probably close to a thousand in a ten-year period. Occasionally, but rarely, she would land a job. To date, after living in New York for fifteen years, Lisa had landed three well-paying television commercials, and two small speaking parts in major motion pictures, one of which was cut from three lines down to two words, and where she was not credited, and another where she did end up with two lines and a credit. Most of her acting career was to remain in the realm of extra work. She had appeared on Law and Order some twenty-seven times, and never once spoke a single word. Extra work, along with her other jobs, is where she was able to eke out a living, barely making enough to survive in New York City.

Lisa was thirty-one when she met Charlie Lindel on the set of a television commercial for a large car dealership in New Jersey. Charlie had written the jingle that Lisa was to sing, although even here she was to lip sync to a prerecorded studio track. Two years later, they met again, this time at a large industry party, and struck up a relationship. At this point, Lisa was thirty-three and Charlie fifty-four, twenty-one years her senior.

Lisa did very much like Charlie, who, although now worth millions, was still at heart an average guy from Ohio. But she was also an opportunist. Never did she truly love Charlie; she had always been a shallow human being who lived in a fantasy where she dreamed of her own fame and fortune. Charlie was an exceptionally talented and successful individual, even though he kept a low profile in the entertainment industry where he basically served as a journeyman. His only fame came from a couple songs he had written before Lisa was born. For Lisa, this was a marriage of opportunity, a marriage that would set her up financially for the rest of her life, and a marriage where she also hoped she could use Charlie's vast connections in the entertainment industry to help forward her career as an actress.

Unfortunately, during the four years of their marriage, Lisa's career did not move forward a single inch. Now that she lived in an elegant Manhattan brownstone on the Upper East Side, where every need was taken care of, the need for a paycheck was gone. She no longer had to do extra work and slowly she stopped going on auditions. As the wife of a millionaire, she now felt somehow that her agent would be sending her on bigger auditions for bigger jobs, but being a rather mediocre actress, never having landed any serious jobs in her past, and now not even taking the small jobs and extra work, the phone simply stopped ringing. And over the last four years she became nothing more than another good-looking, Upper East Side trophy wife, to a man who never treated her as such.

Charles Lindel had fallen in love with a woman who was, for the most part, nothing more than a dazzling empty vessel, like an expensive vase he could place on the mantel and where guests could comment on how beautiful it was.

Lisa did, however, have enough acting ability in Jenny's opinion, to lead Charlie, and all their friends and family, in believing that she was indeed in love. The only critic Lisa couldn't win over was Jenny Lindel. Jenny, from the start, believed her father's new girlfriend, was never in love with, or going to be in love with, her father. A fact that made Jenny more sad than angry. She loved her father and wanted him to be happy but believed the happiness he found with Lisa was based on nothing more than the biggest role of Lisa's acting career - that of a loving wife.

Two years later they were married, and now four years after their wedding Charlie was dying of cancer. He had recently moved from his bed in his home of over thirty years to a bed at the Memorial Sloan Kettering Medical Center, where his prognosis was dim. The doctors were to try one more surgery, but it was without question a Hail Mary pass if ever there was one. Charlie was thought to have only a twenty percent shot at survival.

But despite what Jenny thought of her stepmother, Lisa did prove herself to be a good and doting wife throughout Charlie's illness. Whether she was madly in love with her husband when they were married, or if this was indeed a marriage of convenience, she did, very much, tow the line for her husband Charlie. When he was bedridden at home, she took care of his every need; she fed him and cleaned him, and whenever he was admitted to the hospital, she visited him at least once a day, sometimes twice. Lisa Lindel without fail stood by Charlie when he needed her most, through the best times, and the absolute worst.

And now she was going to identify the body of her stepdaughter, her husband's one and only child. What would she say to Charlie? How in the world would she, could she, tell him that Jenny was gone?

***

Tommy parked on 26th Street outside the City Morgue which is attached to Bellevue Hospital.

As they exited the gray Crown Vic, Lisa Lindel paused and looked up at the building, stopping momentarily on the sidewalk.

"Are you okay, Mrs. Lindel?" Jimmy asked.

Tommy turned to see what was happening and echoed what Jimmy asked, "Are you okay, Mrs. Lindel?"

"Yes, yes, I am. It's just all becoming real to me right now," she said, wiping a tear from her cheek.

Tommy approached her and put his left hand on her upper right arm.

"I'm not going to say this is going to be fine, Mrs. Lindel, these things never are. It is something that needs to be done though. It may be a time for you to say goodbye as well if that helps you out at all. It will be only a minute, but you may take as long as you like, if you need, okay? And we'll be here for you, we can be right by your side, and we can also leave you alone if you like. It's all up to you, dear."

"Thank you," she said through her sniffles, "Thank you." She straightened up, silently braced herself, and started towards the entrance.

The three of them entered the morgue. Tommy identified himself to the person at the front desk, who nodded and pointed toward the hall. Tommy joined the others, and they made the long, slow, walk to the room where the bodies were kept in stainless-steel refrigerated coolers that stood in rows like giant filing cabinets.

The attending M.E. directed the trio to stand near a large glass window that looked into this room. He went through the door and entered the room. Once inside he pushed a table, with a black nylon body bag on it, up to the other side of the window, where the trio stood in wait. He unzipped the bag and exposed Jenny Lindel's head and shoulders, and as he did, Lisa Lindel let out a gasp and began to go weak at the knees. Both Jimmy and Tommy grabbed her by her arms to hold her up as she buckled.

"Okay. Oh God, our Jenny, our Jenny," she began to sob, then stood up straight and apologized, "I'm sorry, I'm so sorry. I'll be alright - I'll be alright."

The M.E. unzipped the bag a bit more to Jenny's waist and showed Jenny still dressed in the clothes she was found in. The M.E. exposed just enough of her to identify the jacket and face which lay facing up, still in the same position she was found in, and still defrosting, her eyes open, staring up at the ceiling.

"Oh my God! Yes, yes, yes, oh our poor Jenny. Oh God, no. No, no. Yes, yes, that's our Jenny."

Lisa Lindel turned abruptly, buried her head in Tommy's shoulder and began to sob, again going weak at the knees so Tommy had to put his arms around her to keep her from falling.

"It's okay, Mrs. Lindel. It's okay. Are you alright? Would you like a minute with her?"

"No. No, I'm good," she sobbed into Tommy's chest, "I'm good, I'm fine, we can go. Goodbye, sweet girl, oh God. Goodbye, I loved you so much. Your father, your father loved you so much."

Tommy nodded to the M.E., who re-zipped the bag, re-covering her face, and pushed away the stainless-steel table that held young Jenny Lindel. Then Tommy, still holding Lisa Lindel in his arms, led her out of the room and back down the hall, and out of the building.

Jenny Lindel had been positively identified by her stepmother, Lisa Lindel, and was officially no longer a Jane Doe.

All Tommy needed now was to get the Medical Examiner's Autopsy Report, which he hoped would be done the following day. Then, hopefully, this case could be closed and the Lindels could make funeral arrangements and begin their grieving.

On the sidewalk, Lisa Lindel paused and took a deep breath. With each hand, she held tightly to both Tommy and Jimmy's forearms, as they both stood by her side. She took another very deep breath and as she spoke, her voice cracked as she fought back the tears.

"Oh my God. What am I going to tell Charlie? Oh, my God, she's so young. How? Why? How? How can she be gone? I can't believe it. She was so young, so beautiful."

She again took a deep breath and exhaled, and simply said, "Okay," and continued toward the detective's car.

The drive back to the Lindel's home on 92nd Street was tense and solemn. For the most part it was silent, with Lisa sniffling now and again from the back seat.

She blankly stared out the side window as the Crown Vic drove north through the traffic, and spoke quietly, almost to herself, "My God, what am I going to tell her father? He's in such bad shape right now with this fucking cancer. What am I going to tell him? Oh Jenny, what did you do? What did you do, you beautiful, sweet girl?

When they arrived at the brownstone, Jimmy double-parked outside of the Lindels' home and Tommy walked her up the stairs of the front stoop.

"Here is my card, Mrs. Lindel, if you need anything, or if there is anything you think we should know, please feel free to call anytime. Jenny's autopsy should be in the next day or two, and you can be certain I'll let you know how she passed, as soon as I find out."

Lisa Lindel leaned in and hugged Tommy, "Thank you, Detective Keane. Thank you for your help. I'm sorry if I haven't handled this well," she said, wiping tears from her eyes.

"Nonsense, it's an impossibly hard thing to have to do. Please, if you need anything give me a call, and I will be in contact very soon."

"Thank you again, Detective, you are so, so very kind."

She then turned and unlocked the door to her house as Tommy headed back down the stairs.

Chapter Fifteen

Tommy and Jimmy arrived at Bellevue at 11:40 AM, about a half an hour before their scheduled time.

They identified themselves and waited for Medical Examiner Marcus to ask them to join her.

The detectives put on their masks and entered the autopsy examination room, where they saw Jenny Lindel's body laid out on the cold, stainless steel examination table. She was naked; her torso split down the middle and cracked open to allow for the Medical Examiner to study her organs, as Jenny's dead eyes stared up at the ceiling.

Tommy hated the morgue, and autopsies, though he knew that they were a necessary and invaluable part of an investigation. He was not squeamish at all, the bodies did not bother him, nor the sight of what they were about to observe, and he had nothing but respect and admiration for the Medical Examiner's Office and its employees.

What bothered Tommy about this part of the job was not only the finality of death for all the victims he had seen over the years, but the lack of dignity there was in death. Tommy, not being a religious or spiritual man in any way, knew that these bodies were now empty, lifeless, meaningless vessels. But that is precisely what saddened him. Here laid a woman, who just days ago was a beautiful young creature, full of life, thoughts, hopes and dreams, and now she lay naked before complete strangers, who would speak clinically over her corpse, as they opened her up with surgical instruments and sorted through her insides in search of a cause of death.

Yes, Tommy knew young Jenny would feel nothing physically, and would have no knowledge of what these strangers would do to her, but no matter how many of these autopsies he experienced, he still could not help but feel as though he had no business trespassing on these lost souls in such an intimate fashion.

And it was at these moments that he envied the religious, who dreamt of a heaven, or an afterlife, someplace that they could make peace with the finality of life on earth. And cling on to the hope that there was more to it all than lying here on a stainless-steel table, or rotting in the cold earth, or being turned to dust in some crematorium.

Tommy and Jimmy did a cursory examination of Jenny Lindel's body, made notes, and took photographs of some of the things they were unable to spot during their initial search of her frozen body on the promenade.

"Okay," Tommy began speaking, as he wrote notes and took photos, "Tattoos, a pair of swallows on her chest, one above each breast each facing in. You see these, Jimmy? These swallows are old sailors' tattoos, and some say they are to help guide a sailor home. Others say they are to take a sailor's soul to heaven if he should die at sea. And here, on her wrists, these are nautical stars, green on the right wrist and red on the left. These were also traditional sailor designs - the red is on the left or Portside of a ship, and the green is on the right or the Starboard side of a ship. On her hands here, notice on her right hand the first bones of the fingers, H-O-P-E, and the second is R-O-M-A, then on her left hand the first bones read L-E-S-S, and the second bones on this hand read N-T-I-C."

"Yeah? I don't get it," Jimmy replied.

"Well, put it together. HOPELESS ROMANTIC."

"Is there significance to that also?" Jimmy asked.

"It's an album title and a song by the band The Bouncing Souls, a Jersey punk band," Tommy said to Jimmy, then he turned his attention back to the corpse, "You look like you were a cool chick, Jenny."

"And this one here, Tommy? The skull and knives?" Jimmy asked, pointing to a tattoo Jenny had under her belly button of a skull with a pink bow, and two crossed switchblades.

"I'm not sure there is anything to it, other than a design she liked, Jimmy."

M.E. Marcus cleared her throat and began.

"So right away we can see here, see? Here round her eye is that bit of petechiae I mentioned at the crime scene. Now that we removed the makeup, see here — we can detect a little more, also here," M.E. Marcus opened Jenny's eye wider with her fingers, "These broken blood vessels around the edge here, these also appear to be abnormal," she continued.

"To look at her here, we observe remarkably little evidence of any immediate cause of death. She has a few marks on her back and legs, which I believe were caused from the fall she took to that odd abutment from the promenade, but looking at them, I believe they are all post-mortem."

"So, she was dead before they happened?" Jimmy asked.

"Correct," M.E. Marcus continued, "Yes, I think she was dead before she went off the side of the promenade. Now, looking at her again as a whole, and seeing this little bit of petechiae, I immediately go here to the neck where at first we don't witness any visible injury, but look closer… here, Detectives."

M.E. Marcus pointed to three spots on Jenny's neck, "You see these here? They are small, almost unnoticeable abrasions; something large and relatively soft made these. Right away I am thinking Ms. Lindel was choked to death from behind, in what is known as an RNC, or Rear Naked Choke. The perpetrator most likely wrapped his, or her, arm around Ms. Lindel's neck and applied a significant amount of pressure. Enough so to cut off oxygen to the lungs and blood flow to the brain. It is possible she was unconscious within ten to thirty seconds of this chokehold being applied, and death within as little as two minutes of constant pressure is certainly possible. So, I think this young woman was choked, in an RNC, then her attacker threw her over the railing thinking he was disposing of her body into the river, but she ended up on the abutment instead."

Marcus moved down the table and continued to address Tommy and Jimmy while looking at the body, "I don't detect any defensive wounds, but she was wearing several layers of clothing to protect herself from the cold. This clothing, if she did fight back, probably protected her from injury as well. She had black leather gloves on, so we found nothing under her fingernails that could help us identify an attacker, and her attacker's jacket, or coat, was probably thick and most likely padded as well. So, all we see are these slight abrasions, possibly from the nylon, or whatever material the outer shell or layer of the jacket was," she pointed towards Jenny's neck.

"I would suggest that whoever applied this choke was fairly strong, much stronger than Ms. Lindel here anyway, who appears to have been a fairly fit young woman. He or she was able to quickly administer this choke with so much immediate force and pressure to the neck that Ms. Lindel barely had time to put up a fight before she was unconscious, and then all he or she had to do was hang onto her until they were satisfied she was dead. Again, back to the attacker's strength, they would have had to be able to lift her 118-pound body and carry it to, and throw it over, the railing of the promenade."

Marcus briefly looked up at the detectives before resuming.

"Now, here is something that I find highly interesting: We found two almost completely dissolved tablets of Methylenedioxymethamphetamine, or Molly, in her mouth along with what appears to be a considerable amount of alcohol still left in her mouth un-swallowed. But no Molly was detected in her stomach or in her blood, and although she did have a 0.09 blood alcohol content, it appears that all we got from her stomach was alcohol consistent with beer. We… I, don't believe she was drinking whiskey that night, at least not much, and certainly wasn't taking Molly. In fact, no narcotics were found other than a trace amount of marijuana in her system. I believe Ms. Lindel was a drinker, but there is no evidence of her ever doing illegal drugs other than some occasional marijuana, and even that appears to have been rare."

"Interesting, so you think the whiskey and pills were postmortem?" Tommy asked.

"Exactly what I think, Detective Keane. It is my belief that someone choked Ms. Lindel to death using an RNC, then put two tablets of Molly in her mouth and attempted to wash them down with some whiskey. The attacker subsequently threw her over the railing of the promenade, and she landed where we found her. Now, on her clothing, which we bagged for you and placed in the corner, and in her hair, I found traces of alcohol, which I again believe to be some of the whiskey that her attacker used in an attempt to wash the pills down her throat."

"So, in the event her body was found in the river, these actions were possibly an attempt to make it appear that she was drinking and drugging, and took her own life?" Tommy interjected.

"Quite possibly, Detective. Now two other things that I found and that will be of interest to you: When brushing out and going through her hair I found three fairly short curly hairs that came from someone who was black. And our victim, Ms. Lindel, was also approximately six to seven weeks pregnant, and at this point, that is all I have for you, Detective Keane."

"Pregnant? Wow, this case has certainly taken a turn. You've again, as always, given me a lot to run with Marcus. I'd like to say it's a pleasure working with you, but sadly every time we meet, we are standing over some poor dead body. That being said, I'm glad you are on the case."

"Well thank you, Detective Keane, I will take that as a compliment. Now, do as you usually do, and go find whatever animal did this to this young woman and bring them to justice."

"We'll do our best Marcus." Tommy said as he stared down into Jenny's dead eyes. And with that, Tommy and Jimmy took all the physical evidence that needed to be vouchered, as well as M.E. Marcus' written report and headed back to the 2-1 where they would now reclassify their Jane Doe D.O.A. into a full-on Homicide Investigation.

***

Tommy and Jimmy got into the car and began to make their way back to the 2-1.

"Wasn't sure what to expect, but I definitely didn't expect that for some reason I don't know. I guess I thought she was going to be a suicide. What did you think?" Jimmy asked as he started the car.

"I didn't think anything. I try not to decide things without any facts. And, from what I had heard from everyone I had interviewed up to, and until her stepmother, Jenny didn't sound like she was going to be the kind of girl to kill herself. But you never can tell with these things, it's why you try to stay as neutral as possible until you get some facts, and some leads to work off. And now, today, we possess both, some facts and some leads, and we owe them all to M.E. Marcus."

"I get we have some facts now. We know she was murdered and how she was murdered, but what do we have going as far as leads?"

"Well, what did we learn today? Yes, we discovered she was choked to death in the middle of the night, right?"

"Yes."

"We also found out her wallet and ID and any cash or cards she may have had on her were missing, right?"

"Right."

"So, what would most people think, if all of her valuables were missing and she was found dead?"

"Robbery/Homicide, right?"

"Right. And I'm going to guess that our killer might have wanted it to seem like she was robbed. I mean, that makes sense, right? But in reality, our perp here actually didn't know what he wanted to stage, because he also, I believe, wanted us to think she was drunk and high and decided to kill herself by jumping off the promenade and into the river."

"Right."

"But now we have some facts to run with: One, we know she was murdered, and two, we know she was basically drug-free. We know that although she was over the limit, blood alcohol-wise, she certainly wasn't drunk, and we know someone made a really lame attempt at trying to force some drugs and alcohol into her system and failed. And I'm going to go ahead and say that number three is that they did this to make it appear as though her death was by suicide rather than the rear naked choke, which was rather skillfully applied, and which we now know is the cause of death. So, are we in agreement with what we know so far?"

"Absolutely."

"Okay. So, taking these facts into account, I will make the assumption that our perpetrator most likely, if not most certainly, knew our victim. So now we have a little bit of a lead. Miss Jenny Black knew her attacker. This is the assumption we are going to begin to work off of. After that, what do we know?"

"He's probably a black guy."

"Well, it certainly may be a black guy. We don't know that, but we can certainly assume it as a strong possibility because the M.E. found three short curly black hairs coming from what we believe to be a black male, yes. But what is more interesting to me, and what I think will bring us right to our killer is the fact that our Jenny was pregnant. Do you remember what the number one cause of death is to pregnant women in the United States is?"

"It's murder."

"You're right, Jimmy. It's murder. So, do you understand what I mean by leads? No, we don't have any names, but we do have a drummer and perhaps a saxophonist we need to find and talk to. As well as any girlfriends she may have."

"Girlfriends? I don't understand?"

"Yeah, girlfriends. If our Jenny was talking to anybody about the guys she has been sleeping with, or about being pregnant, it's most likely going to be her closest girlfriend. Now it may not necessarily be the case, her best friend might be a guy, but dollars to doughnuts, it's going to be a girl."

"Damn, Tommy, we haven't been in the car for two minutes and already you got this case figured out. I don't think I've ever heard such a quick and on the spot Sherlock Holmes type dissertation in my life?"

"Well, we don't possess anything yet. Still nothing but a young dead girl, and a couple of ideas. Hey, hey, turn left here, then make another left on Second. I'll buy you some lunch before we get back to the precinct, and we can go over what we know so far."

"Cool, where do you want to go? Obviously, you have something in mind."

"Yeah, head down 2nd Avenue. There's a little place called Blockhead's between 50th and 51st. It's a tasty little place, you'll like it."

"After yesterday's meal, I'll go wherever you say, Tom. I woke up dreaming about pierogi," Jimmy grinned.

"You liked that polish food, did you?"

"Oh God yeah, that was awesome. I told my girl I'd take her on our next RDOs."

"I love Little Poland, but here, this is what you should do the next time you bring your girl to the City, Jimmy. Right around the corner from Little Poland is an awesome old Italian joint called John's. Been at that location for at least a hundred years. It's got delicious food and great atmosphere, with all these little tables each with a candle stuck in a wine bottle; it's quite a beautiful and romantic little place."

"Sounds first class."

"Oh, it is, and I promise she'll love it. But the trick is, after your meal you don't get dessert there. Instead, you walk down to 11th and 1st and go to Veniero's. It's a little café, they got the best Italian pastries in the City. I don't care what anyone says, Veniero's is the place. I promise your girl will love it and it'll be almost like two dates in one, cuz it kind of breaks it up a little bit, and you get both experiences."

"That sounds like an excellent date night. I'll definitely plan to do that."

"I try to make a trip down to Veniero's around this time each year for some cheesecake and Pignoli cookies for Christmas. They make this Italian cheesecake that my brother-in-law, Tony, goes gaga for. Personally, it's not for me, it's not creamy like regular cheesecake, but those Pignoli cookies? Mmm, I will make myself ill eating those Pignoli cookies, the best in the City."

"I am sold; I love Italian pastries. Hey, that place right? Blockhead's?"

"Yeah, that's the one," Tommy replied as Jimmy pulled into the bus stop and the two detectives exited their vehicle.

***

Blockhead's was a tiny Mexican Restaurant. It looked fun and inviting from the outside. It had a metal exterior that was painted a dark gray with turquoise and inside it was tiny, with a small bar and a dozen or so tables. Colorful Mexican cut-out flag banners known as Papel Picado hung from the ceiling, and colored lights gave the place a bright, festive appearance. Upon entry, they were greeted by a young and small Mexican girl.

"Sit wherever you want, guys."

All but two of the tables were taken at the time, so Tommy and Jimmy took a table near the front, as far away from the other occupied tables as possible, so they could talk with a little privacy.

"Cool place. I love me some Mexican food."

"Yeah, I like this place. It's a little different from your typical Mexican joint. There are a few of these around the City, but I try to stop by this one whenever I'm in the neighborhood. There used to be one on 81st and 2nd that I went to quite often."

When the waitress returned with a couple menus and asked for their drink orders, Tommy asked for a Pepsi and Jimmy an iced tea. Jimmy read the menu, but Tommy didn't bother as he already knew what he wanted.

"No menu necessary? You know what you want?" Jimmy asked.

"Yes sir, my standby, the Steak Chimichurri Burrito."

"Standby, huh? Okay, same for me then. You did right by me yesterday, let's see if you do today. Do you wanna start with something? How 'bout the Nachos Grande?"

"No, we won't need that. These burritos are as big as your head."

"Ha! Okay, I'll take your word for it."

Just as Jimmy finished his sentence the waitress brought their drinks and took their orders.

"So, what's next?" Jimmy asked, "I see where you want to go as far as searching out this woman's killer, but where do you want to start?"

"I guess we'll start with the stepmom, hopefully she can turn us onto some friend and boyfriend information. Then we'll just start bouncing around doing some interviews until something points us in the right direction."

"Right. Just ask around, a man once told me."

"Exactly, Jimmy, just ask around."

Chapter Sixteen

2:52 PM The Lindels home on East 92nd Street.

They parked at the fire hydrant not far from the Lindels' home, made their way up the steps of the stoop, and rang the bell. The young Central American woman answered the door again. She was dressed in a similar manner, a simple t-shirt and jeans, and she invited the detectives in and asked them to sit in the parlor.

Jimmy sat on the sofa and Tommy on a wing chair towards the back of the room, leaving the wing chair at the front of the room open and available to Mrs. Lindel when she arrived, which she did only moments after the two detectives made themselves comfortable. She stepped into the room and both detectives stood up to greet her.

"No, please sit," she said immediately as she saw them rise.

Jimmy sat right back down but Tommy paused for just a second. Mrs. Lindel was dressed simply in tight, blue, denim skinny jeans, high-heeled shoes, and a simple red and blue, floral print, button-down blouse with a semi-ruffled deep cut collar. But the way she stood in the entryway to the parlor from the hallway, with the dappled sunlight bouncing all over her from head to toe, was stunning. She was an attractive woman when they had met the day before when she was in her exercise gear, but today her hair was done, and it fell perfectly over her shoulders. Her makeup was perfect and barely noticeable, showing off just how beautiful her face was. And her clothing, although quite simple, hugged every feminine feature and line of her fit body in such a way to display her fine physique, yet remain classy and somewhat understated. It was obvious at this moment how Mrs. Lindel was indeed Miss Western Massachusetts in her younger years, and a bit surprising that her looks alone did not catapult her into a more successful acting career. Tommy sat, and Mrs. Lindel took a seat in the wingback chair he had left vacant for her.

"Good morning. Or I guess, no, good afternoon, Detective Keane, Detective Colletti. So… So… The autopsy, you are coming from the autopsy?" Lisa Lindel began as soon as she sat, her voice already shaking in nervous anticipation.

"Yes, ma'am," Tommy began, "We don't believe Jenny's death was a suicide. We believe she was murdered."

"Oh my God," Lisa replied in a low, rather astonished voice, her hand rising to meet her chest. "By whom? Who do you think would do such a thing? And, and how?" She asked, her hand now over her mouth and her eyes leaving Tommy's and glancing off into nowhere in disbelief.

"We have no idea. But we are certain she was intentionally killed, and we believe it was very quick and relatively painless. Now, we're going to ask you some questions, ask if we can search Jenny's room and look through some of her things, and hopefully you can point us in some direction with this case. You see, we know nothing about Jenny, and right now you are the only person that we know who knows her at all."

"Of course, of course," she said, wiping tears from her eyes, "Yes yes, yes to all of it, whatever you need, of course. My God, murder, who? What kind of? Who in the world would murder our Jenny?" Lisa Lindel's tears began to run down the cheeks of her surprised, almost dumbfounded face, and faintly she said aloud, "Murder?"

They all sat silently for a moment, to allow Lisa to regain her composure, then Tommy began.

"Mrs. Lindel."

"Lisa, please," she said softly, still staring off into nowhere in disbelief.

"Okay, Lisa, do you have any idea who may have wanted to kill or hurt Jenny?"

"No, absolutely not," she replied, still in that low soft voice, "I can't think of anyone that would or could intentionally do this."

"We understand she did some show promoting. Did Jenny have another job, a regular day job of any kind?"

"No, living here she was well taken care of, and she actually worked really hard with her shows, she loved her music."

"Can you tell me where she went to college?"

"She went to Pace, in Westchester County."

"And high school?"

"Marymount, over on 5th Avenue."

"You mentioned a few names of some friends, Max, Julie, and Jerry. Do you know any last names for these people? Phone numbers, anything at all to help put us in touch with them?"

"No, I'm sorry I don't. Not to my knowledge anyway, but I will certainly try to search everything I can for you. I do believe all of them lived on the West Side. I am not sure why I think that, but I do. I think, I know Julie was probably her best and longest female friend, and Jerry was also a longtime friend. I think, but may be mistaken, but I think that Max and Julie, were a couple. They were all into music, I know that they were all deeply into that punk rock scene and ran around with other punk rockers and musicians. I think they were all in the same circle. Shame on me I know so little about her private life. I'm so sorry, oh God, I'm so sorry," Lisa said through tears.

"It's alright, Lisa, you're helping us already. And soon, more things will start to come to you, believe me, sometimes it takes a little while to get over the shock of an event like this and then you will begin to remember more. And when you do, you'll share it with us. Relax, take your time. May we go to Jenny's room?"

"Yes, of course. Her room is upstairs on the third floor. Please, follow me."

Lisa Lindel stood and walked to the staircase in front of the front door and began to make her way up with Tommy right behind her, and Jimmy right behind him.

Tommy took in everything he could about the Lindels' home. From what he could view, by peering into any open doors they passed on the way up the two flights of stairs, it was an incredibly respectable, well-kept home. Other than that, there was nothing he could see that interested him as far as his investigation was concerned. They reached the door to Jenny's room, which was closed. Lisa turned the knob and opened it, but then hesitated and did not enter. Possibly she felt it was now a crime scene of some sort, or possibly she now felt it was hallowed ground not to be disturbed by her presence. Either way, she stopped short at the threshold.

"This is it; this is Jenny's room. Do you want me to stay with you? Do you want to be alone as you search? What? What would you like, Detectives?" she asked, still standing in the hallway, her hands clasped together.

"Whatever you prefer. You may certainly stay here as we go through Jenny's things, or if you wish you may remove yourself as we look. It's up to you. We will not remove anything without asking you first, and if we think something is evidence, we will absolutely tell you what it is and why we may need to remove it."

"Um. Sure. I think I'll just stand here if that works?"

"Of course."

Tommy and Jimmy entered the room. It, like the rest of the home, was spotless and neat. Possibly it was the way they all naturally lived, but Tommy thought it was more likely because they had a housekeeper who appeared to be in on a daily basis. The walls were painted lavender, up to the picture molding that came down about a foot from the ceiling. From there on up was white, as was the ceiling. The curtains were a heavy, high quality, white cotton fabric, and the shades were also white and pulled halfway down the windows. Tommy expected the room to be covered in band posters, photographs, and stickers, but rather it was decorated almost more like a page from Country Living Magazine. It was a charming, extremely feminine room. The bedspread was a lighter shade of lavender than the walls, and had lovely flowers embroidered all over it. The bed was neatly and tightly made, with the white sheets folded over the top of the bed spread and four white pillows sitting on top, and a darker purple wedding ring quilt, also with a floral motif folded up neatly on the foot of the bed.

Jenny did display a few show posters on her walls, but they were behind glass, in wooden frames. Tommy was surprised when he took a closer look to see they were all signed show posters of hugely popular punk bands, including The Clash, Social Distortion, Rancid, Green Day, H2O, and The Specials. Tommy reached up and touched the glass over Joe Strummer's signature on the Clash poster, almost in disbelief that this young woman would have it here on her wall.

Along with the framed posters were a dozen or so framed photographs of Jenny and her father Charlie, all with musicians backstage at shows, except for three; one at her high school graduation, one at her college graduation, and one of her as a little girl, sitting on her mother's lap with her father leaning down smiling cheek to cheek with his wife and daughter, Jenny, who appeared to be about six. Tommy paused for a second. These photos touched him, and he had to take a deep breath, and swallow, to keep from getting emotional, before continuing his search.

Tommy opened the closet where he found a sea of black clothing. Almost every item was black. He removed all her jackets and went through every pocket. Each one turned up empty. Tommy did the same with about a dozen black hoodies - each with a different band name - and again, only empty pockets. Next, he searched a tall shelf of cubby holes packed with almost all black t-shirts, removing each one in case there was some clue hidden behind or between them, then replaced them all one by one. On the floor of her closet were over a dozen pairs of shoes and boots, all meticulously clean and well cared for: Doc Martens, Converse, Adidas, all black, and each one turned upside down by the detectives in hopes a clue of some kind may fall out, but there was nothing.

There were two stand up dressers and two nightstands. The first dresser had seventeen pairs of black jeans and pants: all of their pockets empty. There were more t-shirts and sweatshirts neatly folded and tucked into them, all black, but no clues.

The second dresser was full of socks and underwear. In the top drawer, among the 50/50 ratio of both black and white cotton socks - the only non-black clothing items the detectives found so far - is where they found a pair of brass knuckles and a couple of photos of Jenny with a group of friends out for the evening at some bar. The second drawer held all her panties, everything from simple cotton underwear to lace G-strings, and these came in a variety of colors but were still predominantly black. Still, no clues. The next drawer was full of bras, but again, no clues.

The next chest of drawers had still more clothing. The top drawer contained stockings and pantyhose, but no clues. The second drawer was night gowns and pajamas, still almost all black but no clues. But the bottom drawer was an interesting drawer; it was filled with seven photo albums and scrapbooks, and dozens and dozens of loose photographs, some small and some 8x10's, as well as a few old stubs from different Broadway shows and larger concerts Jenny had attended over the years.

"Mrs. Lindel? Lisa?" Tommy said rather loudly, getting Mrs. Lindel's attention, "I'd like to go through some of these photos with you please. I'd like to see if you can identify anyone as Jenny's current friends, please."

"Of course, Detective, may we, can we remove them from the room though? I can set them on the table downstairs and go through them. I don't think… her room, I feel, I feel like I'm trespassing somehow," Lisa replied standing in the threshold.

"Absolutely, Mrs. Lindel, whatever makes it easier for you."

"Lisa, please."

"Absolutely, Lisa. Jimmy, can you take all of these photo's downstairs with Lisa, and see if she can identify anyone in them."

"Sure."

Tommy removed the entire drawer from the chest and stuck all the albums and photos back in them as they were found. Jimmy then took the entire drawer down to the dining room table on the first floor, where he sat with Lisa Lindel, who looked through each album and sifted through all the loose photos.

Tommy, now alone in the room as he preferred to be, began to search through everything once again. He looked at everything and into everything, he took the framed art off the walls to observe if anything was taped behind them, he took the drawers out of the dressers to check if anything was hidden in, under, or behind them. He moved the dressers around to check if anything was beneath them, and continually came up with nothing, other than a small push button stiletto switchblade that was in Jenny's nightstand. In her adjoining bathroom, nothing of interest, just the usual toiletries any young woman would own. Tommy did intentionally take a second inspection of the medicine cabinet, the trash, and even behind the towels folded neatly in the small linen closet, for a pregnancy test, or remnants of one, and found nothing.

Tommy sighed and walked around both the bedroom and bathroom one more time until he was satisfied. He had looked at everything, and then he slowly and quietly walked down to the first floor, sticking his head into every open door along the way, but again, seeing nothing that piqued his interest. On the first floor, he found Jimmy and Lisa at the dining room table. Lisa had been crying again, although her tears were now dry. It was obvious by her face, she had again become emotional over the photographs.

"Well, Tom, we have a few faces to go along with our names now," Jimmy said as Tommy walked into the room.

"Alright," Tommy replied, "Please show me what you got."

Tommy leaned over the table where Jimmy had five photographs separated from the dozens that had all now been put back into the drawer from the dresser.

"This one is of her friend Julie. I'm sorry and embarrassed to say I don't know her last name," Lisa said with her finger on a photo of a young woman.

"This one is of Julie, and I am pretty sure this is her friend Max with them," Lisa said as she pointed to another photo.

"This one I am sure is Jerry. They've been friends for years. and again, I am embarrassed and ashamed that I don't know her friends better. I'm sorry, Jenny was never close with me. I loved her but I think she, no, I know she always resented me coming into their lives when she was nineteen. For years she was the only woman in her father's life, and it was like, almost like right after she left for college, I replaced her. It may sound silly, but I don't think she ever accepted the thought of her father loving another woman," she again began to weep.

"It's okay, Lisa, it's okay," Tommy said, and he laid his hand gently on her shoulder, in an attempt to comfort her.

"Thank you," she replied and placed her hand firmly on top of his, in an effort to accept his comfort.

"Here, this is Jenny and Jerry together again," she pointed to one of those photo booth strips that had four black and white photos of the two of them making silly faces for the camera. "And here is one of all of them together with some other friends, at some bar or club somewhere. I'm sorry I don't know any of these other people," Lisa stated as she pointed to the last of the five photos.

"May we keep these, Lisa?" Tommy asked.

"Of course, anything you need, Detective Keane. Whatever it takes to find out what happened and who killed our Jenny."

"Can you tell me about your house staff, please? We'd also like to ask them some questions. I understand you have a maid, or a housekeeper. Is anyone else here in the house, staff-wise?" Tommy asked.

"Yes, yes of course. Well, you met Tina, who let you in and who answered the door for you the first time you visited. She is here six days a week. We also have a chef, Carlo, who comes in on Mondays and shops and does some cooking for the week, then returns another two or three times a week if we ask him to for a dinner or a special event. We also have a gardener named Michael, he is here on Tuesdays and cleans and weeds and tends to the garden in the back and cares for all our houseplants… and that's it. I don't think they will be of any help, but I know you know what it is you gentlemen are looking for from a police standpoint. So, yes, if you'd like to interview Tina now and the others when they are available."

"Yes, if Tina is still here, I would like to ask her a few questions, please," Tommy replied.

"Sure, I think she's in the basement doing laundry or cleaning the gym, let me call for her," Lisa stood up and walked over to the corner of the room and pushed a button on an intercom that was on the wall, "Tina, Tina dear, wherever you are can you come to the dining room, please?"

"Yes, ma'am," was Tina's response. And in less than a minute Tina walked into the room.

"Tina, these two detectives have some questions for you. Our, oh my God, I can't say it. Our Jenny has been killed," Lisa Lindel put her head in her hands and started crying.

Tommy again placed his hand on her shoulder. "Jimmy, sit here with Lisa for a moment, and Tina and I will sit in the living room, and I'll ask her a few questions, okay?"

"Absolutely," Jimmy responded.

"C'mon, Tina, let's go in the living room for a bit."

"Yes sir, Detective," she responded, and as she passed Lisa whose head was still in her hands, she reached out and touched her shoulder.

***

Tommy and Tina sat in the parlor, Tommy in one of the wing chairs and Tina on the sofa.

"Okay, Tina, I want you to know you are in no way in any kind of trouble, so don't be nervous with us, all right? We are here because someone killed Jenny, and that's who we want to find. You may think you don't know anything but maybe you do, and maybe you don't even know what you know, if that makes sense? So, I'm just going to ask you a few questions, okay?"

"Yes, yes please, sir," Tina replied. Her English was excellent, but she still carried a rather heavy Spanish accent.

"So how long have you worked here for the Lindels?"

"Five years, at least."

"Did you know Jenny well?"

"Yes, I think I know Jenny pretty good. She is a very, very nice person."

"How often would you see her? How many days a week?"

"Oh, I don't know, sometimes every day of the week, sometimes no days of the week, but I think I see her at least once or twice every week."

"Did you two talk often? Was she friendly to you?"

"Oh yes, she always talked to me. She was a very nice person, I like Jenny very, very much. She always very kind and very sweet person to me. I cannot believe that she is killed, this is so sad, so, heartbreaking to me," she answered as she wiped a tear from her eye.

"Did you know any of Jenny's friends?"

"Yes, I meet her best friend, Julie, and her best boyfriend Jerry many times, too, and two time her friend Pete, and her other friend Max sometimes, too."

"Do you know any of their last names?"

"No, sorry," Tina answered, shaking her head.

"Who is Pete?"

"Pete is a boy; I think a boyfriend. I see them kiss, tall, skinny, white man with tattoos. You know, a rocker."

"Okay and what can you tell me about Jerry?"

"Jerry is very nice man. Jerry and Jenny are very good friends, since before college I think, maybe from high school? They are friends for a long time, like Julie, she is also a friend for a long time."

"Good, what else can you tell me about Jerry? Was he Jenny's boyfriend also?"

"No. Jerry want to be I think though. I think he love Jenny very much but no, Jenny only like Jerry. No love him more than a friend."

"Did they ever fight?"

"No, I never see that."

"Is this Jerry?" Tommy showed Tina the photo of Jerry and Jenny in the photo booth that Lisa Lindel also identified as Jerry.

"Yes, this is Jerry."

"Can you tell me who is in this photo, please?" Tommy placed the group shot of eight people in a club on the table for Tina to see.

"Yes. This is Jenny, this is Julie, this is Jerry, and this is Max, these is all I know here," Tina said, as she leaned forward in her chair and pointed to each in the photo.

"So, no Pete?

"No, no Pete."

"Okay, you are doing great here, Tina. You are helping me out a lot. Now, what can you tell me about everyone that works here? I know you, how about Carlo, what can you tell me about Carlo?"

"Carlo is nice man, and a really good cook. He comes in on Mondays, sometimes on other different days and nights of the week also."

"Tell me about him."

"Him small and skinny, maybe fifty-five years old, very nice man, very good cook, nice wife. He has two daughters in New Jersey. That's all I know. Nice."

"How about Michael?"

"Michael takes care of the garden on Tuesdays, also maybe fifty-five or sixty. Him also a small man, very nice, very quiet, sometimes I don't even notice him."

"Okay, and that's everybody right? Anybody else work in the house or visit the house regularly we should know of, or I haven't asked you about?"

"Mrs. Lindel sometimes has friends who come for maybe a lunch or a dinner party, and has sometimes a massage lady, a yoga lady, or a trainer to come by also every week."

"Do you know all of these people also?"

"The friends, no. Sometimes I know a little but no, not really. The massage lady is Mary, the yoga lady is Christine, and the trainer is named Amobi. They all come every week to do classes with Mrs. Lindel, and Mr. Lindel sometimes too, before him sick. All nice people, usually they come early in the day before Mr. and Mrs. Lindel take lunch, but sometimes later also, depends on that week's schedule, and now all different times with Mr. Lindel in the hospital."

"Have things changed a lot with Mr. Lindel in the hospital, Tina?"

"Yes and no. It's mostly the same for me, I come in to clean every day, but the schedule does change sometimes. For exercise staff they in and out at different hours now since Mr. Lindel has been sick. We must work around when he is home, work around when he is away, work around the doctors and nurses. When he is in the hospital Mrs. Lindel needs to visit, so it changes things around a little, so yes there are changes but not too much to me, mostly for the other regular staff peoples."

"Okay, Tina, well thank you dear. You have been helpful today. We're all done now, I'm sorry to take you away from your work."

"Oh no, it is okay. I'm very happy to help. We all loved Jenny very much. I can, I cannot believe this, Jenny was good girl. I hope you catch these bad people, and I hope you catch them quick!"

"Thank you, Tina."

Tommy and Tina returned to the dining room, where Jimmy and Lisa Lindel still sat.

"I think we are good to go for the moment, Jimmy. Mrs. Lindel, would you like us to return that drawer of photos back to its rightful place for you?"

"No, Tina or I will put it back, thank you, Detective Keane. Thanks for the visit, and the next time I see you I hope you have some news on who committed this horrid act."

"Yes, ma'am, let's hope that is the case. Thank you again for your time, Lisa, we appreciate it. And thank you, Tina, for your time as well, dear."

"Yes sir, Detective, please find who did this thing to our Jenny, please."

Tommy and Jimmy left the Lindels' home and headed back to their car.

***

"Not a lot there hey, Tommy?" Jimmy asked as soon as they got in the car.

"Well, maybe more than I expected. It was great that Mrs. Lindel let us search the room, so that's done. And although it was pretty fruitless, we do have some images of her friends that we didn't have before, plus maybe a little something extra to look into?"

"You're thinking maybe Jerry, right?"

"Yeah, we're going to have to get ahold of Jerry for sure. He's a longtime friend, he's emotionally attached, and possibly very much in love with a pregnant Jenny. And he's the only black person in the mix so far, so as of right now, he's the one I am most interested to meet."

Chapter Seventeen

Tommy and Jimmy returned to the 2-1, and Tommy instantly started to investigate everything he could, social media-wise, about Jenny Lindel. Now that he knew who he was looking for, he found her on Facebook within minutes. From her page he then found her friends, Julie, Jerry, and Max. And after a little more searching he had all three full names Julie Mayer, Jerry Quick, and Max Spicnic.

Plugging these names into the NYPD's computer system gave Tommy all three addresses, and a phone number for Miss Julie Mayer. Tommy quickly picked up his phone and called. When she did not answer, he left a message.

"Hello, Miss Julie Mayer? This is Detective Tommy Keane from the 21st Precinct. If you would be so kind, please call me back. Your name came up in an investigation I am conducting. Please realize you are in no way a suspect in a crime, but I believe you may be able to help me out. I hope to hear from you soon. Thank you."

Tommy went back to his computer work and in less than ten minutes he received a call from Julie Mayer.

"Hello, Detective Keane, 2-1 Squad."

"Yes, hello. This is Julie Mayer. You just called and left me a message a few minutes ago. What — what do you think I can help you with, Detective?"

"I'd like to come and meet with you, if possible, Miss Mayer. Do you think you can make time for me this evening?"

"Uh, um, yes I might. But may I ask what this is about, Detective?"

"Well, I would rather talk to you in person, but yes this is pertaining to your friend, Jenny Lindel - Jenny Black. Do you think we can meet this evening? I want to ask you a couple of questions about her, please."

"Oh my God! Do you know where she is? Is she alright? I've tried calling her for over a week. We couldn't reach her at all, and we're all worried sick! She just disappeared. Is she alright? Please sir, what can you tell me?"

"Can I come meet you, Julie? If I can, you tell me where and I'll come right over and tell you all about Jenny."

"Oh, sure, um… How about in an hour? I live at 222 West 83rd Street."

"I'll be at your apartment in an hour. Thank you." Tommy hung up and turned to Jimmy.

"Hey, I found a friend of Jenny's to interview in an hour on the West Side. You want to come along or are you signing out for the day?"

"Hell yeah, I'll go. I could use the overtime. Plus, I want to stay with this one through to the end."

"Okay cool, tell the boss and we'll head out in a few."

***

6:28pm 222 West 83rd Street

Tommy and Jimmy arrived in front of 222 West 83rd Street and lucked out with an actual parking spot a few car lengths down from the entrance. 222 was a large, pre-war building of yellowish colored brick, which held one hundred and twenty apartments.

Tommy identified himself to the doorman and told him they wanted Julie Mayer. The doorman rang up to the Mayers' apartment on the third floor and the detectives made their way to the elevator and then up to the third floor.

When the elevator door opened and they stepped out, Julie Mayer stood in the hallway with the door to her apartment open.

"Right here, Detectives, this way," she said.

They walked over to her door and Tommy showed his detective shield, clipped to his belt, and introduced himself.

"Hello, Ms. Mayer, I'm Detective Keane, and this is Detective Colletti, we're from the 21st Precinct."

"Hey, uh, hi. You can call me Julie. Please come in."

Julie stood about five-foot-three. She had a pleasing shade of light brown hair, cut into a bob that was shorter in the back and longer in the front. She wore dark navy denim jeans with slip-on Vans sneakers, and a snug fitting brown t-shirt with a pickup truck that said "The Grizzly Band" in yellow ink. She had a small tattoo of a nautical star on her right wrist and a heart tattooed on her left wrist, a black stud in her nose, and a tiny hole in her lip where she had, at least at one time, wore a lip ring.

Once inside, the detectives saw a young man of about twenty-six. He sat on the couch in the living area and stood up as the detectives entered the apartment. He stood about five-foot-nine, had short hair that was kind of curly on top but tapered down to nothing on his neck and long but close-cut sideburns that ran all the way down to his jaw line. He wore a black t-shirt with a tiger's head on it that read "The Split Seconds, Washington DC," in a Shang Hai font - Tommy took note it was the same band name that Jenny Lindel wore on a guitar pick around her neck - and tight gray tapered denim jeans. It was Max Spicnic.

Both detectives recognized him within a second, and thought to themselves how lucky they were, for this two-in-one interview.

"This is my boyfriend, Max. I hope you don't mind I asked him to come over. I'm, I'm extremely nervous. You're going to tell me something awful, aren't you Detective Keane?"

"No, no, I don't mind at all, Julie," Tommy said as he extended his arm and shook hands with Max, "Please, both of you sit down."

As they did Tommy continued, "And yes, what I need to say is awful. One week ago, your friend Jenny's body was discovered in Carl Schurz Park. She was dead and frozen solid. It took almost an entire week to identify her, and it also took the entire week for her body to thaw out enough to be able to do an autopsy, which was done this morning. We were able to determine that she had indeed been intentionally killed."

Both Julie and Max sat on the brown sofa, intently looking at Tommy's face as he spoke. Julie had tears running down both her cheeks and a grimace on her face as she listened, and Max sat still and expressionless except for his left leg, which shook up and down uncontrollably with nervousness.

"We've already met with Jenny's mother, who positively identified Jenny to us. We've spoken to her at length, but she had no idea who could possibly do anything like this to her daughter. Now from what I understand you are two of her closest friends, and you, Julie, are one of her oldest. So, I would like to ask you some questions, and determine if you can help us find out who in the world would kill this young woman and why."

"God, yes of course," Julie barely squeaked out of her mouth, as she wiped the tears from her face and eyes with her hands and her wrists.

"Okay. Let me let you gain your composure, Julie. Relax a little, dear. How about a glass of water for her, Max?" Tommy asked.

"Yeah, of course," Max jumped up and stepped into the adjoining kitchen. He ran a glass of water from the tap and returned with it and a roll of paper towels for Julie, "Would you gentlemen like some water, or a soda or something? A cup of coffee? We have a Keurig?"

"No, thanks," Jimmy replied.

"No, thank you, Max. Please come and sit and we'll start." And Tommy began. "How long ago did you two become acquainted with Jenny?"

"I have been friends with her since I was about sixteen. We went to different schools, but had mutual friends, and we clicked over music. We were both big music fans. We still are." Julie said.

"And I've known her for about five or six years, ever since Julie and I began dating. These two were best friends, and I… well Jenny became one of my best friends also. We all get along so well the three of us. She's over here all the time. We all enjoy the same music, go to shows together, the movies together, everything. We do everything together," Max added.

"So, Jenny was not a loner then?" Tommy asked.

"A loner? No, she had me and a couple other friends. She was quite selective of who she hung out with, but a loner? No, I wouldn't say that." Julie stated.

"No, in fact I would say far from it. Like Julie said, she was selective in who she hung out with, but I saw her every week, and Julie and Jenny saw each other a few times a week and they talked on the phone almost daily," Max added.

"Well, her stepmother seemed to think she was a bit of a loner and had few friends."

"Well, her stepmother barely knew her," Julie said scornfully. "They never became close, the two of them. Jenny never liked Lisa, and honestly never gave her a chance, and Lisa certainly never tried to make it work with Jenny either. She's not a bad woman at all, but right from the beginning they got off on the wrong foot, and Jenny always resented Lisa. I don't think they necessarily hated each other, but they are two completely different people, and both fought for the attention of Jenny's father, Charlie. He is a kind and good-natured man, but really, well, I guess I'm mostly sorry for him, living with two women who disliked each other. All he wanted was a happy wife and a happy daughter. I'm sorry, that was not what you were asking. No, no, Jenny was not a loner, she had a few friends and she kept us all very close."

"Okay, Julie, I'm going to get a little personal. What can you tell me about Jenny's love life?"

"She had a couple of guys she liked, but no one steady, and she hadn't had a big love since college."

"Can you give me some names? Who was she dating or sleeping with?"

Julie paused.

"She had a couple of guys like I said. One was a guy from Brooklyn named Joe, and a guy from Staten Island named Pete. She would date the both of them semi-regularly, but not seriously."

"How did you feel about these two?"

"I liked them both fine. Friendly guys, sweet to her, she never complained about either of them. To tell you the truth, she never dated assholes. Jenny would rather be alone than date a douche."

"How about you, Max? What did you think of Jenny's boyfriends?" Tommy asked, turning toward Max.

"I liked Pete better than Joe, but only because we liked more of the same things. Joe was fine though, not a bad guy, I guess."

"Is one of them a drummer?"

"Yes, Pete was. Why, does that mean something?" Julie asked excitedly.

"No. No I'm sorry. I heard she dated a drummer from The Hudson Falcons, and I was not aware of who he was. No, I didn't mean anything by that, I'm only asking," Tommy replied, shaking his head.

"Oh, oh got it," Julie stated flatly, "No, Pete wasn't in The Hudson Falcons, that was Jeremy, I think. And that was only a one-night thing, no romance happening, no nothing. Just a one-night stand, a couple years ago."

"Ah, okay. Now what can you tell me about Jerry?"

"Jerry Quick?" Julie asked, "Jerry is a long-time mutual friend of mine and Jenny's. His name came up also? It should, if you have my name, I'm sure you heard his. Jerry is our friend since we were about seventeen. I think he started hanging around with us about eight or ten months after Jenny and I became friends."

"And Jerry plays saxophone?"

"Yes, he can play any brass, but he mostly likes the trombone, he's also a decent piano player."

"Have Jenny and Jerry ever been an item? Did they ever date?"

"No! Absolutely not. But he wishes. He's had it bad for Jenny since we were teenagers."

"Never a love connection?"

"No never, and I would know. Jenny tells me everything."

"So never a love connection, but he was, can I say, in love with Jenny?" Tommy asked.

"I would say yes, undeniably in love with her," Julie answered.

"I would say madly in love with her," Max added.

"I'm not sure about madly in love with her," Julie said turning her attention to Max. "He for sure had a big crush on Jenny, and for years, yes, but he was not obsessed with her."

"He was! He was definitely obsessed with Jenny, Jules, c'mon. He was infatuated with her. The guy followed you two around like a puppy dog. I mean seriously, the guy was relentlessly in love with her."

"C'mon, Max, you're making Jerry sound like a stalker now."

"No, no I'm not. I'm simply stating a fact. Jerry was infatuated with Jenny, and he would do anything to be with her. I'm not saying his feelings are a bad thing, that was just how it was."

"Well, I don't like the way it sounds," Julie continued, switching her attention between Tommy and Max. "Jerry is a fantastic friend to all of us. He's always been available for Jenny and me, and you too, Max. Anytime we needed anything, Jerry's dependable. He's a truly good and decent guy, and yes, he is, was, in love with Jenny. But it never got in the way of our, or I guess I should say, their friendship."

"Okay. I would like to hear a little more about Jerry, but please understand, Julie, and you too, Max, I'm trying to put together a picture of someone, of your friend, Jenny, who I never met before, okay? Understand, I have nothing to go on other than your friend was killed seven, maybe nine, days ago. It took us almost a week simply to figure out who she was, and so now, we are trying to piece together her life."

Tommy looked from Julie to Max and back to Julie, and continued, "Anything that may help lead us to her killer. And anything I may ask is in no way accusatory. I am searching for some clarity, and some truth. You guys understand?"

"Yes, sir," Max answered.

"Yes, yes of course," said Julie.

"Okay, so you told me that Jerry was in love with Jenny, and for many, many years now. And, well, it sounds to me that Jenny never had any feelings for Jerry. Am I correct?"

"Yes, that is true," Julie answered.

"Has Jerry ever, or often, been jealous of Jenny's boyfriends or lovers?"

"Well… yes, he has. Well, he is, you know, an artist, a musician, and he can be quite emotional at times, and quite, well I mean, he can be a bitch. And sometimes, on occasion, he would become quite depressed that Jenny did or when she would, have a boyfriend or even a one-night stand. He would sometimes be upset about it, yes. It did, would, hurt him," Julie explained.

"Did he ever act out, or confront her? As in, would it ever be an issue between them?"

"No. Well he would kinda… act like a bitch, like a bitchy high school girl who was jealous of some boy. But never act out."

"C'mon, Julie, he could act out. Remember that night outside of The Dublin House?" Max interjected.

"What happened at The Dublin House?" Tommy asked.

"It was nothing," Julie answered, giving Max a look of disapproval.

"Tell him, Julie," Max said.

Julie let out a little sigh and said, "We were all hanging out late one night after coming home from seeing the band Gogol Bordello at Irving Plaza. We were all having an outstanding night, and had been drinking a bit, quite a bit all night, and Jenny and our friend Mike were hanging all over one another. They had been making out at the show and then well, later at the bar, at the Dublin House, when Mike went to the bathroom, Jenny told us, all of us out loud, how she was going to take Mike home and fuck his brains out. And well, well after Mike came out of the bathroom, Jenny and him said goodnight and left. They, they caught a cab back to her place and Jerry, poor Jerry was… well he didn't take it well. He went outside after they left and put his fist through a van window, after which he picked up a garbage can and threw it onto the hood of a car. He went a little nuts, is all. I think, well he could handle her dating guys, but couldn't handle it being thrown in his face like that."

"Do you think she said that intentionally, Julie? To make him jealous or angry on purpose?"

"Oh no definitely not," Julie shook her head, "She was just having fun, and we were, we were all drinking and partying, and she basically announced to all of us that she was going to go fuck Mike, and well, Jerry didn't take it well."

"Did Jerry and Jenny ever fight?"

"No, never."

"Any other violent outbursts like that, that you can tell me about, that were related to his relationship with Jenny?"

"No, Jerry isn't a violent man, he really isn't. He's… God how do I say this? Well, like I said before, he's more of a whiny bitch. He never acted out like that, before or after that night, but he would often call me or text me to whine and complain that she, Jenny, that she would be so happy if she was with him, instead of any of the other guys she would date."

"He isn't a violent man, but he was a martial artist, so I mean he was capable of violence though," Max added.

"A martial artist? Do you recall what he studied?" Tommy asked.

"Yes, he did Aikido for a while, and Jiu Jitsu also. He was a pretty confident guy and was particularly proud of his training with the martial arts."

"You've been friends with him the longest, Julie. Was Jerry a fighter? Did he fight often?"

"I've never seen him fight, but he would talk about fights and fighting when we were teenagers. But mostly I think it was talk, like he was trying to impress us, macho stuff more than real stuff I think?"

"Max? What more can you add to that?"

"That kinda sums up my experience with Jerry also. Other than that night at The Dublin House, I've never seen Jerry be violent, but I have heard him tell some stories about fights, and about training in his dojo, and about how tough he is. But, once, one time, we were at the club, Arlene's Grocery down on Stanton Street, and a bit of a brawl began. Jerry grabbed a guy from behind and choked him almost unconscious. But he was not seriously involved in the brawl, he only stepped in to help the doorman, who was a little outnumbered. I've never actually seen him fight with anyone other than that, and over the years we have spent a lot of time together."

"Got it, thank you. Let me ask you, when was the last time you saw Jenny?"

"Well, it has been exactly… eight days," Max said.

"Indeed, so it would have been the day, the same day of the homicide?"

"Oh Jesus!" Julie said louder than she had spoken during the interview so far and began crying again. Max placed his arm around her to comfort her.

"Gee, uh yes… It sounds like that is correct," Max replied.

"Please, tell me what you guys did, that day or night?"

"Well, we all met up at The Storehouse, on 23rd. It's a bar on West 23rd Street," Max said.

"I'm familiar with the place," Tommy replied, "Who was we?"

"Only the four of us. Me and Julie, Jenny and Jerry. I was — I had worked late that day, and I work a couple blocks over and so we decided to meet at The Storehouse that evening. Nothing special that night, some drinks and some pub grub. It was getting a little late, around midnight or so, and Jenny got a phone call. I didn't ask from who, and she told us she was done for the night, and she was going to head home. Nothing weird or unusual, I didn't think anything of it. Did you Julie?"

"No, nothing, nothing at all," Julie said softly as she wiped her tears and nose with a paper towel.

"So, what? She just left?"

"Yeah, nothing rushed really. She just said she was done for the night, dropped $80 bucks on the table for her drinks and kissed us all goodnight. And we… well, we haven't heard from her since, and we were getting, truly worried," Max began to choke up as those final few words left his mouth and the reality of Jenny's death hit him.

"And that was it? She left alone then?"

"Yes. She left alone," Max said, wiping a tear from his eye.

"And you three stayed and drank some more?"

"Well… No, Jerry left immediately after she did."

"Immediately? How soon is immediately?"

"Oh, um, extremely soon. Literally like less than two minutes. She walked out the door and he got up and put his jacket on and walked out behind her. Couldn't have been more than a minute or two after she left that he left."

"Okay and you guys were all having a good night, right? Nothing unusual?"

"Yeah, we were having a great night. We usually do, just hanging out, having some laughs, some beers, just having a great time."

"Alright. Now can you two think of anyone, anyone at all that might want to hurt Jenny for any reason?"

"God no. Jenny was the greatest, and everyone loved her," Max replied.

"Julie?" Tommy asked.

"No. Definitely not. Jenny was the best person I have ever known. She was nothing but decent. She was my best friend, my best friend in the whole world. Oh God, can't believe she is gone, we shared everything. She can't be gone. Who? Why?"

"Julie. I need to ask you… Did Jenny tell you that she was pregnant?"

"What?" Julie replied slowly in a downcast, disbelieving voice. "Pregnant? No, you must be mistaken."

"No, Julie, I'm not. She was six, perhaps seven weeks pregnant. Can you tell me who she may have been having sex with, six or seven weeks ago?"

"Christ! This is all way too much to take in," Julie moaned, curling over in a tight ball. She looked up at Tommy as she quietly asked, "You're telling me someone murdered her, and now you are telling me she was pregnant?"

"Yes, that's what I am telling you. Whose baby do you think it might have been?"

"This is too much. Fuck! — It could have been Pete or Joe's. It could have been another guys also… Aaron. She had recently hooked up with a guy named Aaron. I don't remember his last name and I don't have any idea if they, if they, actually did it. Had sex at all, or yet. I, we, never met him. Oh God, I just know she met him and they had gone out a couple of times, and she… she said he was an amazing guy. But he was from Massachusetts, so she wasn't going to hang out with him anymore because she didn't want to start a relationship with someone from so far away."

"And? Any more? Do you remember anything more about this Aaron?"

"I really know nothing but his name," Max said.

"Not much more," Julie replied. "I believe she was or sounded impressed with him. She told me he wasn't a musician or an artist, he did engineer work of some kind and he was visiting for business. Something, sounded like his work would bring him to New York and other cities from Boston."

"And you two never met him? Any idea of what he looks like?" Tommy asked.

"No, she said he was beautiful though," Julie replied, "But I think Jerry met him? Jerry said, 'he wasn't all that beautiful.' Yeah, he said 'he wasn't all that beautiful,' I think. So, you'll need to talk with Jerry about him. I do believe that Jerry met Aaron at the Starbucks on Madison Avenue. Yes, yes Jerry met him at the Starbucks on Madison a few weeks ago. About six or seven weeks ago."

"Can you give me Jerry's phone number please? Also, Jenny's number? We never recovered a phone from her."

"Yes, of course," Julie answered and rattled both numbers off as Tommy and Jimmy jotted them down in their notebooks.

"And how about Pete, and Joe's? Do you have their numbers as well?"

"Yes, we do," Both Julie and Max said in unison. Max looked up both numbers and read them off to the detectives from his phone.

"And anything on Aaron?"

"No, no nothing," they both said together.

Tommy took a deep breath and stood up. He reached into his pocket and then handed a card to both Julie and Max.

"Thank you. Thank you both. You've helped us out a lot here. I'm certain I will probably end up with more questions for the both of you in the future, but at the moment I think we can leave you and let you two take it all in, and well, grieve for your friend. For whatever it may be worth, Jenny seemed like a genuinely decent person to me, and I'm very sorry for your loss."

"Thank you, Detective Keane, Detective Colletti," Max said as he stood and shook Tommy's then Jimmy's hand.

"Yes, thank you. Find him… them… whoever did this, please," Julie said as she also rose from the couch to shake the detectives' hands.

Chapter Eighteen

The detectives made their way out of the apartment and to the elevator.

On the way down, Tommy opened the conversation, "You were pretty quiet again, Jimmy. You know if you have any questions, you can ask them, too."

"Sure, I realize that, but you seemed to be covering everything, Tommy. I didn't think of anything you hadn't already asked, and I also didn't want to break the conversation."

"Okay, well don't be shy. If you think of something that you feel may be important always speak up."

"Of course, yes, I will," Jimmy replied with a hint of embarrassment. "So, what next? I assume we want to interview these men, Jenny's boyfriends, yes?"

"Yes, this was a productive interview for us. Julie and Max giving us four names and numbers was terrific. Now all we need to do is get with each of them for some questioning. Hopefully we can have them all come into the precinct. Currently all four are possible suspects, and Jenny being pregnant could certainly be the motivating factor in her death."

"Yes, homicide is the number one cause of death for pregnant woman… a disturbing fucking fact, isn't it?"

"Yes, it is. That's why I'd like to get all these guys to come in for their interviews. I want to get them all in the box so we can have the cameras on and record everything we talk about. No way to know anything at this point, but I'm going to say there's a solid chance one of these four men is the man we're looking for."

"You're including Jerry Quick in these four? Even though he never slept with Jenny and would have no pregnancy link?"

"Absolutely, in fact he may be our most interesting person of interest. As of right now, he's the one with the most evidence pointing his way, just do the math."

"Yeah, you're right. He's one of the last people we know to have seen her alive. He was in love with her, so it may be a jealousy-love triangle kind of thing. And the pregnancy, if he knew, could have sparked some sort of angry outburst, which we learned he was prone to. He also knew how to choke people, which isn't saying much but, we do have this statement from his closest friends. And he is our only black suspect, and Jenny had three hairs from a black person, most likely a man since they were short, in her hair."

"There you go. After doing the math our man Jerry Quick is looking like someone we need to speak to right away. But let's not get ahead of ourselves. Not only do we have three more possible suspects, but there are also still some unanswered questions that we need to place. First one that is gnawing at me is why our little Jenny Black would go to Carl Schurz Park after midnight. Is this something, Jimmy? What is the reason this happened in the park? Why did she go to the park? What brought her there? It just seems unusual to me. Something about it feels so remote, and I don't know, almost planned."

The conversation continued as they passed the doorman and left the building.

"You mean like it was a setup?"

"Yeah, exactly. Again, this is just unanswered stuff in my head, but that's a question that could change this investigation, and maybe nail our perpetrator. Why was she in the park? Why did she leave the bar and go to the park? Or go home and then to the park? After all, we still don't know what time this occurred, but we are going to assume this happened in the early hours of the morning, relatively soon after leaving The Storehouse on 23rd."

"Yeah, what's with the park? Why the park? I didn't think of that. So, what's next? You said you want to bring all four of these guys in for questioning, right?"

"Yeah, that's what's next. What time is it?" Tommy asked as he looked at his phone to find out. "Almost 7:30, so about five hours since we ate. What say rather than go back to the precinct we sit down for a meal, and I call these fellas from the restaurant and see what I can set up with them."

"I like your style. I assume you have some new culinary adventure in mind for me tonight as well?"

"No, I was thinking a little Italian Village? Back in the 2-1."

"Okay, that's fine," Jimmy replied, almost disappointed that there was not something new on the menu. Italian Village was tasty, but the last couple days Jimmy had really enjoyed eating at Tommy's suggested restaurants, and the thought of another meal at Italian Village seemed a little lackluster to him.

"Italian Village not doing it for you, Jimmy?" Tommy asked.

"No, pizza is fine," he replied in an almost boyish manner.

"Well, we could also do a little China-Latina if you like? One of my favorite places is just a few blocks away."

"China-Latina?"

"Yeah China-Latina. Chinese-Spanish food. Never had it? It's awesome."

"Now that sounds a bit more interesting than another night of pizza, let's do that," Jimmy replied.

"Okay, you drive. La Dinastia, 72nd between Amsterdam and Columbus."

***

Jimmy parked the car in the middle of the block, and they walked over to La Dinastia, located on the north side of 72nd Street. From the outside it was a small unassuming place, with a white stone façade, and a maroon awning that read in white letters "LA DINASTIA CHINESE-LATIN CUISINE."

"Chinese-Latin cuisine," Jimmy said as they approached, "Never heard of it."

"Well, you don't know what you're missing, kid," Tommy replied.

As they entered the restaurant Jimmy took the place in. In the front of the space there was a long bar counter with a larger rectangular room behind it that had about twenty, four-top oak tables. The tables lined the walls and ran down the center. The ceiling was a typical white, low hung drop ceiling, and the walls had ugly

80's tan-on-tan striped wallpaper over oak wainscoting. The staff were all Chinese men in white button-down shirts and black pants.

Tommy and Jimmy took a table in the rear right corner of the room and sat down. An older Chinese man with black framed glasses approached with two menus in one hand, and two glasses of ice water in amber tinted glasses in the other and set one of each in front of each of the detectives.

Staring at the table and not making eye contact, the waiter spoke, "Long time since you been here. Welcome back."

"Thank you," Tommy replied.

"You take time now, I be back," the waiter said and walked off.

"So, I'm just going to follow you again. You order what you like best, and I'll have the same thing."

"Well here the portions are huge, and everything gets served on separate plates, so we'll do the share-share thing. Let's order a few items and take what we like, cool?"

"Sounds terrific to me. I'll just let you order whatever you like then."

"You got it," Tommy raised his eyebrows to the waiter who came back across the room to take their order.

"What you like?" The waiter asked.

"Give us one boneless chicken crackling, yellow rice, black beans, one tostones, and one maduros, please."

"Okay, to drink?"

"Water is cool for me," Tommy replied.

"Coffee for me, please," Jimmy answered.

"Okay. Good." The waiter said, never making eye contact or writing anything down.

Tommy pulled out his phone and his notebook and called the first number on his list: Jerry Quick.

The call went straight to voicemail, and Tommy left a message: "Hello Mr. Quick, this is Detective Keane from the 21st Precinct. Your name has come up in an investigation. Let me let you know you are in no way in trouble, but I do need to talk to you, sir. If you would, please give me a call back so we can see if we can schedule a time when you can come in and answer a few questions please. Thank you and have a good evening."

"One called. Let's move onto number two," Tommy said as he punched in the next number.

"Hello, Peter? Yes, sir, how are you? My name is Detective Tommy Keane, I'm calling from the 21st Precinct in Manhattan. Yes, sir. No, you're not in any trouble, sir. But your name has come up in an investigation and I need to ask you a few questions. Again sir, you're not in any sort of trouble, but I will need to talk to you as soon as possible. When can you come by the precinct? Yes, sir, yes, sir. Okay great. So, I can expect to see you tomorrow at 1:00 PM. Outstanding. Yes, I'll see you tomorrow."

"Okay, two called, one interview set. Let's move onto number three."

Tommy dialed and reached Joe. Having basically the same conversation as with Pete, he arranged a meeting at 6:00 PM for the following day.

"And that's all we got for the time being since we have no info on Mr. Aaron Massachusetts, as of yet."

"Well done. Do you think Jerry will be calling you back? Or do you think you may have spooked him?"

"I think he'll call back. If he doesn't it will raise our suspicions. And if he is involved with Jenny Black's death or not, he won't want that."

"True."

"Tomorrow, we'll have to get a line on Jenny's phone. I'd like to see what calls and what texts she made or received the day of her death. I'm sure that will be a helpful bit of evidence to add to this mystery as well."

"Definitely," Jimmy added as the waiter placed the food on the table, "Ooh this looks delicious."

"It is. This is some of the best chicken you'll ever have, I promise you that."

"Damn, that is tasty," Jimmy exclaimed after swallowing a large bite.

Tommy and Jimmy finished their meal and continued to discuss every facet of the Jenny Lindel case from beginning to end, then left the restaurant and headed back to the precinct to sign out for the evening. In the car during their drive, Tommy felt his phone go off.

"Keane," he answered, "Yes, Mr. Quick, how are you, sir? Thank you so much for getting back to me so quickly." He continued with the conversation and arranged for Jerry to meet them at the precinct at 10:00 AM the next morning. "Outstanding. Yes, sir, I will see you then. Thank you," he finished with and hung up.

"There we go. Three possibles and three interviews, all lined up for tomorrow. Excellent."

"Very nice!" Jimmy replied, rather impressed with how smoothly the case was now moving.

Detectives Keane and Colletti parked outside the precinct and made their way upstairs to the squad room, where they both signed out for the day. Then they headed home for the night, both fairly satisfied with the day's work.

Chapter Nineteen

Tommy was happy with how well the day had gone, and how quickly things had begun to fall into place, now that they had identified Jenny Lindel and were able to question some of her friends and family.

But there were still questions to be answered and now four suspects. Was one of these four men the father of Jenny's unborn child? And did he kill her to be rid of her and the baby? Tommy knew this was a common motive for murder. Was it a love triangle? Did one of these men act out in a jealous rage towards Jenny because of her involvement with one of the others?

'What evidence do we have?' Tommy asked himself as he turned the corner north on Lexington Avenue. 'Jenny was choked to death, but whoever did it tried to wash pills down her throat. Why? Only explanation is to make it look more like a drug-infused suicide. Was this planned? Or done in a panic to try to cover up the crime? Planned? I bet our killer planned this,' Tommy thought.

'Yeah, planned. There is next to zero evidence of the choking or of any fight. Whoever did this did it quickly and deliberately, and Jenny never saw it coming. She had little to no chance to fight back before she was unconscious, and then dead.'

'Yeah Tommy-boy, I believe whoever did this decided to do it before they reached the park. The murder is just too clean, too smooth, and neat to have been a fight. Her clothes weren't a mess, she hadn't been beaten up beforehand and the staged drug use - whoever did this planned it. Let's hope I can draw it out of one of these three fellas tomorrow. Let's hope I can get to the bottom of this tomorrow, Jenny, you poor young thing. Whoever did this to you, you certainly didn't deserve it, and I'll figure it out Jenny, I promise you.'

***

Tommy headed straight home, and as he did, he continued to run the different possible scenarios of Jenny's murder through his mind. He, for the moment, had decided her murder was planned, premeditated as they say. Most murders are not random; there is almost always a link between the murderer and the victim, and this is even truer with premeditated homicides. Now all Tommy needed to do was find the link.

As he entered his mother's apartment on 88th Street, his new little friend JoJo sat patiently waiting for Tommy to finish unlocking the door and open it.

"Hey, little buddy, how you doin' today?" Tommy asked, when he spotted little JoJo sitting at the entrance to the apartment, with what almost appeared to be a smile on his face.

"Hi, Tommy, how was your day today, Tommy?" His mother asked loudly. She sat in her recliner, where she exhaled cigarette smoke and kept her eyes glued to the TV screen, intently watching an old episode of The Odd Couple.

"Not bad, Ma. Actually, it was pretty good, got some productive stuff done today, I think. How was yours, and my little buddy's here?"

"JoJo's was wonderful, Tommy, and mine was too, Tommy. Well, except your little buddy there got a hold of one of my slippers and chewed it all to bits, Tommy, and now I need new slippers."

"I'm sorry. Does this bad little guy need to go out?"

"No, Tommy, I just had him out before I started this program. I think he's done for the night, Tommy. And he's not bad he's a little naughty is all."

"Okay, well I think I'll clean myself up and head to bed. Would you like him tonight or would you like him in with me tonight?"

"No, Tommy, you take him, Tommy. You know he wants to be with you when you're home, he loves to be with you, Tommy."

"Alright, Ma, I love you. And I love to be here with you." He leaned over and kissed his mother on the head.

"Ahh, you're a sweet boy, Tommy," Maria Keane replied, as she took a drag of her cigarette, her eyes still not leaving the TV screen.

"C'mon, JoJo. C'mon buddy, let's hit the sheets, pal," he said to the dog who playfully bounced off the hardwood floors as he followed Tommy into his room.

***

American Pinup's "Strongbow" woke Tommy. He felt JoJo sleeping on the pillow and pressed up against the top of Tommy's head, breathing with a slight whistle to each exhale.

Tommy sat up in the darkness of his room, gave JoJo a pat, and got onto the floor for his 50 morning push-ups. Tommy awoke with optimism this morning. He felt fairly hopeful that this may be the day he would find something which would help him close the case on Jenny Lindel. He had no idea which one of these four men may have killed her, but he felt it would be one of them, and he felt it most likely would be the father of her unborn baby. This was a statistical probability. But Tommy always liked to quote his old partner and mentor, Detective Samuel Isaacs, "We don't know nothin' till we know it, kid." And with those words indelibly marked in his mind he was not going to rule out anything, or anyone.

Although the only evidence Tommy had pointed to Jenny's longtime friend, Jerry Quick, it was all strictly circumstantial at the moment and for some reason Tommy wasn't liking Mr. Quick for this crime, not yet anyway. Although he had nothing to go on, it was Pete, Joe, and Aaron, that Tommy looked forward to interviewing and learning more about.

The pregnancy, and the statistical probability that the father would be the killer, is what Tommy had on his mind as he dressed for work. Would he meet Jenny's killer today during one of his scheduled interviews? Or was it this new Aaron? Aaron the Beautiful from Boston — would he be the one who did this to young Jenny?

Tommy finished dressing, walked little JoJo, kissed his mother goodbye, and headed out the door for work. As he stepped out the door of his building, he scanned the block from left to right and then began his walk to the precinct. It was a cold morning but not a bitter one, and on this day, he walked up 88th to Lexington and headed south. As he passed Tal Bagels right off 83rd Street, he did an about face and stepped inside to get a dozen assorted bagels, with sides of butter and cream cheese, for the rest of the squad. Tommy was feeling positive about the day and the need to spread a little positivity befell him as he passed the shop. Plus, it was nice to warm up inside about halfway through his walk to the precinct.

Tommy entered the squad room at the 2-1 and found Detective Mark Stein sitting at his desk, flipping through one of his case folders.

"Hey, morning, how you doing?" Tommy asked.

"Pretty good, you?" Stein replied never taking his eyes off what he was reading.

"I got bagels today, pal, hope you didn't eat yet."

"I did, but I'm sure I'll be having one in a bit. Thank you. You stop by H&H?"

"No, I got these at Tal."

"Over on 86th?"

"No, Lexington and 83rd," Tommy answered as he laid out the bagels and sides on the table in the back of the room.

"Right." Stein said, still never looking up once from his folder as they spoke.

"You in the house today? Or will you be heading out?"

"Little of both, why? What do you have going on? You need something?"

"Not really. I have a few interviews today for this Lindel homicide. If you're in I'd like you to watch, see if you catch anything I may miss. I'll have Jimmy in the box with me, but I always like a seasoned pair of eyes like yours, and perhaps the Lu's, on the lookout as well."

"Sure, if I'm in I'll definitely help out. Do you have a solid suspect?"

"No. I have four possibles, three are coming in today for interviews, the fourth I have nothing on but a first name and that he may be from Boston.

"What times are these interviews today?"

"Ten, one, and six."

"Well, if nothing gets in the way, I'll absolutely help you with these."

"Thanks, I appreciate it." Tommy replied as he picked up the phone and called the District Attorney's Office. He needed to speak to the Assistant District Attorney assigned this case, Jessica Lokietz.

"Hello, Detective Keane calling for ADA Lokietz, please? Thank you."

"Good morning, ADA Lokietz, how you doing today? Good, yes, I am well also, thank you. Listen, about our Lindel case, I want to let you know I have three interviews with possible perps today and I also want to ask if you can obtain a warrant for a trap and trace on the victims' phone, please? If you can write one up, I'll shoot down there sometime today to swear it out. Yeah? Okay cool. Yes, thank you so much. I look forward to seeing you later."

Once Tommy got off the phone with the ADA, he fixed himself an onion bagel with a little butter and began preparing some questions for his upcoming interviews. He took a walk around the block a couple times to empty his mind, grab a little air, and meditate on everything he knew so far about the Jenny Lindel case.

***

9:49 AM

PAA Charice Tate, today wearing a bright orange cardigan, stepped into the squad room from her desk that was situated just outside of it, "Hello, handsome Detective Keane, you have a visitor waiting for you downstairs, a mister Jerry Quick."

"Thanks, Charice," Tommy replied, "And a couple minutes early," He followed with, in a lower voice directed at Stein.

Tommy made his way down the steps to the precinct's lobby, where he saw Jerry Quick.

Jerry stood about six feet tall. He was a handsome, light-skinned, black man with short, cropped hair. He wore a gray, hip-length wool coat, a white shirt, black tie, dark gray slacks, and black Oxfords. It was decidedly business attire, and he looked as though he may be arriving at a job interview, the way he nervously stood near the entrance next to the stone benches, cautiously observing his surroundings.

"Mr. Quick?" Tommy asked as he approached him.

"Yes, yes sir," Jerry replied.

"Pleasure to meet you, Mr. Quick. I'm Detective Keane, the one you spoke to on the phone. Thanks so much for making it in today."

"Sure, of course."

"Please follow me. Right this way."

Tommy led Jerry up the stairs to the squad room. As they entered the squad room Tommy introduced Jerry to Jimmy Colletti, "This is my partner Detective Colletti. He'll be joining us for our interview. Before we start can I grab you a cup of coffee or maybe a bagel? We have some warm fresh bagels this morning."

"No… uh, no thank you, Detective," Jerry replied nervously.

"Well, how about we get started. Please, let's step into this room over here where we won't be interrupted."

Tommy led Jerry into "The Box," the interview room, which was situated to the left of the cage, and down a noticeably short corridor, to the rear of the squad room. It was a small room, with a table, a couple chairs, and a bench against one of the walls. There was a camera in the corner up against the ceiling that would record the detectives' interviews.

Opposite the table was a two-way mirror where observers could watch the interviews from a smaller adjoining room. Stein and Doyle both stood behind the glass and watched Tommy and Jimmy as they interviewed Jerry Quick.

Tommy had Jerry sit at the table at the far wall of the interview room, so Jerry was facing the entrance, and the camera, and Stein and Doyle had full view of him and his facial expressions.

Tommy sat opposite Jerry at the table and Jimmy sat on the bench against the wall with the two-way mirror.

"Okay, Jerry. First let me thank you again for coming in to see us today, we do appreciate you giving us your time. Do you know why you are here today, sir?"

"Ahh, no? You said my name came up in an investigation you were doing. I, I have no idea how, or why my name would be part of anything you gentlemen may be looking into, but I wanted to make sure I came and saw you right away," Jerry replied in a calm and cool manner. He was visibly nervous, but in no way did he appear to be defensive. Instead, he sounded genuinely concerned as to why he was there.

"Okay, well, yes. I'm sorry to tell you, your friend Jenny Lindel's body was found a week ago."

"Her Body? You mean her… her dead body?" Jerry asked, rather flatly.

"Yes, Jerry, her dead body."

"What? What happened to her?" He asked again, still in a rather flat, stoic manner.

"Someone killed her."

"Killed her? Who, how, was it a robbery?"

"We don't know, Jerry What we are doing is talking to the people who knew her best. Trying to create a picture of who this woman was, her lifestyle, her habits, who she knew, who may have wanted to do something like this… and well, sir, we understand you are one of her closest friends, and we're hoping you can help us out a little?"

"Anything," Jerry answered.

"Okay fantastic. That is what we like to hear. Well, let me start with, when was the last time you saw Jenny, Jerry?"

"Uh, eight, maybe nine days ago? We were hanging out at The Storehouse for some drinks and food on West 23rd Street. And that… that was the last time I saw Jenny."

"And did you speak to her at all later in the week?"

"No, no. And I did call her a couple times, but no sir, I didn't, hadn't, spoken to her since that night."

"Did she text you, or email you, at all after the night at The Storehouse?"

"No, no sir. I haven't heard from her at all."

"But you did call her?"

"Yeah, a couple times," Jerry stated and shifted in his seat.

"And she never returned your calls, correct?"

"Correct."

"Is that unusual? For her not to call you back?"

"Well, with Jenny, no. She could be moody, and if she wasn't in a good mood, she could definitely blow you off for a few days before she returned a call or message."

"Was she in a bad mood at The Storehouse that night?"

"No, sir. She was in a good mood, we all were."

"And who is 'we,' Jerry?"

"Me, Jenny, and another couple we hang out with a lot, Max and Julie."

"Okay. So you four got together regularly?"

"Oh yes sir, all the time. I would say we hung out with Max and Julie at least once a week, sometimes more."

"And what would you four do together?"

"Everything. We're all into music, so we'd do a lot of music-related things, you know, shows, go record shopping, hang out at clubs, maybe hang in the park on a weekend afternoon. We did just about everything with Max and Julie."

"So, it sounds like you are all quite close?"

"Oh yeah, we were all very close. Jenny and Julie, I think, spoke on the phone every day."

"And you and Jenny were an item, I take it?"

"An item?" Jerry asked.

"Yes, you were dating? You were boyfriend-girlfriend?"

Jerry paused. "Yeah, well, we had an on and off kind of relationship."

"I'm not sure I understand," Tommy replied, "Were you currently dating Jenny?"

"No, sir, not currently. But we are still best friends."

"Okay, I'm going to get a little more personal here. Were you recently having sex with Jenny? I realize this may sound like I'm prying into your personal life, but we need to know everything we can about Jenny, in order to find out what happened to her the night she was killed."

"Do you not think this, her, her killing was random? Like during a mugging?"

"We don't know, Jerry, that's why we are trying, like I said before, to paint a picture of Jenny's life. You see, we know nothing about Jenny, which is why we want to interview you. You are one of her closest friends, and we need to know everything about her, do you understand?"

"Yes, yes, sir, I do," Jerry replied lowly, still in a particularly flat and stoic manner.

"So, let me ask you again, Jerry, and please, sir, forgive my intrusions into both your and Jenny's lives, but when was the last time you had sex with Jenny?"

Jerry paused, looked down at the table, taking his eyes away from Tommy's, "I'm not sure? Two to three months ago?"

"Okay, so that was an on period for the two of you. Would you consider this, or a week ago, to be an off period of your on and off relationship?"

"I guess you could say that, yes," said Jerry, still staring at the table, "She, we, we were, or had a very on and off relationship."

"Okay. Can I ask if Jenny… did Jenny date other guys?"

"Sometimes, yes. When we were on breaks, we both would go with other people. Yes."

"Okay, do you know anybody else she may have been seeing?"

"I have met one or two on occasion, yes."

"Do you remember their names?"

"Yes… Uh… there was a, a Pete, and a Joe, and recently she dated a guy named Aaron."

"And can you tell us anything about these men?"

"Not much, no. Just guys, average guys."

"C'mon, that's all you know? I thought you and Jenny were best friends?"

"We were!" Jerry raised his voice and for the first time showed a bit of life. "But we never talked about any other guys. That part of her life was hers, and my personal life was mine, and we respected that."

"Okay. So, and again understand, I'm trying to get to know Jenny here, she did see other guys, but you never spoke about them. But you have met these guys, yes?"

"Yes. Yes, I have," Jerry replied returning to his subdued and stoic demeanor.

"Tell me a little about Pete, whatever you got, whatever you think?"

"Pete's a bit of a dummy. Definitely not smart enough for Jenny. Punk rock guy, you know, lots of tattoos, different colored hair, nice enough, I guess."

"That's it? How long have Jenny and Pete known each other?"

"Maybe two years?"

"And Joe?"

"Joe? Maybe three years?"

"And what do you think of Joe?"

"He's alright. I guess, kind of a lovable loser. He's another rocker, or a wannabe rocker. I think he's a plumber during the week but tries to live like a rock star on the weekends."

"A poser?"

"Nah, not so much a poser. Just a guy who wanted a career in music, but didn't have it, you know? So, he lives it on the weekends, looks the part, dresses the part, but fixes toilets all week."

"Okay and Aaron. What can you tell me about Aaron?"

"He's an engineer from Boston. He's boring, too boring for Jenny."

"Boring huh? Is he good looking? Is that why she dates him?"

"Nah… I don't see it, he's just an average looking guy, I think. I have no idea what she sees in him," Jerry became visibly agitated while talking about Aaron.

"Do you think any of these men could, or would, be able to hurt Jenny?"

"Do you suspect one of them?" Jerry asked, sitting up anxiously for an answer.

"I don't think anything, Jerry. I'm just looking for some answers as to what happened and to who could have possibly done something like this to Jenny."

"Well, if it was any of these three, I would bet it would be Aaron," Jerry stated with a bit of a damning tone.

"Aaron? And why Aaron, Jerry?"

"He… he has something cold about him. You know when you look into a man's eyes and they look cold, maybe a little hateful? I don't know, it's his demeanor. And I didn't like the way he spoke to her either."

"How? How did Aaron speak to Jenny?"

"He was, I don't know, too confident, too arrogant. He thought he was incredibly cool, you know? And that Jenny wasn't, well wasn't as cool as he was. When in reality she was way too cool to be with some jock asshole like him. She was way too cool for him."

Jerry's sentence ended on a somber note. It was obvious speaking about Jenny in the past tense hit him hard.

"Let's go back to The Storehouse, Jerry. What can you tell me about that night? Take a second to think and tell me what happened that night."

"Not a lot. Nothing unusual anyway. We — Jenny, me, and Max and Julie agreed to meet there for some dinner and drinks because it was close to Max's job. We had a good time like we usually do, eating, drinking, and bullshitting about nothing really. Honestly that was it."

"Okay and how did the night end?"

"Jenny got a phone call, and suddenly hopped up, threw a few bucks on the table and said she had to go. And that was it, she left."

"And the rest of you?"

"I paid up too, and we all left."

"Together? Did the three of you leave together?"

"No, I don't think so –" Jerry paused for a moment, "I put my money on the table, then I left, and Max and Julie stayed to pay the tab."

"Then what did you do?"

"I left. I caught a cab home, and that was it."

"And there was nothing in your conversations with Jenny that night that would lead you to believe anything unusual was going on in her life, or possibly distressing her in any way?"

"No, sir, she was perfectly normal."

"Who do you think called her?"

Jerry paused for a moment, "Well… I don't know, she didn't tell us, and seemed a little secretive, so I, I thought it was probably Aaron. He's the most recent person she had been seeing, but I can't tell you it was him, that's only what we thought."

"Okay Jerry, you've helped us to understand Jenny a lot better today. I think we're about done here, but I would like to ask you, sir, and it may seem a little odd but let me explain please… We plan on going over Jenny's clothes for any physical evidence the killer may have left. It would be easier if we had a sample of your hair to eliminate from any other hair fibers found, since you were in such close proximity to her. I'd also like to take your fingerprints if we may? Now again, please understand me when I tell you you're not in any kind of trouble at all, and by giving us your fingerprints and a hair sample we can immediately rule out some of this evidence, if we know it comes from you. Does that make sense? You see, we know you two were together, so we want to be able to rule you out as a suspect when this evidence comes back to us from the lab work."

"Uh, yeah sure, I don't see why not. Sure, you can do whatever you need to do, Detective."

"Great, thanks for understanding." Tommy took a sheet of paper from the back of the yellow notepad he was writing on and placed it on the table in front of Jerry Quick. "Please, Jerry, if you would, hang your head over that sheet of paper and vigorously scratch your head for me, please."

Jerry did what he was asked and about eight hairs fell onto the sheet of paper. Tommy took the sheet and folded into an envelope. As their eyes met it was obvious Jerry was having second thoughts about what he had just done.

"Thanks again, Mr. Quick. You've helped us out a lot this morning. Now let's get those prints done and then we can say goodbye for today."

Tommy took Jerry Quick's fingerprints and talked some small talk about his personal life and music, just to help put him at ease. Then he shook his hand and thanked him again after walking him to the front door of the precinct.

***

When he returned to the squad room, Tommy found the rest of the squad working on their other cases. Tommy sat on one of the unoccupied desks and asked out loud.

"Alright squad, let's have a little sit down here about what we all think about our Jerry Quick?"

Doreen was the first to speak up, "Seems awful unemotional for a man who was just told the love of his life was murdered a week ago, dontcha think?"

"Exactly. Fucker was stone-cold," Jimmy replied, "You didn't let on at all that we already interviewed Julie and Max. He looked clueless about that, but he still didn't seem shocked when you told him Jenny was dead. Seemed kind of matter of fact about it."

"Yeah, cold, matter of fact. The only emotion he seemed to show was jealously about the other guys, and especially the one named Aaron," Doreen added, "I mean, that's to be expected, but it strikes me as odd that the only emotion — which was little, was from his jealousy, not her death. That I find very off-putting."

"Mark? What's going on in that head of yours?" Tommy asked.

"Well, Tom, there was nothing damning about his interview, but I have to agree with these two. I found Mr. Quick to be remarkably unemotional about the death of his friend, lover, whatever she was. He said they were best friends and occasional lovers, and like Doreen said, the only glints of emotion came from his jealousy and not from her loss. Are you liking him for this, Tom?"

"Not just yet, but what we have so far on Mr. Quick is: He was one of the last three people we know of to see her alive, he has held a torch for the victim since they were teenagers, he has trained in Jiu Jitsu and Aikido, and certainly knows how to apply a Rear Naked Choke, and now I think he is also a liar, in that I am inclined to believe Julie and Max's account of Jenny and Jerry's relationship more than I am to believe his. So yes, I think we need to dig deeper into Mr. Jerry Quick.

"Okay, I'll see what I can dig up on the computer," said Doreen.

"Thanks, Doreen, I appreciate it."

"You got it, Tommy," she replied.

"And thanks for watching," Tommy said to both Mark and Doreen, "I appreciate the extra eyes, and the input. I have the next contestant on The Dating Game showing up in about an hour or so. If you're still in the office, I'd love for the two of you to watch that one as well."

"I'll wait. Maybe I'll go grab a sandwich around the corner first, then return for your interview," said Mark. He turned and asked Doreen, "What you say, Doreen? You want to take a walk over to Neil's Coffee Shop and grab lunch?"

"Sure, sounds good," Doreen replied.

"Can we bring something back for you two?" Mark asked of Tommy and Jimmy.

"No, I think I'm good, Mark. Why don't you take a walk with them, Jimmy? We don't have much to do here. I'll just look over my notes and wait in case our next guy shows up early."

"Yeah, sure, sounds good to me. An hour, right?"

"Yeah, you got an hour and ten to get back here."

"Okay, we'll see you later."

The three detectives grabbed their coats and then took a walk for some lunch as Tommy sat alone in the squad room and went over his notes and everything he knew about this case to date. He did his best to study everything he had so far, yet still remain neutral as far as any leads or hypotheses. It was still too early for that, and he knew making any pre-determinations on the case may cause him to overlook any new evidence or clues that may present themselves.

Tommy stood and walked over to the little coffee station they had near Lieutenant Bricks' office. He was disappointed there was not another onion bagel for him, so he chose a poppy seed instead, cut it in half and buttered it. As he bit into the bagel, he looked out the window and thought again about Jenny and what he knew about her short life.

***

1:06 PM

Everyone was back in the squad room. Doreen tapped away at the computer as she searched out everything she could find about Jerry Quick. Tommy and Jimmy went over what they both knew about Jenny's case and where it was going, and Mark worked on one of his own cases, a grand larceny that was getting old and needed closing before Sergeant Browne began the daily needling to have it done.

PAA Charice Tate stuck her head in the door of the squad room. "Detective Keane, you have another visitor waiting for you downstairs, a Mr. Peter Hobbson."

"Thanks, Charice," Tommy said and got up from his seat and announced to the group, "Here we go, contestant number two on this episode of The Dating Game."

Tommy made his way down the stairs and immediately knew which one of the men in the lobby was there to be interviewed.

Peter Hobbson stood about five feet, ten inches tall. His hair was short, but bushy. The left side of his head was bleached to an almost platinum blonde and the right side was dyed black. Although it was relatively cold outside, all he wore as an outer garment was a black zip-up hoodie with a sleeveless denim jacket over it that was festooned with band patches and small buttons, all with the names of different bands on them. He wore a tight, faded pair of blue jeans and black Converse All-Stars sneakers.

Tommy called out to him about halfway down the stairs, "Mr. Hobbson, Pete, right this way, please." He made eye contact with the officer at the desk, letting him know it was okay for Pete to join him and head up to the squad room.

Tommy shook Peter Hobbson's hand, and then lead him up to the squad room and into the interview room just as he had with Jerry Quick. He had him sit in the same spot, as he and Jimmy took the same seats they had before. Mark and Doreen likewise took their positions in the small room behind the two-way mirror to observe the interview.

"So, Mr. Hobbson, I guess you are wondering what this is all about and why I've called you down here for some questions?" Tommy began.

"Yeah. I am really wondering, like, a lot. I'm a little nervous what you guys could possibly want with me?"

"Well, sir, we want to ask you some questions about your friend, Jenny Lindel."

"Jenny? What's up with Jenny? She's not in any trouble, is she?"

"Well, Pete, yes. Jenny is no longer with us, she's dead."

"What? Dead?" Pete said loudly. He paused and began again in a much softer tone, "My God, my God, I didn't picture this coming. What, what happened? How, how did she die?"

"She was murdered, Pete. Someone killed her."

"Why? Who would kill Jenny? She… She… Jenny was nothing but good. Who would, who could kill Jenny?" Pete said, his eyes filling up with water, and his voice cracking in disbelief.

"We don't know, Pete, that's why we asked you here. You see, we don't know much at all about Jenny, and we're trying to paint a picture of her life, see if we can get to know her, and in doing so, figure out who did this."

"Wow. Wow. I can't believe what you're telling me. Yeah, go ahead, ask me anything you want." He finished as he wiped a tear from his cheek.

"Can you tell me the last time you saw Jenny?"

"Yeah, uh, about three, three and a half weeks ago. It was a Thursday and we had a show in Brooklyn. She came out to watch us."

"Where in Brooklyn, Pete?"

"A little place called Legion on Metropolitan Avenue."

"I'm familiar with the place, bar in the front, little room with a stage in the back. And that was the last time you were with her?"

"Yes, and yes, sir."

"And the last time you spoke to her?"

"Around two or three days later. We texted one another. She wished me luck on tour and said we'd meet up for dinner or drinks when I came back."

"So, you've been away?"

"Yes, sir, we were on tour. I was with my band on tour down to Gainesville, Florida and back."

"And how long were you gone?"

"Sixteen days total. New York to Florida, looped out to Memphis and Nashville, and made our way back one city at a time."

"And when did you arrive back?"

"Four or five days ago. I actually called and texted Jenny like two days after I got back but didn't hear from her."

"No, Pete, you wouldn't have. She's been gone for about nine days now. Let's talk about Jenny a little, and I may get a little personal, Pete, but I want you to know we're trying to get to know Jenny, okay? And the more we know, hopefully the easier it will be to find who did this to her," Tommy said, and Pete nodded his head. "How close were you and Jenny? Can you tell us a little about your relationship, please?"

"We were good friends, that's all, and we dated on and off, but never seriously. I've known her for maybe two or three years. I really, really liked Jenny. She was a really cool girl, smart, truly kind, super sweet."

"You say you dated, so you were romantic?"

"Yeah sure. If you mean sex, yeah, if you mean love, well not really. I think it was just fun for her. I think I liked her more than she liked me, to tell you the truth. But I can't say I was in love with her. In the last two years we've gotten together like ten to twelve times. So yeah, I wouldn't say we were a couple at all, just friends, with occasional benefits."

"Are you friends or friendly with a guy named Joe Martinelli?"

"Sure, I know Joe. Not really well but I know him. You don't think he had anything to do with Jenny, with her, with her dying, do you?"

"I don't think anything, Pete. I'm just trying to put a puzzle together here – You know they dated, yes?"

"Oh yeah, I have seen them together."

"What do you think of Joe?"

"I think he's a good guy, hardworking guy. He's in the trades, a plumber I think, was in a couple bands years ago, but nothing now that I know of."

"You say a good guy, but have you ever seen him lose his temper, act out violently, anything at all that might make you think he could in any way be capable of something like this?"

"No, sir, never. I didn't know Joe well, but he always seemed like a good guy, a nice guy. No tough guy bullshit, always very respectful."

"Okay, do you recognize the name Aaron? An Aaron that would relate to Jenny, of course."

"No, I don't know anyone named Aaron at all."

"Okay and how well do you know Jenny's friend Jerry?"

"I only know Jerry through Jenny. I know he's a musician, does a lot of studio work. From what I understand he gets paid pretty well as a studio guy. I've only met him maybe six or seven times, and always in bars and clubs, so I really never got to know him very well."

"Okay, I get that, but can you tell me what you think of him, even if they are just your first impressions?"

"I, well, I don't particularly like Jerry. He told me once if I ever hurt Jenny, he'd kill me, like he was her father or big brother, but really more like he was just a big asshole. I mean we're all adults man, relax with the macho bullshit, you know?"

"Really? So, he threatened you over Jenny."

"Yeah, I think he had a big crush on her, to be honest, and he was a little jealous of us getting together."

"How often did he speak or act this way towards you?"

"Just the one time, but he seemed really, I don't know, really serious and angry with me when he said it. Like you know, like a real threat, not like a joke."

"Did he scare you?" Jimmy interjected.

"I wouldn't say I was scared," Pete said, turning his head to face Jimmy, "But I would say he definitely put me off. I mean, really, we're all adults now, and we were all having a good time just hanging out, and he pulls me to the side to say that. Who does that shit?"

"Do you know, or think, that Jerry and Jenny have ever had a sexual relationship at all?"

"No, I don't. And not just because I don't think it, but because Jenny told me so. I had asked her about Jerry and how he seemed jealous around us, and she said he comes off like that because he's protective of her, because they were such good friends for so long. I asked if they were ever a couple and she said no, and

I'm embarrassed to say I even asked if they ever had sex, and she again said no, they never had."

"Okay, can you tell me how well you know her friends, Julie and Max?"

"Pretty well. I've seen them over a dozen times over the last couple years. I really like the both of them, super nice people, super nice couple. We've double dated a couple times, and met up at bars and shows, good people. Jenny and Julie are like best friends from high school. I think that's how far they go back, with Jerry too, back to high school."

"Again, I'm sorry I have to ask a rather personal question - when was the last time you and Jenny had sex?"

"Uh, okay, I'm going to say September. I can't give you a day, but it was back in September. Does that, does that mean anything? I mean what does our sex life have to do with her being murdered nine days ago?" For the first time during the interview, Pete seemed annoyed by the question.

"Did you know, Pete, did Jenny, or anyone else, tell you that she was pregnant?"

Pete paused and his eyes widened in surprise, "No, no. Do you, do you think it could have been mine? Is that what? Oh man, could she have been pregnant by me?"

"I don't think so, Pete, not if the last time you two were together was in September. This pregnancy would have happened about two months ago, not four."

"Oh man. And you're sure about that right, Detective? I hate to think - God, I hate to think that it was mine and she never told me."

"Was the last time you were together in September?"

"Yes, sir, I'm sure of it. I'm sure of it."

"Okay then it wasn't your child. And I think we're done with you for now, Mr. Hobbson, but I may have to call you back at some point."

"Yes, sir, I understand. I really can't believe Jenny is dead and I'll help if I can. Thank you both."

"No thank you, Pete. C'mon, I'll walk you out."

Tommy took Peter Hobbson down to the lobby, shook his hand and thanked him again for coming in. He said goodbye, then headed back up to the squad room.

"Any thoughts? Any thoughts at all on Mr. Peter Hobbson?" Tommy asked the four detectives as he stepped back into the squad room.

"He wasn't even in town," Jimmy said.

"Not in town doesn't mean he couldn't have had anything to do with this, Jimmy. However, overall, I don't see him being involved at the moment. The fact that he was out of town frees him from personally killing her, if that story checks out, and I assume it will. Plus, I felt he was truly sincere in his surprise and visible sorrow about the victim's death. So yes, I don't think you'll find Mr. Hobbson to be your man," was Mark's reply.

Then Doreen added, "I think he strengthened any suspicions you may have for Jerry Quick though. Could definitely be a jealousy angle here, Tommy. Maybe she told Jerry about the pregnancy, and he snapped and choked her, then panicked and tried to make it look like a suicide. He was with her that night, right? They were together that night, and he left right after she did?"

"Yes, Doreen," Tommy jumped in, "Jerry Quick is certainly our number one person of interest now, there's no denying that. If either of you two are still around at 6:00, our next contender should arrive, and I'm curious to find out what his story will be. In the meantime, I need to run down to Centre Street and sign out a warrant for Jenny Lindel's phone. Hopefully that trap and trace I'm asking for will land us some solid evidence on one of these guys."

"Are you're doubting it's Jerry Quick?" Jimmy asked.

"I'm not doubting anything, Jimmy. Thing is we have nothing on anyone yet, nothing solid, and just cause we have interest in him, doesn't mean we got him. We need something solid and right now we still got nothing."

***

Tommy made it down to Centre Street and managed to get his warrant signed out, delivered to Jenny Lindel's phone provider, and make it back to the 2-1 all with time to spare to properly prepare himself for his final interview of the day, with Joe Martinelli.

As he entered the squad room, Mark greeted him with "Doreen's got some interesting news for you, Tommy. She's in the ladies' room, but you're gonna wanna hear this." He grinned at Tommy as he sat back in his chair.

"C'mon, don't do that to me, Mark. What's she got?"

"No sir, I won't tell and have to deal with her after spilling the beans."

As Mark finished his sentence, Doreen walked into the room, "Tommy, Tommy, Tommy, do I have news for you!"

"Yeah, that's what I understand. What you got, kid?"

"Okay well it's not damning, but it is interesting. So, our friend Jerry Quick is clean right? We can't find anything, no arrests, no moving violations, nothing. But wait! I did find that while in college he was caught by campus police, not once, but twice, in possession of… are you ready? In possession of a controlled substance, Ecstasy, Molly, MDMA. Now of course I know this doesn't mean shit as far as him killing your victim, but I think it does show Mr. Quick is no complete stranger to the narcotic that was found placed, forced, planted into your victim's mouth. Like I said, I know it ain't much, but if you end up collaring Mr. Quick for this one, the ADA assigned will certainly like to add this fact to the case somehow."

"Thanks, Doreen. It's not going to help me put cuffs on him, but it certainly is another mark against Jerry Quick. Thanks again, Doreen, I love unleashing you on that computer." Tommy grinned at her.

"Anytime, Tommy."

***

5:44 PM

PAA Charice Tate stepped into the squad room, "My goodness, you are a popular man today, Detective Keane. Downstairs you have another visitor, a Mr. Joe Martinelli."

"Thanks, Charice," Tommy replied and headed down the stairs to the lobby, where he saw Joe Martinelli waiting on one of the stone benches.

Joe was a handsome man. He had just turned thirty, and when he stood, he appeared to be about five feet, nine inches tall. He was dressed in navy blue Dickies, from head to toe, with black boots. "Martinelli Plumbing" was embroidered on the left chest of his jacket, and "Joe" on the right chest. His hair was slicked back in a retro-styled pompadour that gave him a very rockabilly look. He had a Japanese style red demon tattoo visible on the left side of his neck, and both his hands were also tattooed - his right with a black panther's head surrounded by flowers, and the word HARD across his fingers, his left with a tiger's head, also surrounded by flowers, and CORE across the fingers.

"Hello, Joe. I'm Detective Keane. Please sir, follow me."

And for the third time that day Tommy escorted a man upstairs to be interviewed about Jenny's case. He sat Joe Martinelli in the same seat as the others, and everyone again took their same positions as with the others interviewed, and again the interview began.

"Thanks for coming to meet us today, Mr. Martinelli. I understand you had a long day, sir, but we need to ask you a few questions about a friend of yours. I'll do my best to make it quick so you can head home. I'm sure you have work again tomorrow, and the trip back to Bensonhurst with the traffic at this time will be a pain."

"Yeah, thanks. Well, I always like to help, but you got me, Detective, I don't know why I'm here yet. You said something about a friend? My name is part of an investigation, and it's something to do with a friend?"

"Yes, sir. May I ask you, Joe, when was the last time you saw Jenny Lindel?"

"Jenny? Jenny Black? Um, I don't know. We went out maybe like three weeks ago? Met up for some dinner, and then went to a show over at the Grand Victory, why what's up?"

"And when was the last time you talked to her?"

"Day or two after the last time we saw each other. In fact, we was supposed to go out like a week ago, but she never returned my calls. What's going on here, Detective Keane? I don't like this. Something happen to Jenny? What happened to Jenny?"

"Jenny's dead, Joe. Someone killed her."

"Oh! What! Someone killed Jenny? Holy fuck! Who do you think did it? Do you got the motherfucker? Or you still looking for him?"

Joe Martinelli became extremely animated and was almost yelling at Tommy as he asked, "Who would kill her? Someone do this on purpose or was it some random street shit? You don't, you don't think I had anything to do with this, do you?"

"I don't think anything, Joe. I'm trying to figure it all out. Please, relax. I have a few questions I need to ask you, okay?"

"Yeah, yeah sure. I'm sorry, go ahead, Detective, please go ahead. Fuck me, dead and murdered. Holy fuck, who would kill that sweet girl?" Joe said softly, and he slumped a bit in his chair as he took in the news.

"How long have you known Jenny, Joe?"

"Maybe three years?"

"And you two dated that whole time?"

"Dated, yeah, but not like we was an item or nothin'. Just like — you know, we got together a lot."

"You got together romantically, yes?"

"Romantically? Like sex? Yeah. We dated on and off, every once in a while, yeah. Sometimes I'd see her four times in a month and sometimes we wouldn't get together for maybe two months."

"So, you weren't boyfriend and girlfriend then?"

"No, not really. I mean, we got along great, but she wasn't interested in that, Jenny wasn't."

"You liked her, right?"

"Fuck yeah. I loved her. She was great - good lookin', smart, nicest person I ever met. I loved everything about her."

"But you weren't committed to one another?"

"Listen, I was down, Jenny wasn't. She thought she was too young to be serious with anyone yet, and I got that, kinda respected it too. She was one of a kind that Jenny. Fuck, I can't believe you're tellin' me she's gone, and fuckin murdered. Holy fuck this is crazy."

"So, were you two close? Sounds like you got together regularly. Did you two talk about things, you know, about her life?"

"Yeah, what you think? Of course we did, we talked about just about everything."

"Do you know a fella named Pete?"

"Sure, I know Pete. Pete the drummer, right? Yeah, I know Pete, decent guy. Why? Is he mixed up in this?"

"No, Joe, we're just trying to paint a picture of Jenny's life, and well, we really have nothing to go on. We're just trying to find as many pieces of a puzzle as we can fit together. To try and figure out who Jenny was and hopefully who's responsible for her death."

"Yeah, well okay, I get that. Well, if you're lookin' at Pete, I would think no, not him, as far as I would guess. Pete's a mellow guy, I can't picture that… But hey, you never know? Am I right?"

"How about a guy named Aaron. Do you know him?"

"Aaron? Nope, I don't know no Aaron. Why what's his story?"

"Nothing, no story, just a name. Back to your relationship with Jenny, Joe. Can you tell me how many times you've seen her recently, let's say in the last three months?"

"Last three months, okay. Well, let me see that was, October, November, December, right? Maybe a little of September too. Okay, let me think," Joe's eyes went up to the ceiling as the months ran through his head. "We went out a couple times in September. I'd say around four or five times in October and November, around once a week steady. I only saw her once this month, December. I'm gonna say that's probably ninety percent accurate, but I can check if you need exact dates or anything."

"I don't think that will be necessary, Joe, but if we need them, we'll ask. Do you know how many of those dates you had sex with Jenny?"

"Every one. Why? What's that got to do with anything?"

"Did Jenny ever tell you that she was pregnant, Joe?"

Joe's face went white as all the blood seemed to drain from him. He paused momentarily before he was able to reply. "What! Pregnant? No. No, she never told me she was pregnant. Fuck, do you think that? Holy fuck. It could be mine? You think it could have been mine? Man, this is a crazy day. First you're telling me my best girl was murdered, then you're telling me she's carrying my baby. What the fuck is going on man?"

"Relax, Joe. I know it's a lot to take in."

"A lot to take in? That's an understatement!"

"I know it is. Tell me, Joe. Tell me, did you often hang out with Max and Julie?"

Joe let out a deep breath to try and calm down, "Yeah sure, quite a bit. Jenny and Julie was best friends and Max was always along for the ride."

"What do you mean?"

"Well, he was Julie's guy. Wherever Julie went, he went. Not that he didn't want to half the time, but it was just a thing. I don't think I ever saw Julie without Max."

"Okay I got it; they were inseparable."

"Yeah right, inseparable."

"And how about their other friend, Jerry? Did you spend much time with him?"

"As little as possible."

"Really? Okay, tell us about that."

"Not a lot to tell really. He had it bad for Jenny. They was friends since high school, good friends, the three of them. Three little punk rockers running around the city together. I like Julie just fine. In fact, I like her a lot, and Max is a decent guy, too. But that Jerry, well, he had it real bad for Jenny. Followed her around like a puppy dog, did anything for her, was always showing up uninvited and from what I understand, always getting involved with her personal life and her boyfriends."

"He ever try to interfere in your relationship with Jenny?"

"All the fuckin time, you kiddin' me?"

"Like what?"

"Well, he was always a pain in the ass, you know, pullin' that third wheel shit. Then one night this guy tells me if I ever hurt Jenny, he's gonna kill me. So, I tells him, if he ever talks to me like that again, I'm gonna break his fuckin' face, and shove his fagotty little karate black belt up his ass."

"And then?"

"Best thing I ever did. Guy completely avoided me after that, tried to convince everyone I was a homophobe cause I called him fagotty. But it was a small price to pay to get him to avoid me whenever we ended up in the same room together. And you know what? I can't think of anyone that would want to hurt Jenny. But if you're looking for a weird, obsessed guy with anger issues, I would definitely check out Jerry. And that's not me being spiteful cause we had some beef, that's me saying if anyone she was close to did this shit, you should look at him."

"Well thank you, Joe. I think we'll end this here. We may have to call you back in the future, but as of right now I think you've answered everything we wanted to ask. C'mon with me and I'll walk you down and out."

***

Tommy returned to the squad room and once again polled his colleagues, "Okay, so what did we all think of Mr. Martinelli?"

"I'm not feeling him, Tommy," Jimmy said.

"No, me either, Tommy. I mean he's got the best motive if it is his kid, but I really believe he didn't know she was pregnant. Actually, he seemed pretty upset at the thought of it possibly being his and being killed along with Jenny," Doreen added.

Then Mark began, "I agree with Jimmy and Doreen in that I don't think Martinelli is going to be your man. I don't think he had a clue of what he was in for when he walked in here today. He seemed genuinely surprised that Ms. Lindel was pregnant. Of course, that being said, you can't rule him out. He, most likely being the father could be the motive, and if we do rule out Pete Hobbson, since it looks like he's got a solid alibi, then that leaves us with Quick and Martinelli. Now I may not be feeling Martinelli, but it wouldn't be the first time I was wrong."

"Yeah, I'm right there with you all, and stuck with nothing. We'll just keep digging into both of these men, and hopefully be able to find something a little more solid. Anyone want to stay late with me for a bit? I want to go to 23rd Street and see if we can get any leads from the pub they were at," Tommy replied.

Jimmy nodded.

"Fuckin' Tommy, if there is a pub connected to a case, you certainly want to investigate it, don't you?" Doreen exclaimed with a grin.

"Hey, just part of the job, Doreen," Tommy winked at her.

"Well, I already told the wife I was coming right home, so you can count me out," Mark replied.

"I don't think we should all be heading down there on overtime, Tommy, so maybe you and Jimmy go. I'll tag along and then leave for home from there," Was Doreen's way of saying, Yes, I'll have a Jack and Diet.

***

8:12 PM

The three detectives entered The Storehouse Pub located at 69 West 23rd Street. It was a well-lit pub that had a long bar on the left, and a double row of tables to the right, with solid wood floors and dark red walls. It was a simple and clean establishment that Tommy had been to on at least two occasions in the past.

The bar side was packed with people, so they took a high-top table towards the back of the pub. There they were greeted by a short, blonde girl with an Irish accent, who asked if they would be needing menus or if they just wanted drinks. Tommy asked for menus, and ordered a pint of Smithwick's Lager for himself, Jack Daniel's and Diet for Doreen, and then turned to Jimmy.

"I don't know, I guess I'll take a Magners, please."

As they removed their coats and settled in, the waitress returned with their drinks and their menus. As they looked them over Doreen commented, “I don’t know, it’s a little creepy. I almost feel disrespectful sitting here, knowing that Jenny Black had her last meal here with her friends just a little more than a week ago.”

“Yeah, it is a little weird, right?” Jimmy replied.

And then they all fell silent as they read the menus.

“Are ye’s ready ta order yet?” The waitress asked as she passed the table.

“I think we’re ready,” Tommy answered.

Tommy and Doreen both ordered the Crispy Chicken Sandwich and Jimmy ordered a cheeseburger.

“Can I ask your name, dear?” Tommy asked.

“I’m Caitlyn,” the waitress answered.

“Really? That’s my daughter’s name,” Tommy replied.

“Imagine dat. Two Caitlyn’s in yer life now, what are da odds,” The waitress said, stone-faced and loaded with sarcasm.

“Let me ask you, Caitlyn, is this place wired with cameras?”

“Lookin’ ta rob da place, are ye?”

“No, not exactly, love. We’re detectives from the 21st Precinct, and we are actually hoping you have some footage of a group that was in here a week and half ago.”

"Da cops huh? Yeah, ye's looks like cops ta me. We got cameras, da managers not here douh. Let me put yer orders in and I'll give 'im a call and get ye's into da office to see em."

"That would be great. Thank you dear."

A few minutes went by and Caitlyn returned.

"Aw'ight I can get ye's in. Tell me what day it was, and I'll be cue-in' it up for ye's while ye's eat, so we won't be wastin' yer time."

"Ahhh you're a doll, Caitlyn. It was a Wednesday night, two Wednesdays ago, and I'd say line it up to about 11:30 at night, please. Thank you so much."

Caitlyn soon returned with the detectives' meals, "Take yer time. I'll come get ye's when it's cued and ready."

***

After their meals were finished Caitlyn led them to the pub's office, where she had the footage ready to go.

There were several screens from each of the cameras, but one immediately showed the foursome sitting and drinking at the table right next to where the detectives were sitting themselves just moments ago.

They sped the cameras up a bit, until they saw Jenny get up and put her jacket on.

"Can you back that up a bit?" Tommy asked. "There — right here, she's answering her phone. What time does it say there? 11:49… That's going to be our caller. She stands up, puts some bills on the table, puts her jacket on and kisses everyone goodbye. Watch our boy, Jerry. He does the same, drops his money, picks up his jacket and doesn't even put the jacket on and he is right out the door after our Jenny. Can we jump to that camera there? That shows the entrance. Yup, there you go. She's hailing a cab there at the fire hydrant, and as it pulls up, he stops her…

"Look at that… That lying fucker… They got in the cab together," Jimmy finished up with.

"Wow," Doreen added, "He got in the cab with her. He said they left separately, and he went straight home."

"This dirty fucker," Tommy said in a low and irritated voice.

The three detectives all thanked Caitlyn for showing them the video footage and both Tommy and Doreen recorded it onto their phones. Then they returned to their table and discussed the case over another round.

"Should we go grab him now?" Jimmy asked.

"No. I think we'll call him and try to get him in for another interview tomorrow. I don't want to spook him and have him flee or be on the defensive when we interview him. Plus, even with this little bit of video, all it proves is that he's a liar. Other than that, we still have no solid evidence on this kid."

"We have them leaving in a cab together and we have his hair recovered from her body, don't we?" Jimmy replied.

"Don't get ahead of yourself, Jimmy. Yes, we have them getting into a cab together, and we're still waiting on the hair to come back from the lab. But even then, their meeting isn't in dispute. They spent a couple hours together right here, hugged and kissed one another hello and goodbye. I'm surprised the Medical Examiner only found three of his hairs on her body. No, we have nothing solid enough to take to the D.A.'s office yet. And if we spook him, he may cover something up that we haven't found yet, or even take flight. So, we gotta play this one cool and see what more we can get out of him before we can make an arrest."

"Yeah, you're right. I know you're right, I'm just getting a little anxious. I'm really looking forward to seeing his face when we do make the arrest though. This creep, killing this girl because, why? Because he couldn't have her for himself? If that was common practice, shit I'd be doing multiple life sentences for every time I've been turned down by a girl."

"Turned down? Handsome fella like you, Jimmy?" Tommy asked in a sarcastic tone.

"Looks ain't everything, Tommy. A girl needs a little personality also," Doreen added.

"Ouch! What did I do to you to get that knife in the side?"

"I saw an opening, sorry! It was an easy one," Doreen replied laughing.

The three of them finished their round and then said goodnight. Doreen and Jimmy both headed home to their apartments in Queens and Tommy returned to the 2-1 to sign both he and Jimmy out for the night. While at the precinct Tommy put in a call to Jerry Quick.

"Good evening, Mr. Quick. Detective Keane again from the 21st Precinct. I'm sorry to call so late. Listen, I'm sorry to ask, but we forgot to ask about a few details about Jenny's case earlier today, and

I also need a signature. Do you think you can make it in tomorrow, preferably in the morning? … Well, what's too early for you? … You can make it that early? Excellent, we'll see you at 8 AM then sir. Yes, yes, thank you very much, Mr. Quick, we appreciate it."

Chapter Twenty

Tommy awoke about an hour before his alarm was to sound. He laid on his side, staring into the complete darkness of his room at his mother's apartment on 88th Street. Step by step, he went through the Jenny Lindel case in his head. It had only been a couple of days since the Medical Examiner had ruled her death a homicide, and he already had a suspect. The questions bouncing around his head right now were about how to proceed. (There was little physical evidence so far, and what he had could easily be accounted for at trial.) The hair meant nothing; they were together all night. Lying about sharing a cab? More nothing. Jerry's lawyer would say he was drinking and simply could not remember correctly. And motive? Sure, Jerry was known to be jealous and known to act out on it, but that does not prove he killed Jenny. No, Tommy needed more. He needed something that put Jerry in the park with Jenny, something irrefutable. But what?

Tommy rolled out of bed and onto the floor. He did his fifty morning push-ups, then sat up on his knees, turned the lamp on and turned off the alarm on his phone. He then looked over at JoJo who sat at attention, waiting for Tommy to acknowledge him. Tommy turned to face the little dog and pet him with both hands down his face and sides, and JoJo gave Tommy one big lick, catching him right in the middle of his face.

“No, no, no. You know I hate that, JoJo. No dog kisses, you dirty dog,” Tommy said softly to him in the poorly lit room. When Tommy spoke JoJo immediately got excited and started jumping around the bed in a happy, frenzied way, knowing it was time to start his day.

Tommy took the dog out for a quick walk, came back in, and showered and dressed for the day. He stepped into the living room where his mother, still in her nightgown, and JoJo watched television. He said a quick good morning and goodbye in the same sentence as he kissed her on the head. As her cigarette smoldered in the ashtray, next to a cup of coffee, she waved goodbye.

It was early and not bitterly cold as Tommy walked to the precinct. While he walked, he lulled himself into a thoughtless, meditative state. He cleared out everything in his head to look at the Jenny Lindel case with a fresh perspective.

Tommy arrived at the squad room about forty-five minutes before his shift was to start. The place was empty, which he liked. He removed his coat and hung it up, then sat at Doreen’s desk, where he found a large manila envelope with his name on it.

Tommy expected it to be the hair comparison and analysis from the lab confirming it was Jerry’s hair that was found on Jenny’s body. But that is not all it was.

The analysis showed one positive match to the suspect, and two hairs belonging to a yet unknown person.

‘An unknown person? Someone else? What the hell, Tommy? Someone else’s hairs, two hairs, from another black person. Could it be? Is it not Jerry after all? Or is it Jerry and another perpetrator? Could there be two killers? Was he acting in concert with another individual? Or could this be someone totally unrelated?

Could it be a random robbery in the park after all? All of her personal things were missing. Is that possible?'

Tommy's clear head began to spin. He was never one hundred percent sold on Jerry's guilt, but the process of elimination, combined with the ever-mounting bits of circumstantial evidence, were certainly leading him in that direction. But now this tiny bit of physical evidence was shedding new light onto this case. Two tiny hairs, who did they belong to? And why were they found in Jenny's hair?

Tommy sat silently. He pondered. He spun around in his chair and thought, and thought, and thought.

"Morning, Tom, how are you today?" Tommy's train of thought, and the morning quiet, was shattered by the voice of Sergeant Browne entering the squad room.

"Doing okay, Boss. You? How you doin' today?"

"Just fine, Tom. How you making out on that Lindel murder? I know those CUPPIs (Case or Circumstances Undetermined Pending Police Investigation) are a bitch, but I heard you had several interviews lined up yesterday. You get anywhere with them? Love to close that case before COMPSTAT (COMPSTAT was a weekly meeting where police commanders compared crime statistics) next week."

"I was hoping to get somewhere yesterday, Boss. But they, for the most part, all fell flat. And now some lab stuff arrived that has possibly changed the direction of this case as well."

"Oh yeah? What you got?" Sergeant Browne asked, stopping by the desk.

"Not a lot, just some strange hairs that we weren't counting on. Could be something, could be nothing. I don't know."

"You'll find 'em, I know you will, Tom. Keep banging away at it, I have faith," Sergeant Browne replied as he continued into his office and shut the door behind him.

"Thanks, Boss."

Next in was Mark Stein, followed by Jimmy Colletti, Lieutenant Bricks, and Doreen Doyle. As they all walked in together there was a sea of greetings and good mornings. As soon as everyone settled, Tommy let the squad in on what he had just learned, and the discussion of different possibilities began.

PAA Charice Tate entered the room with her usual loud and cheerful greeting, "Good morning my beautiful B-Squad! How are all my lovely, lovely detectives today? It was a quiet one in the old 2-1 last night, so here is two cases for you, Detective Doyle, two for you, Detective Stein, and two for you, Detective Colletti. Charice has no new cases for you handsome Detective Keane because you are still out of rotation with your homicide, but I do have this for you. Not sure what it is, some paperwork from a phone company. You expectin' something from a phone company, Detective?"

"Yes, I am, Charice. Thank you so much."

"You got it, honey. Hope it's what you are waiting for." She turned and sashayed out the door.

Tommy opened the envelope and Doreen and Jimmy each sidled up next to him to see what it was.

"It's the trap and trace from the warrant on Jenny's phone. There are a few numbers on here but here, this one at 11:48, it's from an Amobi Adebayo… Amobi Adebayo? That sounds familiar somehow. He called at 11:48 and then again at a quarter after midnight."

"The plot thickens," Doreen said with a rather positive tone.

"Amobi Ade-what?" Jimmy asked, "That could be our new black guy, that name sounds African-ish to me."

"Yes, Amobi Adebayo is definitely African," Mark said from behind the newspaper he read at his desk, "Dollars to doughnuts, he's a Nigerian."

"Dollars to doughnuts?" Doreen repeated, "Stop dating yourself, Mark. When was the last time you could buy a doughnut for less than a dollar?"

"Fair enough, Doreen. But the smart money says he's a Nigerian."

Tommy paused for a minute as the wheels turned in his head. "Doreen, my love, would you please run Mr. Adebayo in the computer for me, every which way you can? And please, if you can, work some of your social media magic. I'm sure we'll end up with numerous hits, but the sooner we get started the sooner we'll have something to narrow down from whatever we find along the way."

"My pleasure, Tommy," Doreen said, and turned to go back to her desk.

"Jimmy, our friend Jerry Quick will be coming back in at 8 AM to be re-interviewed. This time I think we'll dig a little harder, and more aggressively. We don't have much to go on with this guy, but we have proof that he lied to us. We also have the hair analysis back from the lab. We'll throw his Jiu Jitsu training in his face and see if we can catch him in some more lies. Then we'll see if he knows this Amobi Adebayo as well, and if they know one another well, this could turn interesting."

"Okay cool. I assume I'll be quiet for the most part, unless I have a question, right?"

"You know what, Jimmy? I think we'll do just a tiny bit of good-cop-bad-cop here. We'll run through the interview same as yesterday, but when you see me run my hand over my hair," Tommy ran his hand over his hair as he said it, to illustrate what he was talking about, "I want you to jump up and say something like 'Bullshit! He's Lying' in a loud and menacing way and we'll see if we can rattle him a little. This kid has never been in trouble except for some Molly in college, and he doesn't seem to be a hard guy at all to me either. So maybe, maybe, if we shake him up a little, we can crack him, and get something out of him."

"Cool, so I'm the bad cop, and I'll wait for your signal, got it."

"Detective Keane?" Charice asked from the entrance of the squad room, "There's a Jerry Quick downstairs waiting for you."

"Thanks, Charice." Tommy headed down the stairs and saw Jerry waiting for him, dressed almost the same as he was the day prior, only with a blue button-down shirt rather than the white.

"Morning, Mr. Quick. Follow me, please." Tommy led Jerry up the stairs and back to the interview room, where he, Jerry, and Jimmy all took the same seats they had the day before. Mark observed from behind the two-way mirror, but Doreen continued her search for Amobi Adebayo on the computer.

"Thanks for coming in again this morning. We had a few more questions for you, Jerry. You're truly helping us out today by coming back in right away, and so early. We appreciate it," Tommy began the interview.

"Absolutely, Detective. Like I said, anything to help." Jerry replied.

"Okay. We think we have a pretty good timeline of the night all of you were at The Storehouse, but we really want to make sure we are a hundred percent accurate. So let me read you what I have, according to what you told us yesterday."

With that, Tommy read through his notes from the day before, and had Jerry agree to each point he made as they went along. They went over everything from the beginning to the end of their evening at The Storehouse; From where they sat to what they ate to what they drank, and whatever they talked about that evening. Jerry agreed with it all and even added bits he remembered as they went along. All of the night's events only took about ten minutes to go through.

"Okay and then Jenny got a call, right?" Tommy asked.

"Right. She got a call, and that was when she said she had to leave," Jerry replied.

"Right, that's what you said yesterday. So she gets a call? From whom you don't know, but she says she has to leave?"

"Correct," Jerry answered.

"And then?"

"She dropped her money - I think it was $80 on the table, put her jacket on, hugged us all goodbye and left," Jerry answered.

"Right, and then you left?"

"Yeah, then I left."

"Right away? How long after Jenny left?"

"Oh, I don't know for sure. A couple minutes? Four, possibly five, minutes after?" Jerry answered, shifting in his chair, looking a bit restless.

"Four or five minutes after she left? Okay, and what? You caught a cab home?"

"Yeah, maybe four or five minutes and I took off. I gave Julie and Max some money for the tab, then I left and caught a cab home."

"Alone?"

"Alone?" Jerry asked.

"Yeah, alone. You were by yourself when you left and caught a cab?"

"Yes sir, I was alone."

Tommy ran his hand over the top of his head.

"Bullshit! This kid's a fucking liar, Tommy! A fucking liar!" Jimmy yelled out, and stood up from the bench, so loudly and aggressively that Jerry Quick jumped about four inches out of his chair, a look of panic appearing on his face.

"Whoa, sit down, Detective Colletti," Tommy said in an authoritative voice.

"No. No, Detectives, I promise I'm telling the truth. Why, why would I lie to you?"

"Exactly what I'd like to know, Jerry. Why would you lie to us?"

"I wouldn't, Detective Keane. Sir, I wouldn't. What I told you is the truth, I swear."

Tommy leaned into the table. He moved slowly, locking eyes with Jerry until his head was as close as the table would allow him to get. His face turned from the nice, understanding Detective Keane, to the soulless dead-eyed Detective Keane, and in a low almost whisper of a voice he said, "But it's not, Jerry. It's not the truth and we know it."

Jerry Quick sat up straight. His eyes were wide, and they bounced from Tommy's to Jimmy's and back to Tommy's. "I'm, I'm telling you the truth. I swear," he repeated.

Tommy, still in the same position, spoke again in his flat and profoundly serious voice, "No, you're lying. And your lies will bury you, Jerry."

Tommy paused and then he continued, "You lied because you left immediately after Jenny did. You left so immediately after she did that you met her near the fire hydrant right in front of The Storehouse Pub, and you got in the cab with her. We know this, Jerry, because you are on video. You are on video getting into the cab with Jenny. What else have you lied to us about, Jerry? What else?"

"No. Noth – Nothing. I mean yeah, uh, we, we did share a cab, I remember that now. But we went up the West Side to my place and I got out and she continued home, I swear. I swear. I must have been mistaken."

Tommy ran his hand over his head again.

"Bullshit! You fuckin' liar. No way you were mistaken, no one makes a mistake like that. Either you took a cab alone or you didn't you lying fuck!" Jimmy shouted, once again frightening Jerry and making Mark jump in the observation room.

"Sit down, Detective!" Tommy said in an angry tone.

He continued to question Jerry, who was now beginning to shake in his seat. Again, in his restrained, deadpan voice, Tommy said, "Jerry, you knew. You knew Jenny was pregnant."

"Pregnant?" Jerry repeated.

"You knew. You knew, Jerry. You said you had sex with Jenny eight weeks before she died, and she was exactly eight weeks pregnant. And that's why you killed her, Jerry."

"What! You think—"

"That is what you told us. You told us you fucked Jenny eight weeks before she was found dead, Jerry. Pregnant. Pregnant and choked to death by a Rear Naked Choke hold. You're a Jiu Jitsu guy, aren't you? You didn't want the baby, did you? Thought you were too young, thought it would get in the way? So, you killed her. You choked her to death and stuffed some Molly into her mouth, so it'd look like a suicide and then threw her in the river. Didn't you, Jerry?"

"What? What? No, no, no. No, no, no, Detectives, no. I didn't do any of that. Yes, yes, I lied, okay? Yes, I lied. I did share a cab with her, but I swear, I swear, I got out of the cab in front of my building and Jenny went home, and I swear, I swear, I never ever have had sex with her. I loved Jenny. God oh God, I loved Jenny more than anything. I would never ever hurt her. No. No, I never ever would hurt her I loved her so –"

Tommy ran his hand over his head.

"Bullshit, you lying fuck. You killed that beautiful young girl because she was pregnant. You're a lying piece of shit, and you're gonna rot in hell for this you—"

"Detective! Sit down!" Tommy yelled angrily at Jimmy.

At this point Jerry was in complete shock and crying out loud, tears running down his face and drool beginning to come out of his mouth.

"Why, Jerry? Why, Jerry? You two could have aborted the baby. Why did you have to kill her, Jerry?"

"No!" Jerry shrieked. "I didn't. I loved her, I loved her, I don't know why I lied about those things, but I swear, I swear I didn't kill her. I loved Jenny so much. I'm sorry I lied, I'm so sorry!"

"Who's Amobi, Jerry?" Tommy shouted "Who's Amobi? Amobi!"

"What? What? Amobi? Amobi?" Jerry answered, confused by the question.

"Who the fuck is Amobi, Jerry?" Tommy said loudly and firmly but not shouting anymore.

Jerry froze for a second and stuttered as he tried to get the words out in disbelief. With his brow furrowed he stated in a much lower, less frantic voice.

"A, A, Amobi… Amobi, is, is their trainer. Their, their personal trainer, he, he trains Jenny and the Lindels'. He, Amobi…" Jerry went silent as the events of the last few minutes took hold.

Tommy gave him a second to process his thoughts. He felt there was something about to break.

"Who is Amobi, Jerry? It's obvious you know. He a friend of yours?" Tommy asked in his usual low stern way.

"Amobi is Jenny's trainer. He, he teaches her kickboxing," Jerry answered wiping tears from his eyes, still visibly shaking. Something clicked in Tommy's mind… 'The trainer.'

"Stand up, Jerry, give me your phone. Jimmy, pat him down please, and make sure he's got nothing on him. Jerry, listen to me, and listen to me good. You're going to sit here and do nothing while we step out of the room for a minute. Don't be stupid, you're being taped and recorded, and for Christ's sake don't piss me off, Alright? We'll be right back. Do you understand me?"

"Yes, yes sir, Detective Keane," Jerry answered tears running down both cheeks.

Both Tommy and Jimmy left the box. "Fuck, Jimmy, I knew that name sounded familiar. Tina, the maid, she mentioned him when she was telling us about the staff that came into the Lindel house."

"Shit, Tommy, you're right. He's on the list of house staff. Could he be involved?"

Mark met up with them as he came down the corridor from the observation room, toward the squad room.

"I'd say you two tore that boy a new one. Every time Jimmy shouted at him, I jumped out of my own shoes," Mark said when they met.

"Yeah, this thing has taken a sharp turn. I think this Amobi is who we may be looking for. I'm not sure our pal Jerry here is innocent, but I'm beginning to think my suspicions may be wrong. We'll have to see how connected he is to Amobi, and if they have a history."

"Hey, Tommy, come here," Doreen called out from where she was clicking away at the computer. When he arrived, she continued, "Pull up a chair, Tommy. 'Kay so we're looking pretty good so far. I have a couple Amobi Adebayo's in our system for past arrests, but nothing juicy. Seems to mostly be collars for peddling without a license—"

"Nigerians," Mark said from across the room.

"A couple of these arrests in the Bronx, a few in Queens, and a few in Brooklyn. A few different dates of birth so these aren't helping us a lot at the moment, but on Facebook I found a total of 54. Of those 54, most live in Nigeria!" She said loudly and in Mark Stein's direction.

"Told you," He replied still standing near the doorway.

"But three live here in New York. Well, two in Brooklyn and one in the Bronx. Now our Bronx guy looks to be about 14 and has arms like spaghetti noodles. One of our Brooklyn Amobi's looks to be in his mid-twenties, but also has spaghetti arms. Now look at number three here, he's built like Superman. He's got the name, and he's definitely got the muscle to choke your victim out and throw her over the railing into the river. Let's read more. He loves football, of course that's soccer to us, he was in the army in Nigeria, he loves America, and he works as a personal trainer here. Unfortunately, that's all I have so far but I'm still looking into this guy."

"That was quick, Doreen. Yeah, this is our Amobi, and I think this guy is connected to this case. Fuck yeah, Doreen, you rock, kid. Thank you so much for the help."

"No problem, Mister Man. Give me a little time and we'll see if I can rock your world."

"Okay," Tommy replied with a little laugh, "Hey, do you think you could print me a photo of Amobi, please?"

"Oh wait. I don't know if you're going to like this," Doreen replied in a somewhat sullen tone.

"What Doreen? What is it?" Tommy asked, suddenly serious.

"All I could find… is a confirmation on the phone number, along with this photo, and his current address on Livonia Avenue in Brownsville, Brooklyn," She replied with a childish smile.

"Doreen, I love you. I absolutely love you," Tommy relaxed and laughed.

Tommy walked over to Lieutenant Bricks' office and knocked on the door.

"Come in."

"Hey Lu —"

"All okay, Tommy? I could hear you from in here."

"Yeah, Lu, I wanted to keep you up to date. We have a good idea who's responsible for the Jenny Lindel homicide. I'm going to try and get a little more out of this kid we have in the box, and if it checks out, I'm going to try and scoop this guy up today at his apartment in Brownsville. What I'd really like though is to be able to keep this kid in the box until we return.

"Do what you gotta do, Tom. Just be careful and be smart."

"Thanks, Lu."

Tommy left the office and was handed a photo of Amobi Adebayo by Doreen. "Thanks, Doreen, listen, I'm going to try and get this kid to stay here in the box while we try and grab this Amobi. He's not under arrest so I can't hold him, but if it turns out he's mixed up with this Amobi, I don't want to have to go find him again, especially now that he knows what we're up to. Do you think you can keep an eye on him while Jimmy and I go find Amobi?"

"Of course, I got plenty of paperwork to get through here. I'm sure I can fill hours typing through these cases until you get back."

"Thanks, Again, you rock kid."

Tommy opened the door to the interview room and Jerry looked up at him. His eyes were now dry but completely bloodshot from the tears and the stress of his morning.

"Who's this?" Tommy asked in a very severe way.

"That's him. That's Amobi."

"And you're certain."

"Yes, a hundred percent."

"Okay, listen. Listen to me, Jerry, I'm not placing you under arrest. You are free to go. However, what I'd like you to do is to wait right here. I'll be gone for at least an hour, maybe two, maybe even three, I don't know. But I'd like you to wait here for me. Will you do that? Can you do that for me? Can you do that for Jenny?"

"If it helps, Detective, I'll do whatever you ask."

"Okay then. You understand, you're not under arrest, but you're going to wait here for me to return?" Jerry nodded yes. "Good man. Come with me, please." Tommy led Jerry out to the squad room, "Detective Doyle, Detective Stein, this is Jerry Quick, you may remember him from yesterday. He's going to be staying with us for a couple of hours here in the interview room. He's free to leave but he really wants to stay and help us out if he can."

"Hey, Jerry. Can I get you a coffee or a soda? A candy bar or a bag of chips?" Doreen asked in a friendly and comforting tone.

"No, no, ma'am, I'm good right now, thank you," Jerry replied.

"You're doing the right thing, Jerry. Thank you. Now go have a seat and we'll be back as soon as we can."

Chapter Twenty-One

Tommy and Jimmy drove out to Brownsville. On the way Jimmy asked, "So why are you having Jerry Quick wait for us? I'm a little confused. We're going to grab this guy Adebayo right, so why is Quick waiting for us?"

"I know it's a little unorthodox. But you see we have Jerry, and we have him currently of his own free will. After this morning we may never get him to come back in and we still don't know if he's a part of this homicide or not. He's a fucking liar, and we don't know if we can trust anything he says, but if he's dumb enough to wait for us to go scoop up this Amobi fuck, well that's just fine with me. If they're in on this together I'd rather lock them both up today then have to chase Jerry down at a later date. I don't have enough to arrest him yet, but I certainly don't want him walking just yet either. So if he's willing to wait for us to connect some dots, then good for us and shame on him."

"You're a clever bastard, Tommy Keane."

"Well, let's see if it works. He can leave anytime he wants."

They found Amobi Adebayo's building on Livonia Avenue. It was a beat up, small red brick home that had been cut up into three small one-bedroom apartments. Jimmy found the name Adebayo on the bell of one of the two doors on the concrete front stoop of the home.

"You ready?" Tommy asked.

"Sure am."

Tommy rang the bell, paused, then knocked.

"Yes? Who is it there?"

"We're from Housing and Urban Renewal, Mr. Adebayo. We have some questions for you about possibly improving your living conditions, either here or in one of our nicer buildings on Dumont Avenue, if you're interested."

The locks on the door tumbled, and the door opened. Amobi Adebayo stood shirtless in front of the detectives in a pair of Adidas track pants and black rubber sandals. He was built like an Olympic gymnast and stared at the detectives with a puzzled look on his face.

"A new apartment? Nicer? What are you from, the City?"

"Yes, sir, we are from the city. But actually, we are detectives from the 21st Precinct and we'd like to ask you a couple questions about Jenny Lindel, if we may."

Amobi Adebayo stood silently staring into Tommy's eyes for a second, then suddenly tried to slam the door closed. Tommy jammed it open with his left leg as Amobi struggled to close the door. Then he took flight, running into the back room, leaping over the couch like a gazelle. As he began to unlock the window, Tommy was able to grab him around the waist from behind. As he did, Amobi threw a left elbow at Tommy, catching him just above his left eye. Both men fell to the floor between the bed and the wall. Tommy managed to get one arm around Amobi in a half nelson while Jimmy punched Amobi twice in the head. Jimmy was then able to get a cuff on his left wrist and immobilize his arm.

"Spin him around to the left, Jimmy," Tommy shouted, and in one move both detectives managed to roll him over, so Amobi was face down on the floor, allowing them to force his other wrist into the cuffs.

"Oh, you dirty fucker," Tommy exclaimed, feeling the lump growing above his left eye with his fingers, as all three men sat on the floor catching their breaths.

"All we wanted to do was talk, Amobi. What's with the running and the fighting?" Tommy asked in a surprisingly soft and kind manner. Amobi did not reply. "So, now you're gonna make us be tough guys, and take you into the precinct to talk to you instead of sitting here on your couch like gentlemen. So, what do you got to say for yourself? Nothing?" Amobi remained silent. "That's okay, pal, we have all night, time you see, is on our side, Amobi."

Tommy hopped up onto his feet and put out his hand to help pull Jimmy off the floor, "Let's get our friend Amobi a shirt and a jacket there, Jimmy, and we'll take him home to the 2-1," Tommy said.

When Jimmy went to open the top of Amobi's dresser in search of a t-shirt, he could not believe what was sitting in plain view on top of the dresser. "Tommy! Look at this, I can't believe it!" Atop the dresser lay three credit cards and a driver's license, all in the name of Jennifer Lindel.

"Amobi, Amobi, Amobi, shame on you," Tommy said in a sarcastic tone, "Amobi…you got some explaining to do." He added, mimicking Desi Arnez as he said it. "But nothing just yet, we're going to get you dressed and take you back to the precinct where we'll have a nice long conversation. Now I'm going to tell you this now, and I'll repeat it when we get to the station house, okay?"

Then Tommy began, again with a rather kind and lighthearted voice, "You have the right to remain silent. Anything you say can be used against you in a court of law. You have the right to an attorney. If you cannot afford an attorney, one will be provided for you. Do you understand the rights I have just read to you? Now that you have this info, understand this works if you wanna talk now, or anytime in the future."

Tommy continued in a friendly, pleasant manner, "And when we get to the precinct, we'll go over this again and I'll have you sign a form for me, okay? Now listen, listen to me good, okay? You and I are about to spend a lot of time together. If you act like a gentleman, I'll treat you like a gentleman, and I'll get you a slice of pizza or a candy bar and a soda to help you make it through the night. But if you wanna play it hard, and make my night difficult, believe me I can be difficult as well, and neither of us want that, Amobi. So, what say we both act like gentlemen for the next eight to ten hours we are together, okay?" Directing his attention to Jimmy he said, "Here Jimmy, help me get him on his feet."

Together Tommy and Jimmy hoisted Amobi up. Leaving his hands cuffed behind his back, they pulled a t-shirt over his head and shoulders, and over that they wrapped a hoodie around him and zipped it up to his neck.

"Grab our friend two pairs of socks and some underwear, Jimmy, and stuff them into his pockets. He'll be happy he has them later, although I doubt they'll let him keep them at Central Booking."

And with that, they collected the credit cards and driver's license, as well as a smartphone that sat next to them, and led Amobi

Adebayo to their car. Jimmy drove while Tommy rode in the backseat with Amobi, who remained silent.

***

Once back at the 2-1, they led Amobi into the station house and checked in at the desk with Sergeant Ruffalo. They then brought Amobi up the stairs to the squad room and stuck him in the cage and closed the door.

"I see you boys got your man there," Mark said staring at Amobi through the iron bars of the cell that sat against the far wall of the squad room. "Looks like he got you too, Tom." He added, motioning with his eyes and brow to the bruised lump over Tommy's eye.

"Yes. It was an eventful trip out to Brownsville this morning, but I'm happy to say a fruitful one," Tommy replied as he made his way to Lieutenant Bricks' office. He knocked twice and cracked the door open, "Hey Lu, wanted to let you know we got our guy, and he had some of the victim's personal affects in his possession. So, pending any unforeseen nonsense this should be a closed case in a couple hours."

"Excellent, Tom. Good to hear. Looks like your perp gave you a little trouble," Bricks replied, pointing a finger at Tommy's forehead.

"Ah, nothing to it, Lu," Tommy replied.

Tommy made his way back toward the interview room where Jerry Quick still sat waiting. He tapped Jimmy on the shoulder, signaling him to follow.

"Jerry, my friend, how you makin' out here the last couple hours?" Tommy greeted him, as he and Jimmy walked in the door.

"Oh, thank God! I have been losing my mind in here waiting for you."

Well, we're glad you waited. I want to ask you about your friend, Amobi." Tommy said as he sat down in the chair.

"My friend? He's not my friend at all, Detective Keane. I just know who he is, is all," Jerry replied.

"Okay, well tell us everything you know about him, please."

"Why? You think it's him? You think it's him, don't you?"

"Don't worry about what we think, Jerry. Just tell us what you know about Amobi Adebayo, and don't leave anything out."

"Uh, okay, well I don't know a lot. I didn't even know his last name. I know he's a personal trainer, I know he's from Africa and he would go to the Lindels' and train the family there in the gym they had in the basement. I know, or think, he worked in a fitness club also but no idea where. I know, I know Jenny liked him. He taught her kickboxing, right there, right there in their house, in their basement, and, and that's it."

"So, he trained the whole family?"

"Well, Jenny and her stepmother. I don't think the father ever worked out, but yeah, he worked for the family, you know like as a regular job. Like Tina the maid, or their chef, whose name I can't remember."

"And Jenny, she liked him?"

"Oh yeah, she thought he was great. You, you think he killed Jenny, don't you?"

"No, Jerry, I don't think anything yet. Do you think he could kill Jenny?"

"I don't know why he would. They seemed to like each other a lot, but I don't know. Was he capable? I'm sure he was. He was in the army in Africa, I know that, so I guess he was trained to be a killer, but I don't know why he would."

Tommy paused for a moment, "Jimmy, would you like to ask Jerry anything?"

"No, Tommy, I think I'm good."

"Okay, unless you have something to add, Jerry, you're free to go. We may need to call you back, but I think we're finished with you for today."

"Really? Okay great, thank you, thank you."

"Jimmy, can you do me a favor and go have Amobi turn around in the cage so he can't see Jerry when he leaves, please?"

"He's here? Amobi is here? You caught him? Did he do it? Did he kill Jenny?"

Jerry began to cry again, and with his tears he washed away any lingering suspicions Tommy had for him. He now knew Jerry was guilty of nothing more than being a foolish bragger, and a liar, a sin most young men are guilty of from time to time.

"We're not sure just yet, Jerry. But it looks that way, thanks for coming in," Tommy stuck out his hand and shook Jerry's firmly.

Before he let go, he said in a nonthreatening tone, "Don't ever lie to the police again. In fact, try and give up lying as a whole, it does no one any good."

"Yes, sir. Thank you, Detective."

Tommy stepped out of the room and made sure Amobi was facing the corner of the cage, then motioned to Jerry that it was alright to leave. Jerry left the 2-1, never to return.

***

"Jimmy, my friend, my partner, my colleague, we have a long road ahead of us today. What say you order up a pie or two from Italian Village and we'll settle in on our interview of Mr. Adebayo, and then process him for the murder of Miss Jenny Lindel."

"Sounds good to me. What would you like on it?"

"Never mind me. I'll eat anything. Ask these two, as well as the Lu and the Sarge, if he's in."

Tommy checked the interview room to make sure it was clean, and nothing was left behind from Jerry, before he unlocked the cage and had Amobi turn around so he could remove his cuffs.

"Remember our conversation over at your place, Amobi? If you act like a gentleman, I'll treat you like a gentleman. I understand you used to be a soldier. If that's the case, you should be able to act like a soldier, and if you're cool with me, I'll be cool with you, Understand?"

"Yes. I understand. I will be cool with you, Officer."

"Alright, look at that, we're talking now. That is more like it. Go ahead fix your shirts."

Amobi slipped everything he was wearing off over his head, then put his t-shirt on properly, next his hoodie. He sat on the bench in the cage, then took a pair of socks out of his pocket and put them on as well. Then he looked up from the bench at Tommy and gave him an approving nod, in a way to say, 'We have an understanding.'

Tommy called ADA Jessica Lokietz and let her know an arrest was made in the Lindel case, and that he would be interviewing and processing the perpetrator now. After he hung up the phone, he took $50 out of his pocket and went to see Charice, who sat at her desk outside the squad room.

"Charice, can I ask a favor? We have a couple pizzas coming and if you don't mind, could you pay for them when they arrive? We'll be interviewing our perp, and Mark and Doreen will be observing."

"Why of course, Detective Keane. You know Charice is here for you, honey."

"Thanks, Charice, I appreciate it."

Tommy gave her the money and returned to the squad room, "You ready, Jimmy?"

"Yup," Jimmy replied.

Tommy unlocked the door to the cage, "C'mon, Amobi, we got some talking to do."

Tommy led him into the interview room and the three of them sat the same way they had earlier in the day with Jerry. And it began.

"You have the right to remain silent. Anything you say can be used against you in a court of law. You have the right to have an attorney present, now or in the future. If you cannot afford an attorney, one will be provided for you. Do you understand the rights I have just read to you? And with these rights in mind are you willing to speak with me today?"

Amobi nodded, "I think so."

"Okay, sign here saying I told you what I just told you," Amobi signed his Miranda form. "Alright, so I'm not going to ask you anything until I tell you some stuff, okay? Then I want you to think about it for a bit, now you haven't said much, but from what I heard it sounds like you speak English very well, so I'm not worried about understanding you. I want to make sure you understand me. I know some people think I have a strong accent, and I don't always talk so well, so please if you don't understand anything I am saying, or asking, please speak up."

"My English is perfect, Officer. In Nigeria, we speak English, it is our national language."

"Hey, again, I want to make sure you understand me, Mr. Adebayo. You need to understand every word I say, okay? Sometimes people don't always understand everything that comes out of my mouth, but it's important that you do."

Tommy paused, then continued, "So, Mr. Adebayo, Amobi, we know enough to have you here. We know you killed Jenny Lindel. We know you called her just minutes before you last saw her a week and a half ago in Carl Schurz Park, and that you met her on the promenade. There you grabbed her from behind and choked her to death, then for some reason attempted to wash some tablets of Molly down her throat with some whiskey. After that you robbed her dead body of her phone and belongings, which we recovered from your apartment. And after taking her things you picked her up and threw her over the railing into the East River. Now, let me repeat the important part of all of this, and it is that we know these things. Understand that, Amobi. We know this all to be true. We have evidence that puts you there, we have your phone calls, we have physical evidence proving your body touched her body that night. We have it all, everything that we need to book you for Murder One. And that, my friend, is as big as it gets."

Amobi Adebayo sat silently staring into Tommy's eyes as he spoke, taking in every word he said.

"Now, here in New York State, a Murder One conviction — and trust me, with everything we have on you, you will most certainly be convicted - carries a sentence of twenty-five years to life in prison, and usually without parole. But to give you a little hope, Amobi, I want you to know that with a conviction of twenty-five to life with parole, the average prisoner serves forty years."

Tommy sat back in his chair and continued, "Now, I've said what I want to say, and to be honest I don't care if you want to talk to us at all. With all of the physical evidence we have on this case, I don't need to waste my time talking to you. I know for a fact we already have everything we need for a solid conviction on the Murder One, and that the District Attorney's office is going to throw me a party when I bring you to them."

Tommy paused for a moment for effect.

"But once all this sinks in, what I want from you, and what the District Attorney is going to want to make their job easier, is for you to tell your side of the story, why did you do this, why you had to kill Jenny. And if you do, if you can tell us why you killed her and put it down on paper, Amobi, I know for a fact that the District Attorney will most likely be willing to lower your charges a bit. And do you know why? Do you know why?

"No," was Amobi's one-word answer, while he stared at Tommy from an equally dead-eyed stare.

Tommy leaned back in his chair, still locking eyes with Amobi, "Because you'll make it easy on them and because they are lazy. They don't want to do the extra work it takes for a full conviction. You see it's not about Jenny. You think they care about Jenny? Do you know how many people get killed every day in this City? It's a lot of work man, and even with a slam dunk case like this, if you make it easy on them, I can all but guarantee, they will take it easy on you."

Tommy again took a pause.

"Now we're going to give you a couple minutes, Amobi. And again, I don't care if you talk to me or not, I really don't. I have all I need on my end, and you talking to me doesn't make my job any easier. We got you, and you know we got you. So just think on it for a bit and we'll be right back."

Tommy and Jimmy got up and left Amobi in the box alone.

"Nice job, Tommy," Jimmy whispered after they left the interview room.

They both joined Mark and Doreen in the adjoining observation room.

"Good job, Tom. I liked your approach. Look at him. He looks cool, but his wheels are turning," Mark said pointing to Amobi, who sat against the wall with his arms folded, staring straight ahead at the wall in front of him.

The four of them watched Amobi stew for about five minutes.

"Okay, round two," Tommy said as he opened the door to the observation room.

"Go get 'em, Champ!" Doreen said in a low voice as he and Jimmy left.

Tommy and Jimmy reentered the room and as they began to sit, Amobi spoke.

"Officers, I can tell you my story, and I can tell you more, but I need assurances. I need assurances that one day I will again be free. For that, I promise you, your District Attorneys will throw you a party. Because what I have will make them salivate for justice."

Tommy sat down and cocked his head to the side. This interview had not only turned out to be easy, but now it had become interesting. He looked at Jimmy, whose eyes widened for a moment when they met Tommy's, and then he looked back at Amobi.

"Really? Alright, I'm interested. What you got for us?"

"Ahh no, I need assurances first."

"Fair enough. Give me an idea of what we're talking here so I can call the District Attorney and see if they'll make a deal with you. I'm sure they will, but I have to give them a taste first."

"Ahh yes. Fair enough, I understand. Well, tell your District Attorney that I, Amobi, did kill Jenny Lindel, but tell them it was a contract killing, and that Amobi Adebayo will tell you everything. But no Murder One. No life without parole."

"Let me see what I can do for you, Amobi. Give me a minute."

Tommy stepped out of the interview room, pulled out his cell phone, and called the D.A.'s office.

"ADA Lokietz please. Okay, thank you. Hey, Jessica, how you doing? Tommy Keane here from the 2-1 again. Okay, we made the collar on the Lindel case, and he has confessed. However, he says it was a contract killing, and he's willing to give it all up and name names if he can get a guarantee to no Murder One... Yes, yes, so far, I find him to be highly credible... No, he hasn't asked for a lawyer yet... Yes, how soon can you make it up here? Outstanding. Yes, yes, okay... We'll see you in a bit."

Tommy returned to the interview room.

"Good news, Mr. Adebayo. The ADA in charge of this case is on her way up here to talk to you right now. She says if she believes what you have to say, and everything checks out, she is willing to make a deal with you to ensure you are eligible for parole in the future."

Amobi nodded with a somewhat satisfied look on his face.

"What I will tell you now, and please understand, because I have been through this before, you must be one hundred percent honest with this woman. If she, or we, think you are lying, or you send us on a wild goose chase, I promise you, she and the judge assigned will take it personally and hammer you as hard as they can. You got that?"

"Yes, I understand, and I will tell the truth," Amobi answered.

"Okay great. We should all get along just fine then, please excuse us again, Detective Colletti and I are going to step out and wait for the District Attorney to arrive."

Tommy and Jimmy stepped out and into the squad room. Tommy grabbed a can of Coke from the machine and took a slice of pizza from the box and brought them to Amobi, who thanked him. Then he got the same for himself and he and Jimmy ate in the observation room as they all awaited ADA Lokietz to arrive.

***

When ADA Lokietz arrived, she announced herself in a small, mousy voice and with a heavy Long Island accent, "Hello, I'm ADA Lokietz, and I'm looking for Detective Keane, please."

She was short, even in her high heeled shoes. She was no more than about five-foot-two, young, with jet back hair that was pulled up on the sides in a banana clip and allowed to flow freely down her back. She wore a well-tailored, gray suit jacket and black skirt, and carried a briefcase, which she clutched to her chest with both arms wrapped around it, as she made her announcement.

"Follow me and I'll take you to him," Doreen said and led the ADA to the observation room.

"Hello, Jessica," Tommy said immediately, as Doreen opened the door and allowed ADA Lokietz to enter the room ahead of her.

"Hi, Detective Keane, nice to see you again. So, this is our man here, hey?" Jessica said, as she looked through the two-way mirror. Amobi Adebayo sat as he did earlier, with his arms folded, staring straight ahead at the wall in front of him.

"Yup, this is the guy. We scooped him up a couple hours ago, it was the trap and trace you helped us out with, and Detective Doyle's computer work, that led us right to his apartment. Lucky for us we caught him before he left for the day."

"Is he the one that put that lump on your head, Detective?" Jessica asked as she turned around and looked up at Tommy.

"Yes, ma'am, he's the one."

"And you believe what he's told you about this being a murder for hire, and that he's willing to give us everything he knows?" She asked as she again stared through the glass, studying Amobi Adebayo.

"Yes, I do. I also made it perfectly clear not to jerk you around or you would hammer him with the full weight of the law."

"Good, thank you, I like that part," she said, looking over her shoulder at Tommy with a large smile on her face. She knew she was tiny and unimposing, but also knew she held Amobi's life in her hands at this moment.

"Are you ready, Jessica?" Tommy asked.

"Yeah, let's do this. I'll follow your lead, Detective, and if I like what I hear, we'll make a deal."

"Very good. Let's do this."

Tommy, Jessica, and Jimmy all entered the interview room. Jimmy sat back on the bench where he had sat all day. Tommy this time, deliberately sat against the wall opposite and to the left of Amobi. Leaving the seat directly across from Amobi, for Jessica Lokietz, giving her a more commanding and authoritative position during the interview.

Tommy began, "Okay, Amobi, here we go. This is ADA Lokietz. She is the one with the power to decide if we can make a deal with you or not. I have informed her of your desire to cooperate with us in furthering this investigation, and that we think it would be beneficial, to both us and to you, for you to do so."

"Good afternoon, Mr. Adebayo. I'm not going to repeat everything Detective Keane just said, but yes, if we like what you have to tell us, and it all checks out, I do have the power to charge you with a lesser crime than the Murder One you are currently looking at, which I am sure you have been told by these detectives comes with a sentence of life without parole. Are you willing, sir, to cooperate with these detectives and with us at the District Attorney's office?"

"Yes, I am. I am willing to cooperate, and I am willing to tell you everything. But I must have assurances, no Murder One."

"Very well. I have the ability to bring lesser charges sir, but you will have to give us something, something that says, something that proves, what you are telling us is indeed the truth, sir. Then, and only then, I will agree not to assign the maximum charge of Murder One to your case. What may I ask, Mr. Adebayo, do you have that will convince these detectives and myself that you are willing to work with us honestly?"

"My phone, Miss. Detective Keane may I have my phone?" Amobi answered, still locking eyes with ADA Lokietz, who stared straight back at the musclebound killer without a blink or a worry, as she knew he was at her mercy now.

"Jimmy, do us a favor please and get Amobi's phone. It's in the top drawer of Doreen's desk."

"Sure thing," Jimmy hopped up from the bench, went and retrieved the phone, and handed it to Tommy as he reentered the room.

"Here you go, Amobi," Tommy said, as he passed the phone.

Amobi tapped away, then turned it to face both Tommy and Jessica, "Here. Do you see this? Go ahead and read it."

It was a text message. No name on the top, just initials "LL1" In the blue bubble it read, "It's Done!" and in the gray bubble it read, "Oh God, Thank you."

Amobi continued, "Push it over to see the time. What time does this tell you?"

"12:54," Jessica read.

"That is when I was done with Jenny. Can you detectives tell me who LL1 is?"

Tommy leaned back in his chair, folded his arms, and exhaled. He pursed his lips, and as Jessica and Jimmy both looked to him, he stated flatly in a disappointed tone, "Lisa Lindel."

"Yes, Detective Keane, you are right."

"Why?" Jimmy asked, a bit surprised.

"Why does anybody do anything, Detective? For money, for greed."

"What does Lisa Lindel have to gain from her daughter's death, Mr. Adebayo?" Jessica asked.

"Everything. Millions. When her husband dies, which could be any day now."

"And what did she give you for the murder?"

"$25,000, plus she promised to sponsor my family to come to the United States."

"And can you prove this?"

"Yes. She paid me with a check, and I kept $5,000, and sent $20,000 to my father in Nigeria. I have receipts, I have proof," Amobi replied.

"Okay, okay. Mr. Adebayo I will no longer seek a Murder One for the death of Jenny Lindel. Please, sir, tell us everything you can about what led you to commit this crime," Jessica said.

Amobi began to tell them about himself, the Lindels, and the death of young Jenny Black.

***

Amobi Adebayo was born and raised in a middle-class family in Port Harcourt, Nigeria. His father was a manager at an oil refinery and his mother was a homemaker who raised him and his three younger siblings.

Amobi performed well in school and excelled in sports as a youth, football (soccer) in particular. After school he enlisted in the Nigerian Army and when his time of service ended, he returned home to Port Harcourt and worked for a short time in the same oil refinery as his father. Approximately a year later he received a student visa to come to America, where he was to attend Long Island University's Brooklyn Campus, in pursuit of a degree in physical therapy.

While going to school at LIU, he worked in several health clubs, and privately as a personal trainer. This is how he met Lisa Lindel.

His first encounter with her was at the gym, where he filled in on occasion as her trainer. Later he became her full-time personal trainer.

Although New York City was an unbelievably expensive place to live, Amobi could not believe the amount of money he was able to make, simply by telling foolish rich people how to lift weights, and by counting their reps for them. New York was a dream come true for Amobi, who, in his home country of Nigeria lived a relatively good life. Here in New York he could see that the possibilities to make money, and not have to work extremely hard to make it, were seemingly endless.

Amobi Adebayo had been training Lisa Lindel for approximately six months when she asked him for some private training sessions at her residence on 92nd Street, where she had a complete gym set up in the basement.

Lisa had no romantic interest in Amobi. This was a professional relationship, where he was asked to visit her home four times a week for weight training sessions and kickboxing classes.

Soon, Lisa had Amobi running errands for her and began treating him more and more like a personal valet, which Amobi encouraged. The more he worked for Mrs. Lindel, and the more he ingratiated himself to her, the more she would pay him both in cash and with gifts.

When Charlie Lindel became too sick to leave home, Amobi would occasionally escort Lisa Lindel to a Broadway show. Once he accompanied her to a Rangers game at Madison Square Garden, and another time to a Yankee game at Yankee stadium in the Bronx.

Lisa Lindel and Amobi Adebayo had somehow struck up a rather odd relationship. Lisa had become a benefactor of sorts for Amobi. In him she could tout herself as some kind of hero by helping out an underprivileged African immigrant, exposing him to things an average immigrant of his standing would never be able to afford. By doing so she could feel morally superior to others in her circles. To many of her acquaintances, it seemed as though she began to keep Amobi more as a pet than as an employee, and the rumors of a sexual relationship between the two were ever present, even if they were in fact unfounded.

For Amobi, well he was just enjoying the ride. Less than three years prior he was fresh out of the Nigerian Army and working a hot and miserable job in a Port Harcourt oil refinery. Now he was taking a beautiful white woman out to dinner, sporting events, and Broadway shows and being paid to do so. America truly was the land of opportunity for him.

Amobi also slowly became Lisa Lindel's confidant. She confided in Amobi the way a young child would tell her pet puppy all her childish problems. Amobi, of course, took full advantage of this, and would encourage her paranoias and self-doubt, simply so he could turn around and build her back up again.

When Lisa Lindel learned that her husband, Charlie, had only left her with a one-million-dollar life insurance policy and one million out of his portfolio, she was beside herself with contempt for him, and for his daughter Jenny. Jenny stood to inherit approximately four million in cash and investments, as well as the house on 92nd Street and the vacation home on Cape Cod. All in all, it was a fortune to the tune of just over eight million dollars.

This is when the virtue signaling, morally superior Mrs. Charles Lindel decided something needed to be done to eliminate young Jennifer Lindel and claim Jennifer's inheritance for herself.

And who better to carry out such a diabolical deed than her new right hand and confidant, Amobi? 'He is an army veteran, and came from the inner city,' she thought. 'Surely, he was capable of a simple murder, and after all he owed it to her. After all she had done for him over the past year. Besides, who other than Amobi would understand just how much she deserved this inheritance over that dirty little punk rock freak of a stepdaughter?'

The more she thought about it, the more it infuriated her. And now with Charlie Lindel out of the house and most probably never returning from the Memorial Sloan Kettering Cancer Center, she felt the pressure of immediate action take over her every thought.

Approximately one week before Jenny's body was discovered in Carl Schurz Park, Lisa called Amobi and asked that they meet immediately.

Amobi, ever dutiful, caught a cab from his Brownsville neighborhood in Brooklyn. Upon arrival they sat in the Lindels' living room and, over a bottle of red wine, spoke at length about how to get rid of Jenny Lindel, and why.

It was decided. Amobi would kill and dispose of Jenny's body, something he felt he could easily do, and then he would make it look like a drug and alcohol induced suicide.

In return, Amobi would be paid $25,000 and Lisa Lindel would sponsor his parents and siblings for immigration to the United States via a foundation she would create with her newfound wealth. In her mind again, Lisa was going to be a do-gooder, and through a new foundation be able to prove her moral superiority to others by bringing poor, wretched, underprivileged Africans here to America for a better life. And who could argue with her virtuous actions, even if they were built on the murder of an innocent young woman?

The murder and the disposal of Jenny's body was completely left to Amobi. Lisa would continue to play the concerned wife and stepmother, never knowing for certain what would happen to Jenny.

***

Amobi and Jenny had actually had a good relationship. Amobi was a very kind and charming man, and Jenny was a very curious, and genuinely interested young woman. Over the years that they would pass each other in the house, they would always greet one another warmly.

On five separate occasions Amobi had even given Jenny some kickboxing classes. He was charmed with her genuine interest in his home country of Nigeria, home city of Port Harcourt, and the time he had spent in the military. Jenny, in general, was always interested in people, where they came from, and their different cultures and ways of life. Things, funny enough, that Amobi's benefactor, Lisa Lindel, never showed any interest in. It was not lost on him that Lisa's only interest in Amobi was to enhance her reputation.

But in the end, although he did like Jenny and could see right through Lisa, Amobi saw the murder of Jenny as nothing more than an opportunity. It was a job that needed doing and would greatly enrich his benefactor, Lisa, as well as himself and his family.

Although he thought Lisa was being cheap by only offering him $25,000 for this murder, he also saw this act as a long-term investment. He would now always be attached to Lisa Lindel and in a way, he was now becoming her benefactor, a position he felt he would be able to benefit from again and again in the future.

Amobi had killed before when he was in the Army. He knew of at least two who were suspected members of Boko Haram and there were many more he shot at but never knew for certain if they died.

Other military actions in the northeast of his country, such as razing and displacing entire villages, were things Amobi had taken part in numerous times while serving in the Army. The death of this nice young American woman was a small loss to the world, compared to the benefits he and his family would receive once the deed was done. Now it was just a matter of doing it.

***

Amobi had immediately decided to make Jenny's death appear like a suicide and he hatched a simple plan. Two nights before Jenny's body was discovered on the abutment, Amobi called Jenny and asked if he could meet her privately. He wanted to discuss some disturbing news he had learned about her stepmother Lisa. He said it was important, that it involved her and her father, and he wanted to discuss it immediately in a private setting.

Jenny was a little surprised by the call, and slightly taken aback by the implication of something nefarious at hand involving her stepmother, Lisa. But she was intrigued and said she would come to meet him right away.

At the time of Amobi's call, 11:48 PM, she was hanging out with her longtime friends Julie Mayer, Jerry Quick, and Max Spicnic, at the Storehouse Pub on East 23rd Street. Although she was having a good time, she thought it would not only be prudent, but probably very necessary, for her to go and meet Amobi right away.

So, with no explanation, she excused herself from her friends and caught a cab to meet Amobi in Carl Schurz Park.

Jenny arrived at East End, paid the cab driver, and against her better instincts entered the dark and deserted Carl Schurz Park. She made her way to the Promenade, where she found Amobi waiting for her on a bench, looking out onto the river and Roosevelt Island.

Amobi hoped that Jenny would be drinking and was happy to see she had been when she arrived. It was a chilly evening, but the snow and deep freeze that was on the way had yet to set in, so the two of them were able to talk comfortably on the park bench.

"Hi, Amobi. You have me a little shaken and concerned. What do you think is going on that you had to call me up here like this?" Jenny asked immediately.

"Yes, yes, Jenny. Hello, please come sit here, I too am concerned. I am a little afraid and don't know how to tell you my words right now," Amobi replied in his heavy Nigerian accent, speaking rather coyly. He wanted to feel her out, set her at ease, and take stock of the situation.

"Well? What is it? What do you have to tell me?"

"Come sit here girl. Sit next to Amobi, I will explain."

She sat next to him on the park bench overlooking the river. Amobi looked around suspiciously as if someone might be watching or listening. Jenny then did the same, growing anxious with Amobi's odd behavior.

"I think your stepmother means you and your father harm. I think she sees opportunity in you."

"Really?" Jenny was immediately sucked in by what Amobi had just suggested. He said it with such sincerity, and a hint of fear. "Please, Amobi, what makes you say this? What do you know?"

Amobi stood up and looked around. He leaned against the promenade's railing, looking at her, and began again.

"I hear things, Jenny. I hear what sounds like she don't want you to have no money when your daddy dies, like she wants to keep everything for herself. Do you want a drink? I need a drink." He removed a pint of Powers Whiskey from his coat pocket and took a sip. Coincidentally, it was Jenny's brand.

"Uh, uhm sure." She took the bottle from Amobi's hand and herself took a small sip, "Please, tell me more. What else did you hear? What do you know?"

"I listened to her on the phone, and she said, she said 'whatever it takes, she needs to go' when she was talking about you."

"Seriously?" Jenny replied, sitting up straight in a stance that was not unnerved but defiant.

"Yes really. This woman is serious, I'm telling you. Here do you want a pill? I have these pills; they are for relaxation. Do you like one of these?"

"No, I don't take pills. Please just tell me more about Lisa." She took another tiny sip from the bottle of Powers.

"Well, then… she say something about money too, something about is twenty thousand enough… then twenty-five thousand, is that enough?"

"Enough? Enough for what? What do you think they were talking about?"

Amobi grew more nervous, and he walked around the bench, looking into the trees and up and down the promenade before returning to the railing in front of Jenny.

"To me Jenny, I think. I think she wants someone to rub you out, to get rid of you, so she can keep everything when your daddy dies."

Jenny snorted, "No way, get out of here. You actually think that Lisa is looking to put a hit out on me, so she can keep everything my father has on top of the millions she'll already have coming to her?"

"Yes, I think that is for sure, Jenny. That is what I think she is planning." He again, nervously, started to circle the park bench.

"I don't know man that sounds a little crazy to me."

And those were Jenny's last words.

Amobi stepped behind her while she spoke. He quickly and effectively initiated a Rear Naked Choke lifting her off the bench. He tightened his powerful biceps and forearm around her throat, cutting off all her air, and all blood flow to her brain from the carotid artery, as Medical Examiner Angela Marcus had described. Jenny struggled. Her legs kicked, and her arms flailed, trying to strike Amobi as he choked the life out of her. But she was unconscious in less than fifteen seconds. Amobi held tight for at least another two minutes until he was certain Jenny was indeed dead.

He gently laid her down on the bench and placed her head on his lap. Her open eyes stared up at him and he knew she was gone. He removed the tablets of Molly he had brought from his jacket pocket. He dropped them into her mouth and poured some whiskey after them messaging her throat until it appeared both were gone.

Amobi then looked around one more time and, feeling secure in the fact that only he and Jenny were on the promenade in these wee hours of the morning, he lifted Jenny's dead body up in his arms and heaved her over the railing. He turned quickly, not even waiting to hear her body hit the water some 30 feet below, and he quickly headed out of the park. Upon reaching East End Avenue, he texted Lisa, "It's Done!"

Lisa replied, "Oh God, Thank you."

"He walked to First Avenue, where he caught a cab and went back to his apartment in Brooklyn.

***

After hearing Amobi's confession, ADA Jessica Lokietz thanked him for his honesty and the details he had provided. She then stood up, placed her note pad into her briefcase, and asked Tommy and Jimmy to step out of the interview room with her.

"I am fully satisfied, Detectives. I find everything Mr. Adebayo just told us to be completely credible. And the corroborating evidence on his phone, as well as the promise of proof of a check and money wired to Nigeria, all enough for probable cause for the arrest of Lisa Lindel. I will head back to the courthouse and get you some warrants for his residence in Brooklyn and hers on 92nd Street, as well as anything else you may need for any banks, or to track the money he sent to Nigeria. Great job, Detectives. Next time I see you I hope Lisa Lindel is in custody."

"I think we'll be making that happen within the next hour or so, Miss Lokietz. Thanks for the help, I will keep you posted."

"Very good, Detective Keane, Detective Colletti."

Chapter Twenty-Two

5:54 PM

Tommy and Jimmy made their way up the stairs of the tall stoop of the Lindels' home on 92nd Street and rang the bell.

The door was answered by the Lindels' young housekeeper, Tina.

"Hello, Detectives, welcome back," she said as she opened the door.

"Hey, Tina, how you doing?" Tommy began, "Is Mrs. Lindel home?"

"Yes, I'll get her for you. Please come in." She welcomed the detectives in and motioned for them to go into the parlor to the right of the entrance.

Rather than sit, both Tommy and Jimmy stood in the center of the room and waited. They could hear Lisa's shoes clicking down the steps. She was dressed simply, in tight blue jeans and a white blouse, with high heeled shoes. Her hair had recently been done and she was quite a beautiful sight as she walked into the room to meet the detectives. But Tommy and Jimmy didn't notice her obvious beauty. They now saw her as the vile, murderous creature she was, and as she entered the room the large smile she had on her face quickly left when her eyes met Tommy's. She immediately knew something was wrong.

"Good afternoon, Detective Keane, Detective Colletti. How are you gentlemen? Is everything alright? You look as though you have some bad news to share?"

Tina, who stood in the hall, now looked back and forth nervously between Tommy and Lisa, also feeling as though something was suddenly amiss.

"Tina, can you get Mrs. Lindel her coat, please? She's going to be taking a little trip with us and it's a little cold outside."

"Yes, sir," Tina responded.

"A trip? Detective? What? Where? What is going on Detective? Tommy?" She looked up at him beseechingly.

"You're under arrest, Mrs. Lindel, for the murder of your stepdaughter, Jennifer Lindel." And as he stepped forward, he began, "You have the right to remain silent. Anything you say can be used against you in a court of law. You have the right to an attorney. If you cannot afford an attorney, one will be provided for you. Do you understand the rights I have just read to you?"

Lisa stood motionless, frozen in fear and disbelief, as Tommy turned her around and put the handcuffs on her wrists. When he turned her back around to lead her out the door, she looked at him with a mean, cold hard stare and said, "I want my lawyer."

***

And for the most part Tommy's Jenny Black case was now closed.

Back at the 2-1, Tommy and Jimmy, with a little help from Doreen and Mark, processed both Lisa Lindel and Amobi Adebayo and sent them both to Central Booking.

It was quite late by the time they were finished and both suspects were in the hands of the court system. The following day was the first of B-Squad's RDO's, but Tommy took it upon himself to go to Memorial Sloan Kettering Hospital, where he spoke to Charlie Lindel's doctor. He found out that their Hail Mary pass was a success, and nothing short of a miracle. The exceptionally skilled surgeon performing the surgery on Charlie Lindel had saved his life and removed what they believed to be all of his cancerous tumors. Charlie Lindel would survive, and with treatment, live a normal life with a normal life expectancy.

At the time of this visit, Charlie was in no shape for a conversation, but two days later Tommy and Jimmy returned to Memorial Sloan Kettering and made the longest walk any detective ever has to make. They told Charlie Lindel about the murder of his daughter, and the subsequent arrest of his wife, Lisa, and her trainer, Amobi.

Epilogue

The information Amobi Adebayo had provided, his confession, along with the proof of the phone calls between he and Lisa, and he and Jenny, were enough probable cause to warrant the arrest of Lisa Lindel. As the ADA looked further into their connection, it was found that Lisa Lindel had indeed written Amobi Adebayo a check for $25,000. And he did wire $20,000 to his father in Nigeria, while keeping $5,000 for himself. It still sat in his bank account at the time of his arrest.

***

Lisa Lindel denied having anything to do with her stepdaughter's homicide. The Manhattan D.A.'s Office thought otherwise. They charged Lisa Lindel with Murder in the First Degree and Amobi Adebayo with Murder in the Second Degree.

Lisa maintained her innocence all the way up to and throughout her trial. But the physical evidence, along with the testimony of Amobi Adebayo and the detectives of the 2-1 squad, was more than enough for the jury to find her guilty of the murder of her stepdaughter Jenny.

***

Lisa currently sits in a cell at the Bedford Hills Correctional Facility in Bedford Hills, New York, where she is serving a sentence of twenty-five years to life. Her appeal for a new trial was denied.

Amobi Adebayo pled guilty in return for the lesser charge of Murder in the Second Degree. He was sentenced to fifteen to twenty-five years. He currently sits in a cell at the Attica Correctional Facility, in Attica, New York.

Charles Lindel lived in the same house on 92nd Street for the next nineteen years. He never remarried and only worked occasionally. When he did eventually die of a stroke, it was found that his fortune at the time of his death was worth just over twelve million dollars, all of which he left to his housekeeper of twenty-eight years, Tina.

Jerry Quick went on to be one of the most recorded trombone players in history. Although he did play in several bands over the years, it was his for-hire studio performances that would garner him this small footnote in music history. He became the man anyone would call when they needed a true professional on a recording.

Julie Mayer and Max Spicnic broke up several months after Jenny's investigation was complete, and nothing is known about the rest of their lives.

***

But all this is still to come.

Right now, we must simply wait for Detective Tommy Keane to awake to a new day, and a new stack of case folders, one of which might become one of our next chapters in his story.

Read on for a sneak peek at the next book in the Tommy Keane series:

Li Jun

9:22 PM 439 East 80th Street.

Tommy and Mark drove up 1st Avenue towards 80th Street, where they found police tape stretched across the road, blocking traffic. Officer Ortiz, who stood at the end of the tape, immediately recognized the detectives as they attempted to make the turn. She lifted the tape as high as she could so their car could drive below it, and they continued down the street towards the flashing lights of the awaiting patrol cars.

Halfway down the block, Tommy parked in front of the Caedmon School, which sat on the south side of the street, opposite and a few buildings up from 439. As they approached, they saw Sergeant Diaz, who from about fifteen yards away motioned towards the crime scene with his head. Tommy and Mark looked toward the building and saw what appeared to be a body, impaled on a wrought iron fence, and covered with a white sheet.

They approached and Sergeant Diaz began, "Rios and McCartney were right across the street on a domestic call when it happened. Just as they were leaving they said they heard her land on this fence, then looked over and saw her body."

Tommy stepped closer to the body. The sheet draped over it did little to hide the spikes of the wrought iron that had pierced the woman's midsection and now protruded from her back. She had dropped some thirty plus feet from the window and now hung lifeless over the black fencing.

He looked back at Diaz, who continued, "Rios said people began to exit the building as they ran over, so he and McCartney grabbed everyone and sat them down on the hallway floor until I arrived. We got eight people in total. Five are Chinese—one man and four women—three are Caucasians, one of which is Hasidic. Turns out they're all either staff or clients of what appears to be a Chinese massage parlor… more likely a brothel. They all ran out as soon as this woman came out of that third story window and hit the fence."

Tommy stood silent for a moment before he gently lifted the sheet. A young Asian woman, in her early twenties or possibly still in her teens, dangled lifelessly. She wore nothing but a see-through pink lace teddy over pink panties. Her jet-black hair was tied into two pigtails with matching pink elastic bands. She was tiny; Tommy guessed she weighed less than a hundred pounds. He leaned down to get a better look at her face. She was pretty too, her young face fully made up, and her open brown eyes staring back into Tommy's.

"Ahh, you poor dear thing," he said tenderly to her.

As they watched Tommy examine the young woman's body, Sergeant Diaz informed Mark he had put in a call to the Medical Examiner's office and to the Crime Scene Unit, who had said they would be delayed.

"Delayed?" Mark said flatly, "Well, at least they are coming. We called them for the assault earlier at The Carlow, in case our victim kicks, and they said they couldn't make it at all."

"Hope you got a name—and how's that Joey Macca doing? He gonna make it?" Diaz asked.

"Yeah, I got a name. Looks like he will. He's in a coma but the doctor said he should survive. Unknown when, or even if, he'll wake up, but the doctor sounded relatively positive he'll recover."

Tommy stepped forward and interjected.

"Okay, we have an Asian prostitute, who fell, jumped, or was thrown out a third-floor window to her death, and eight civilians and two members of the service to interview. Crime Scene and Medical Examiner are already notified—Thanks for that, Sarge, we appreciate it. Well, we got hours of work ahead of us. Mark, let's take a look at what's going on in this building, and I guess, fuck me… I guess we'll take all these people back to the station house and do our interviews there."

"That will definitely be our best bet," Mark agreed, "We'll separate them in the meantime; we don't want anyone putting stories together. And we're going to need some help from you, Sergeant Diaz. Do you think you can get us a couple cars, or a van, and some officers to take these people to the precinct and babysit until we can interview them individually?" Mark asked.

"Absolutely not a problem, Detective."

"Thanks, Sarge, that's a huge help," Tommy replied. "In the meantime, while we wait for transport, and Crime Scene and the M.E. to show, what say we separate these people here in the hallway as best we can? Then you and I, Mark, will take a walk through the apartment this young woman came from. If you would, Sarge, have Rios or McCartney keep an eye on our victim here, and the other keep the group inside seated on the floor. Remember, a few feet away from one another and keep them quiet as well, so like Mark here said, they don't cook up some stories."

"Got it. We'll do what we can to help," Sergeant Diaz answered, then turned and barked at Rios, who was on the stoop, "You got that, Rios? You keep an eye on this victim here."

Diaz then climbed the stoop himself and shouted at McCartney, who stood just inside the vestibule, "McCartney! Move all these people about four or five feet apart, and no talking! You hear me people? All of you, please shift yourselves over. I don't want anyone too close to anybody else. And quiet! Is that understood? No talking to one another! In a few minutes we'll begin taking you all, a few at a time, over to the 21st precinct to be interviewed by detectives. We don't want you talking to one another until you are interviewed, am I clear? Does everyone understand that?"

"Excuse me, Officer? Isn't that some sort of violation of our rights?" The Hasidic man spoke up.

"No, it's not! You're being held pending an investigation. And you should have thought about being inconvenienced by the police before you came here to get your dick sucked!" Officer McCartney snapped back.

"What kind of way is that for an officer to talk to a tax paying citizen?" The Hasidic man asked.

"He's right!" Sergeant Diaz responded, "Now all of you, no more talking until a detective is asking you questions. Enough!"

Tommy and Mark slowly walked past the eight people lined up in the first-floor hallway of building 439 and took in as much as they could from their first glance.

All five of the Chinese sat still, with their heads hung low and eyes staring into their laps without saying a word. The Hasidic man, who appeared to be about forty, wore glasses and was dressed in traditional Hasidic garb. As the detectives walked past him, he glanced up and started ranting about his rights.

The other two men sat quietly. One who also appeared to be about forty was dressed casually in jeans and a black and red flannel shirt. He had his eyes shut and leaned his head back against the wall. The other man, who appeared around fifty, wore a suit and tie and an expensive black wool coat. He stared straight ahead through wire-framed glasses at the wall across from him, not making eye contact or speaking to anyone.

The two detectives reached the third floor. There were four possible doors to choose from, but they were sure based on the positioning of the victim on the street that the one they wanted would be towards the front and on the left side of the hallway. With a turn of the knob, the door was open, and all doubts were lifted. As they observed the apartment for the first time, both Tommy and Mark recognized undeniable evidence that the apartment was being used as a brothel.

The door opened into a room which would normally be used as a living room and kitchen combo. A simple desk and chair sat in the kitchen area, opposite a line of eight black metal folding chairs. To the right of this room a door led into what was once a small bedroom with two windows. The space was now divided down the middle by a sheetrock wall, making two tiny chambers, each only about six feet across by eleven feet long. Each chamber had a small window in the far wall. The window in the room to the right led out to the fire escape but was closed and the shade had been drawn. The window in the room to the left, however, was wide open. The shade was up, and it was obvious this was the room where the young woman, still hanging on the fence below, had come from.

Both small rooms were sparsely furnished. In each there was a twin bed with just a simple white fitted sheet against one wall, and a small dresser and chair pushed up against the other wall. On top of each dresser was a bowl full of condoms and a large plastic bottle of K-Y Jelly. Even the walls were bare, painted a plain white and lacking art or decoration of any kind.

The detectives slowly and deliberately walked through the apartment, examining the rooms silently without touching anything. Past the front room with the folding chairs was a small bathroom they examined separately because it was simply too small for them to enter simultaneously. Finally, they reached the last door in the apartment and were not surprised to find another space that was divided into two smaller chambers. Again, the rooms were each appointed with only a twin bed, a small dresser, and a chair.

"Alright, nothing to do here now until Crime Scene comes and does their thing… and that may be awhile. So, what do you think? You want to help get all these people over to the precinct so Doreen and Jimmy can start questioning them?" Mark asked.

"Yeah, we're gonna have to. This is going to be a cluster fuck of an investigation, I can see that already," Tommy replied as he pulled out his cell phone and made a call to Lieutenant Bricks.

"Hey, Lu, how you doing? Listen, we have quite a mess over here on 80th Street. No idea if this is a suicide or a homicide yet, could easily be either, and I have eight possible witnesses and/or perps… What's that? Yeah, it appears to be a brothel on the third floor of a walk up. It's at 438, no sorry, 439 80th… You think you can grab Doreen and Jimmy and come give us a hand? … Great, thanks. Yeah, see you in a bit… Also, Lu, will you do me a favor and put a call into the Asian Gang Unit for me? I don't have the number and I'm sure they'll want to do some interviews once we're done… Yes sir. Yeah, Lu, thanks."

"Alright, sounds like we have some work ahead of us there, Detective." Mark said as soon as he heard Tommy finish his conversation.

"Yes sir, let's head downstairs and wait for the others," Tommy said, before walking back over to the window where he believed their victim had come from. He placed his hands in his pockets, cautious not to touch anything, and visually searched the window trim, the sill, and the floor for a clue of any kind. Tommy then stuck his head out the open window into the cold and stared down at the dead young woman impaled on the fence below. Tommy took a deep breath of the crisp air and said softly to her, "We'll figure this out, young lady. And if there is a debt to be paid, I'll do my best to collect it for you."

About the Authors

Travis Myers and Natasha Myers Marsiguerra are a brother and sister team who both grew up in New York City.

Travis is a retired New York City Police Detective, and Natasha works for the IBEW (International Brotherhood of Electrical Workers) Local 234 in California.

Together they form a perfect team in that Travis, who has more stories to tell than a pub full of Irishmen, suffers from dyslexia and abhors anything to do with reading or writing. Natasha, his beloved little sister, is an avid reader of absolutely anything that is put in front of her and has been blessed with the gift of gab. She can out-story just about anyone, in any room, at any given time, and she can also type 60 words per minute. More importantly, Natasha is able to understand where her older brother is coming from and craft his stories into a readable format.

Together, they weave the Tommy Keane Detective Series into well-braided fictional tales that are nearly all based in actual events. Travis and Natasha deliver on their promise to tell gritty, honest stories that are rooted in the everyday lives of everyday people.

CPSIA information can be obtained
at www.ICGtesting.com
Printed in the USA
JSHW051547160222
22884JS00002BA/11

9 781734 337068